When a
threatens to disho
A YEAR OF LOVING DANGEROUSLY
begins....

Burke Lonigan

Penetrating blue eyes, a powerful build—and a way
with women...

*His wealth had brought him privilege and his work
for SPEAR had brought him honor. But when Burke
married enigmatic Callie Severin, he was about to
learn something about love—and fatherhood....*

Callie Severin

A rare beauty with russet hair and a secret lurking
in her pretty gray eyes...

*She had agreed to be Burke's bride because she
desperately needed his protection. But what would
her sexy husband do when he discovered she was
the mother of his child?*

"Simon"

With his burns and battle scars, this reputed traitor
looked as deadly as rumors made him out to be....

*Simon is steps away from securing the weaponry he
needs to wreak more havoc on SPEAR, but first he
needs to get past powerful
Burke Lonigan....*

Dear Reader,

The 20th anniversary excitement continues as we bring you a 2-in-1 collection containing brand-new novellas by two of your favorite authors: Maggie Shayne and Marilyn Pappano. *Who Do You Love?* It's an interesting question—made more complicated for these heroes and heroines because they're not quite what they seem, making the path to happily-ever-after an especially twisty one. Enjoy!

A YEAR OF LOVING DANGEROUSLY continues with *Her Secret Weapon* by bestselling writer Beverly Barton. This is a great secret-baby story—with a forgotten night of passion thrown in to make things even more exciting. Our in-line 36 HOURS spin-off continues with *A Thanksgiving To Remember,* by Margaret Watson. Suspenseful and sensual, this story shows off her talents to their fullest. Applaud the return of Justine Davis with *The Return of Luke McGuire.* There's something irresistible about a bad boy turned hero, and Justine's compelling and emotional handling of the theme will win your heart. In *The Lawman Meets His Bride,* Meagan McKinney brings her MATCHED IN MONTANA miniseries over from Desire with an exciting romance featuring a to-die-for hero. Finally, pick up *The Virgin Beauty* by Claire King and discover why this relative newcomer already has people talking about her talent.

Share the excitement—and come back next month for more!

Leslie J. Wainger
Executive Senior Editor

Please address questions and book requests to:
Silhouette Reader Service
U.S.: 3010 Walden Ave., P.O. Box 1325, Buffalo, NY 14269
Canadian: P.O. Box 609, Fort Erie, Ont. L2A 5X3

Beverly
Barton
HER SECRET WEAPON

Silhouette ®
INTIMATE ™ MOMENTS ®

Published by Silhouette Books

America's Publisher of Contemporary Romance

To my girls,
Badiema Beaver Waldrep and Jana Parris Beaver

A special thanks to Brian Usher, who helped me with my
London research, and to his aunt, Carol Benjamin, for
putting me in touch with a resident of the U.K.

Special thanks and acknowledgment are given to
Beverly Barton for her contribution to the
A Year of Loving Dangerously series.

SILHOUETTE BOOKS

ISBN 0-373-27104-2

HER SECRET WEAPON

Copyright © 2000 by Harlequin Books S.A.

Visit Silhouette at www.eHarlequin.com

Printed in U.S.A.

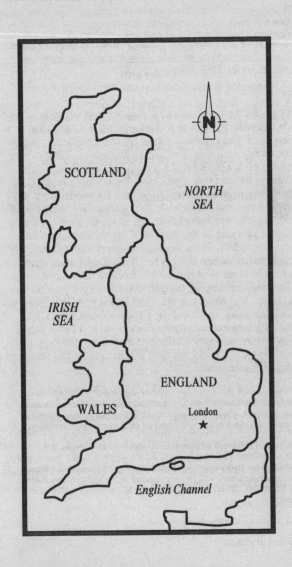

A note from award-winning author Beverly Barton, author of over thirty books, including the bestselling Intimate Moment series THE PROTECTORS.

Dear Reader,

Writing Burke Lonigan and Callie Severin's romance began with a certain process to make the story uniquely my own—a process I undertake whenever I write a book that is part of a continuity series, as *Her Secret Weapon* is. The exciting premise of A YEAR OF LOVING DANGEROUSLY, revolving around characters associated with a highly secret organization formed to protect the world from evil, intrigued me immediately. At first glance *Her Secret Weapon* is simply a secret-baby book, but as we all know, a tried-and-true plot can be the basis of a highly emotional love story—especially if the heroine suspects that the playboy tycoon father of her child is really an illegal arms dealer. As I do with most of my books, I added to the mix a little cloak-and-dagger danger, several unique secondary characters and some hot sex. And in the end I achieved my goal. This story, the fourth in a twelve-book series, took on a life of its own as a Beverly Barton book. I hope you'll enjoy getting to know Callie and Burke and sharing all the emotional highs and lows they experience on the rocky road to happily-ever-after.

During the process of researching London, the British "English language" and numerous other details I needed to know in order to write this book, I became thoroughly absorbed in the setting as well as the plot and characters. Luckily, I had the assistance of a U.K. resident, the nephew of a longtime Heart of Dixie RWA friend who, via e-mail, answered numerous questions for me. The research quickly became almost as much fun as writing the book.

Warmest regards,

Beverly Barton

Prologue

The crisp autumn breeze swirled around Callie Severin as she stood outside the Princess Inn, located in the heart of London's elegant Belgravia. An October rain earlier in the day had lowered the temperature, so that it was rather chilly. Shivering slightly, she wished she'd taken a heavy coat to the office with her today. Hindsight was twenty-twenty, she reminded herself. One of her American father's favorite sayings. And that old saying definitely applied to her love life as well as to her coat!

After Laurence had so cruelly broken their engagement and ripped out her heart only a few hours ago, Callie had resigned her position as a Personal Assistant at McNeill, Inc., where Laurence had been her superior. He'd assured her that her resignation was unnecessary and she had assured him that it most certainly was. And she'd told him that she had no intention of working out a notice. He was a heartless, uncaring cad and she was well rid of him! She had repeated those words to herself so often they were now a litany.

After clearing out her desk and saying a somber good-bye to her associates, Callie had taken the tube home and then rushed down the street to her flat, hoping that Enid would be there. She'd needed a friend. A shoulder to cry on. And who better than Enid, her dearest friend and cousin, with whom she shared the flat in Kensington. But Enid hadn't been there. So Callie had waited and waited, crying for a while and fantasizing about smashing her fist into Laurence's aquiline nose.

After pulling herself together as best as she could, Callie had searched for Enid in all the places she usually frequented, but hadn't found her. Enid delighted in being an artist's model and lived a rather free and easy life, thanks to an inheritance from her paternal grandmother. Men were a disposable commodity to Enid, and she changed lovers frequently. Despite the fact that she and Enid were cousins, their mothers having been sisters, they were as different as day and night. Callie had remained a virgin until she'd become engaged to Laurence.

God! She had to stop thinking about him! *Heartless cad. Better off without him.*

Callie decided that the Princess Inn would be her last stop. If Enid and her new boyfriend, Niles, weren't there, she wouldn't continue searching. She'd go home, have herself another good cry and wait until morning to tell Enid that not only had she lost her fiancé because he was in love with another woman, she would have to temporarily rely on Enid's generosity until she found a new position.

The pub featured a perfect Georgian era facade with Victorian decor. Elegant and probably very expensive, Callie thought, as she scanned the bar area. If Enid were here, her new boyfriend must have plenty of money. Either that or Enid was picking up the tab. Callie searched the place thoroughly, garnering several odds stares and a couple of propositions. But she didn't catch a glimpse of Enid anywhere. Enough of this! Time to go home, she told herself. She would simply have to live through this night alone, no matter how much she needed sympathy and comfort.

Just as Callie turned to leave, she noticed a man sitting alone in a back booth. She wasn't quite sure why her gaze fixed on him—and lingered—or why she couldn't make herself stop staring at him. Oh, he was quite good-looking. Actually more than good-looking. He was devastatingly handsome. In a terribly masculine way. Not young. Not a boy. Probably late thirties. A good ten or fifteen years older than she.

He glanced at Callie and for a split second she stopped breathing. His eyes focused directly on her, freezing her in place. Some inner instinct warned her to run. Now! But his gaze held her hypnotized.

The man's face possessed a world-weary expression and his beautiful blue eyes spoke silently of some deep sadness within him. She had never seen eyes such a brilliant blue or a man's lashes so long and thick. He'd been blessed with black Irish looks—black hair, blue eyes and a fair, ruddy complexion. He was, without a doubt, the best-looking man she'd ever seen.

A heavy stubble darkened his cheeks and chin, as if he hadn't shaved in a couple of days. From the tousled appearance of his stylishly cut hair, she assumed he'd been raking his fingers through it. And his rather expensive-looking navy blue suit was slightly rumpled. She couldn't help wondering if perhaps he'd slept in it last night.

Without taking his eyes off her, he lifted his glass, saluted her with it and downed the last drops of what she thought was probably Scotch whiskey. His lips lifted ever so lightly in an almost smile that never reached his eyes. As if it were a palpable thing, the stranger's misery reached out to her, drawing her to him.

Callie took a hesitant step in the man's direction, her gaze still riveted to his. Somehow she knew he was as unhappy and as alone as she. Could he sense her pain, the way she had sensed his?

He tilted his head, motioning to her, and the almost smile grew wider but remained only a parody of a real smile. As if of their own volition, her legs moved, taking her closer and closer to the stranger. When she stopped at the edge of the booth, the man stood. Unsteady on his feet, he chuckled and grabbed the edge of the table.

With a magnanimous sweep of his hand, he bowed to Callie. "Won't you join me, lovely lady?"

She hesitated only a second before she nodded and slid into the booth. With staggering unease, he slumped onto the seat. "May I get you something to drink?" he asked, but didn't wait for her reply before he tried again to stand. A bit wobbly, he braced his hand on the tabletop.

"Thank you," Callie said. That would be nice, Mr., er, Mr....?

"Lonigan. Burke Lonigan."

His devastating smile did evil things to her stomach, making it tighten and then turn somersaults. Oh, dear me, she thought. Mr. Burke Lonigan was undeniably lethal.

"I'll get myself another," he said, his speech slightly slurred. "And you will have a—"

"Chardonnay," she said, her voice creaky. She cleared her throat, feeling uneasy and uncertain. And breathlessly attracted to a perfect stranger.

Mr. Lonigan made his way across the crowded room to

the bar area, leaving her with her confused thoughts. What was she doing? Had she lost her mind? She'd never been the type to pick up men in pubs. Not until now, a pesky inner voice chided.

He returned from the bar, their drinks in hand, set hers before her and slid into the booth.

"What's a pretty lady like you doing all alone?" he asked.

"I was looking for someone."

"A man?"

"No, actually, I was looking for a friend—a girl-friend."

"Girlfriend, huh? Looking for her to chat her up, I suppose."

"Yes, something like that."

"Good friend, is she?" he asked. "Someone you can trust with your problems?"

"Yes."

"I don't have a friend like that," he said, his eyes piercing her with their intense stare. "Would you like to be my friend? Just for tonight?"

A hint of tears glistened in his eyes. Unshed tears. Agonized tears. She saw the pain and understood—this man was hurting in the worst way. Hurting as she was hurting. Had someone broken his heart? she wondered.

Without thinking about what she was doing, Callie reached over and placed her hand atop his and squeezed gently. "Yes, I'll be your friend, just for tonight, if you'll be my friend."

It was apparent she wasn't going to find Enid tonight, and she desperately needed someone with whom she could share her misery. Why not this handsome man, this stranger she would never see again? She'd often heard that it was easier to talk to a stranger. Perhaps it was.

Suddenly Callie felt him tense as he looked at the whiskey. His hand beneath hers balled into a fist. As he removed his hand from hers, she noted a slight tremble.

"Do you really need more to drink?" she asked.

"If I'm going to drown my sorrows, I do," he told her.

"Can a person really drown their sorrows? If they can, then I'd be willing to give it a try."

"What sorrows could a pretty young thing like you have?" He lifted the whiskey to his mouth and downed half of it in one swallow. The shiver that went through his body was barely discernible.

"The sorrow of having been betrayed by my fiancé," she explained, not really understanding why she was pouring out her heart to this man. "He dumped me this afternoon. Seems he's been having an affair for the past two months with someone he loves *madly.*"

"Obviously, the man's a fool."

"Actually, I'm the fool." Callie lifted the flute of Chardonnay to her lips. The taste was pleasing on her tongue. She sipped the sharp, dry white wine and decided it was the best she'd ever drunk.

Mr. Lonigan downed the rest of his whiskey. His already flushed cheeks darkened. "Why are you the fool?"

"Because I should have known something was wrong. He's been acting odd for quite some time now and I chose to accept his rather weak excuses."

"You were very much in love, I assume. Young girls like you always are, aren't they?"

"I thought I was. You know how it is. He was charming and attentive and he was the first man I'd..." Callie realized she was about to tell this stranger that Laurence had been her first lover. "Well, I'd never been in love before."

Mr. Lonigan's mesmerizing blue eyes opened wide in

an expression that told Callie he had understood only too well the meaning of "he was the first man."

"Love, my girl, is a wasted emotion. Smart people don't need love. They don't give it and they don't expect to receive it. Not from anyone. Not from friends or lovers or—" he paused, sighing loudly "—and not even from parents."

Callie stared at Mr. Lonigan. He looked directly at her, but she knew he was looking through her. It was so obvious that his mind had drifted away to another time and another place. From the expression on his handsome face, she surmised that his memories were painful.

"Mr. Lonigan?"

"Call me Burke." He chuckled. "What shall I call you?" When she opened her mouth to tell him her name, he shushed her. "No, no, don't tell me. I'll just forget it anyway. I could call you *love,* I suppose. But that doesn't suit, does it? Why don't I call you *my darling?* Something just as easy to remember." He inspected her thoroughly. "Besides, you look like a darling to me. So tell me, my darling, what did you do when your fiancé dumped you? Did you scream and cry and call him names?"

"I slapped his silly face and then I resigned my position in the firm where we both worked."

"Ah, so you're without a man and without a job."

"It appears so."

"Mm… If you're as smart as you are pretty, you won't be without either for long."

Burke excused himself for a trip to the bar, but when he asked if she'd like another, she declined. She watched him staggering as he disappeared into the crowded bar area. He returned within minutes, smiling, another whiskey in his hand.

The moment he sat down, he reached for the Scotch.

Callie grasped his hand before he could pick up the glass. "I've told you my sad story," she said. "Why don't you tell me yours?"

"My sad story?" He lifted his eyebrows as if surprised by her request. "What makes you think I have a sad story to tell?"

She tightened her hold on his big hand. "Because you're drinking to drown your sorrows and—" she hesitated momentarily "—you look like an unmade bed."

He tossed back his head and laughed. Genuine, gut-deep laughter.

When he looked at her again, a rather cocky, crooked smile remained in place. "I like honesty in a woman. Unusual quality in most. So, I look like an unmade bed, do I?"

"Yes, you do. And the moment I saw you, I noticed the sadness in your eyes."

His smile vanished. He knocked her hand aside and lifted the whiskey. This time he downed the entire drink in one long swallow. Afterward he coughed several times.

"Observant little thing, aren't you?"

"Please, don't drink any more. You've had more than enough."

He deliberately pinched his cheek. "I'm afraid I can still feel, so that means I haven't had enough."

"Want to tell me what's wrong?"

"Why is it that women always want to poke and probe into a man's business? If you really want to help me, then why don't you come closer and I'll tell you what will really make me feel better."

She noted that he'd begun to slur his words more and more. Another drink and he might not be able to walk. *So, why do you care?* an inner voice asked. *This man doesn't mean anything to you. He's a stranger. But he is a stranger in pain. He needs someone tonight. Someone to ease his pain. And you need someone, too,* that inner voice reminded her. *Someone to ease your pain.*

Callie slid closer to him so that they were shoulder to shoulder. Then she draped her arm around his waist and cuddled to his side. "Don't drink any more and we'll discuss what we can do for each other...how I can ease your pain and you can ease mine."

She had no intention of giving this man anything more than sympathy and caring. The two things they both needed. But first she had to find a way to stop him from drinking, didn't she?

He grinned at her. The bottom dropped out of her stomach. She'd never had such a strong physical reaction to a man—not even Laurence, and they had been lovers. It was as if she and this stranger, this Mr. Lonigan, were somehow connected. She couldn't explain the odd attraction she felt for him. Did he feel it, too? she wondered. She thought that perhaps he did. Right now he was looking at her as if he could see straight through her clothes. His intense scrutiny made her feel completely naked.

"Would you come home with me, my darling?" he asked, his voice a deep, sensuous invitation.

"I'll make sure you get home safely." She made a counteroffer.

"Will you now?"

Callie's heartbeat quickened when he stared at her, his eyes twinkling with devilment. "I'm not really into casual sex," she admitted. "I've just lived through one of the worst days of my life and obviously you have, too, so perhaps—"

"No sex, huh?"

"I'll get us a taxi," Callie said. "And I'll see you home."

Burke glowered at her. "Take-charge kind of girl, are you? Well, I don't need anyone to take charge of me, thank you kindly." With that said, he tried to stand. After swaying right and left, he quickly sat. "I seem to be quite blotto."

Callie couldn't suppress the giggle that escaped from her throat.

"You won't get an argument from me. You, Mr. Lonigan, are most definitely blotto."

Within ten minutes Callie, aided by a pub employee, eased Burke Lonigan into a black cab, then slid in beside him. While she rummaged in her purse for money to tip the young man who had helped her, Burke handed the man an overly generous twenty quid.

"Where to, governor?" the driver asked.

When Burke gave the driver his address, Callie gasped. His home was in Belgravia? Only the extremely wealthy lived here. Multimillionaires. Was her Mr. Lonigan that rich? she wondered. *Not your Mr. Lonigan,* an inner voice scolded.

Burke slipped his arm around Callie's shoulders and pulled her against him. His whiskey breath was warm and soft against the side of her face. A tingling shudder rippled up her spine, and her stomach fluttered with sexual awareness.

Burke nuzzled her ear and laughed when she trembled. "You're as jumpy as a virgin, my darling."

"I'm not a—"

"Of course you're not. You had a fiancé, didn't you?"

"Yes, I did."

"Engaged long?" Burke asked.

"Nearly a year," she said. "What about you?"

"What about me?"

"Are you married or engaged or anything?"

"Never married. Never engaged. But a great deal of *anything.*"

His teasing manner helped her relax just a bit. "Have you ever been in love?"

"Depends on your definition of love."

"I suppose what I'm trying to ask is why you're so sad tonight. I thought perhaps you had a broken heart, too." She cuddled against Burke Lonigan's large, strong body. Oddly enough, being encompassed in this stranger's arms made her feel safe and comforted.

"Ah, I see." He released her, scooted her toward the opposite side of the taxi and then laid his head on her lap as he stretched his long legs across the seat. "You don't mind, do you?"

"No." And she really didn't. Unable to stop herself, she threaded her fingers through his wavy black hair, which felt incredibly soft and silky to the touch.

Burke lifted his right arm. Reaching up, he caressed the back of her neck with his fingertips. He lowered his left hand to begin a similar maneuver with her knees.

She could stop him. She should stop him! But she didn't. His touch somehow soothed her as, at the same time, it excited her. An odd combination, but she knew no other way to describe the sensations fluttering inside her body.

"My father died." Burke's voice was low and quiet, as if he were talking to himself.

"Oh, I'm so very sorry."

"Nothing to be sorry about. The old bastard lived to be nearly eighty!"

Callie didn't understand the bitterness in Burke's voice or the sudden tenseness in his body. Why would anyone refer to their father as an old bastard? Although she and her father didn't always agree on everything, they got along rather well. Arthur Severin had been a strict but loving parent who had done his best to bring up his only child after his wife's untimely death when Callie was twelve.

Burke chuckled. "Actually, I'm the bastard. My parents were never married. He was an older married man and she a young Irish maid. My mother married a Yank soldier when I was ten and we moved to America. I only became acquainted with my real father when I returned to England as a grown man."

"Did the two of you never reconcile?" Callie asked.

"In a way, I suppose we did." Burke halted his caress of Callie's knees, allowing his hand to cup her kneecap. He lowered the hand at her neck until it rested at his side. "I'm afraid Seamus Malcolm didn't have room in his life for an illegitimate son, so in all the years I knew him, he never actually acknowledged me. Just kept me on the fringes of his life. Tossed me a crumb from time to time."

"He sounds like a beastly man." Callie's heart ached for Burke Lonigan, for the little boy inside him who still longed for a father's love and attention.

"Not really. He was just a man of his time." Burke harrumphed. "Old Seamus died last week. I was out of the country. On business. His family—his legitimate children—didn't even bother to try to contact me. I wasn't here for my own father's funeral. I returned to London this morning and when I telephoned him, as I often did after I'd been out of the country, I was told that he had died."

Burke lifted his head from her lap, then slowly pulled himself into a sitting position. "When I stopped by the house this afternoon to pay my condolences, I was told I wasn't welcome."

"Oh, how dreadful for you." Callie wrapped her arms around him and hugged him to her.

Engulfing her in his embrace, Burke melted against her. "The maid who turned me away followed me out into the street and told me that Mr. Seamus had asked for me on his deathbed and they had told him I wouldn't come."

"Oh, God!" Callie held Burke, offering him sympathy and comfort and tender care.

He buried his face against her neck. She caressed the back of his head, then turned and kissed him sweetly on his temple. He lifted his face to her, and his breathtaking blue eyes glistened with moisture.

"It's all right," she said. "It really is quite all right to cry for your father."

"I don't cry," he told her, the tone of his voice hard, even if his words were slightly slurred. "I've cried only once since I was a lad of six, when someone called me an ugly name and I knew what it meant. The other time— the last time—was when my dog Skippy died. I was eleven and knew better than to act like a crybaby."

She couldn't bear it, Callie thought. This beautiful, brokenhearted man, who so desperately needed the relief of tears, refused to give in to his emotions. Horrid masculine trait! She wanted nothing more at that moment than to ease his suffering, to erase the pain she saw in his eyes and somehow give him the emotional release he needed.

As if he could read her mind, Burke studied her intently and then without a word he covered her mouth with his. The kiss was wildly passionate, and yet an odd blend of tenderness and savagery. He devoured. Taking, demanding, needing. At first, she simply allowed his plundering, but within moments she responded. Hesitantly she opened her mouth, inviting his invasion. But the second he cupped the back of her head, pressing her deeper into the kiss, she ignited, like dry timber to a lit match. Rational thought ceased. Sensation ruled her completely.

All her bruised and battered emotions clashed with sexual heat and the two melded into raw, primitive need.

"Here we are, governor," the driver said, then hopped out of the cab and opened the door.

Burke ended the kiss, slowly. As if he had all the time in the world. As if some heavyset, gray-haired cabdriver wasn't watching them. As if passersby couldn't see them.

Still lost in a sensual fog, Callie's mind swirled. She eased out of Burke's arms, her body decidedly weak.

"Want me to help you with him, miss?" the driver asked.

"Sir, are you implying that I can't walk without assistance?" Burke demanded, but his tone implied a teasing attitude.

As if to make a point, Burke climbed out of the taxi and stood on his own two feet. Callie slid out directly behind him, then searched in her purse for money to pay the driver.

Burke grabbed her hand. "I'll take care of this." He removed his wallet, pulled out several large bills—twice the cost of the taxi ride—and handed the generous sum to the driver.

"Thank you, sir. Thank you, indeed." The middle-aged man smiled broadly. "I'll be glad to help you inside, governor. No extra charge." When he chuckled, his potbelly jiggled like jelly.

"My darling, do you need any assistance putting me to bed?" Burke draped his arm around Callie's shoulders.

Under the streetlights, Burke's hair shone a rich blue black and his eyes glimmered with temptation and promise.

"Thank you," she said to the driver, "but I think I can handle things."

Callie tried not to let Burke's beautiful period house in prestigious Belgravia intimidate her, but she couldn't help it. The house must have cost him no less than two million pounds! She was far from poor and had been raised quite comfortably by an American diplomat father and a disowned-by-her-family English aristocrat mother. She had friends from every walk of life, including her independently wealthy cousin Enid. But the kind of money it took to live in Belgravia was the kind possessed by oil sheiks and business tycoons. Just who was Burke Lonigan? she wondered. *And what am I doing with him?*

When Callie remained unmoving on the pavement in front of his home, Burke nudged her into action. "You haven't changed your mind, have you?"

Although his steps were unsteady because of the large amount of liquor he had consumed, Callie's movements were shaky for a different reason. Suddenly, she felt very uncertain about going inside this mansion with a man she really didn't know.

When they reached the front door, Burke dove his hand into his pocket and brought out a key, but before inserting it into the lock, he turned and wrapped his arms around Callie. She felt small and vulnerable. With her flats not adding any height to her five-foot-three-inch frame, Burke towered over her a good nine inches.

He pressed his face against her neck, then nuzzled softly and whispered into her ear. "You need me tonight, my darling, just as much as I need you."

He kissed her. A preview of things to come. A hint of the passion they had shared in the taxi sparked, and she knew it wouldn't take much to set them aflame.

When he unlocked and opened the massive front doors,

she went with him into the dark belly of his home. He didn't give her time to assess the situation or to get her bearings before he led her deeper into the cavern of the large foyer. The downstairs area was pitch black, but at the top of the impressive staircase a dim light shone from an open doorway.

On their ascent up the marble staircase, Burke continued kissing her, his lips brushing her cheek, her temple and her jaw. All the while he kept his left arm securely wrapped around her shoulders, he maneuvered his right hand alongside her waist and up to gently cradle the underside of her breast. She sucked in a deep breath when his fingertips brushed her nipple.

The light in the hallway came from a bedroom. Burke's bedroom, she surmised. While her mind instructed her to look at the room, to appreciate the decor and take time out to catch her breath, her senses felt no compulsion to do more than enjoy the ardent attention of the man who kissed and caressed her.

You need this, an inner voice prompted. *You need to be loved tonight. Mindlessly, passionately loved. No commitment. No concerns beyond this one night. Don't think. Feel. Feel what it's like to be with a man like Burke Lonigan.*

Burke shed his coat and let it fall haphazardly to the floor. Then he loosened the buttons on his shirt and tossed the fine linen garment aside. With trembling fingers, he caught the hem of Callie's cashmere jumper and lifted it up and off, then added it to the pile of clothing accumulating on the floor. Before she could catch her breath, he tumbled them onto the massive mahogany bed. His laughter rumbled from his chest as he rolled Callie on top of his long, hard body. She gazed at him, into his sexy blue eyes, and felt her bones beginning to liquefy. Her feminine core clenched and unclenched. Her nipples peaked.

She didn't think she'd ever wanted anything so much in her entire life. Sanity warned her that she was making a mistake. But lust promised her ecstasy beyond her wildest dreams.

She straddled him, the action hiking her skirt to midthigh. At the apex between her spread legs, she felt the large, throbbing bulge of Burke's arousal. Every nerve in her body quivered.

He ran one hand underneath her skirt to cup her hip. "You're wearing tights," he complained. "Take them off."

She kicked off her shoes, then lifted her legs and hastily removed her skirt and her tights, leaving her in only a pair of coral silk panties and matching bra.

"That's better," he said, as he tried to unbuckle his belt. When his fumbling attempt failed, he cursed under his breath.

"Here, let me."

Callie had never undressed a man, not even Laurence, who had preferred to remove his own clothes and be waiting in bed for her. She went at removing Burke's clothes like a madwoman intent upon stripping him bare at record speed. Within two minutes, his shoes, socks, belt, trousers and underpants lay askew across the foot of the bed.

"Eager little thing, aren't you?" Burke teased her.

"Very eager," she admitted.

"Been awhile, has it, since a man pleasured you?"

She covered his body with hers and quickly spread hot, damp kisses over his broad, muscular chest. A soft sprinkling of black hair ran from one tiny male nipple to the other. When she licked each nipple in turn, Burke groaned deeply.

"I've never been with a real man," Callie said. "Only with one very self-centered boy who didn't know the first thing about pleasuring me."

Her confession poured gasoline on an already blazing fire. Burke captured her mouth, thrust his tongue into her waiting warmth and began a sensual assault that soon had her breathless and desperate for satisfaction. His mouth tasted of the Scotch he'd drunk earlier and his skin still retained the faded scent of some expensive men's cologne.

She felt his mouth on her breast and vaguely wondered when he had removed her bra. *Did it matter?* an inner voice asked. No. No! Nothing mattered except that he continue touching her.

His hand crept up inside her scanty bloomers, cupping and caressing her bare buttocks. She writhed against him, loving the feel of his body so intimately entwined with hers. They turned and tossed on the bed, exchanging the dominant position again and again as they caressed, licked, kissed and nibbled each other's bodies. Sometime during their sexual tumble, Burke removed the last barrier between them—her silk bikini panties.

The moment Burke's lips touched her intimately between her thighs, Callie realized she was completely naked. She had no time to protest, no time to think about what he was doing to her. The masterful strokes of his talented tongue treated her to a lush, hot treat that left her panting when release shot through her body like fireworks in the nighttime sky. As the aftershocks of her climax rippled through her, Burke mounted her and lifted her hips. She stared into his face and saw the savage arousal of a primitive man. She cried out when he entered her with a forceful lunge. She clung to him, loving the fullness he created inside her as he filled her completely.

She met him thrust for thrust as the pressure increased. Throbbing, blinding, all-consuming hunger like none she'd ever known. She tensed, her body rioting with sensation, and like a thunderbolt, Callie experienced the most incredible pleasure of her entire life.

As her nails raked his back, her moans of completion sent him over the edge. Burke hammered into her, intensifying her fulfillment. And then he groaned like a wild animal—a roar of masculine triumph—as he shuddered violently inside her damp, receptive body.

He eased to her side but kept his arm possessively draped around her. Callie felt weightless and sated beyond belief. Drained. Sleepy. Deliriously content. Without another thought, she curled up against Burke and fell asleep.

In the wee hours of the morning, with dawn at least an hour away, Callie gathered her clothes and crept into the loo adjoining Burke's bedroom. She washed quickly, refusing to turn on a light or to glance at herself in the mirror. Once she had put on her clothes, she tiptoed across the room, but stopped briefly at the foot of the bed to take one last look at Burke Lonigan.

She couldn't believe that she'd had sex with a man she barely knew. Twice! Unprotected sex, she reminded herself, and groaned silently. Maybe he was the most gorgeous man alive. Maybe they had truly needed each other. And maybe the sex had been the absolutely greatest she'd ever experienced. Scratch that. No maybe about it. It *had* been the greatest sex!

But Burke had been plastered and couldn't be held totally responsible for his actions, where she on the other hand had been perfectly sober and could be held responsible.

She left the bedroom, made her way down the marble staircase and rushed hurriedly through the huge foyer and out the front door. She glanced at the house and said goodbye to her lover. She'd never see Burke Lonigan again. In a few weeks, he would be nothing more than a sweet memory.

Chapter 1

Callie dashed out of the elevator, thankful she'd had several minutes in the lift to catch her breath. The morning had been unusual hectic. Enid had stayed over at a friend's last night and hadn't come home by the time the minder had arrived. Thankfully Seamus adored the plump, motherly Mrs. Goodhope, who had raised four children of her own and had ten grandchildren.

Seamus had been fussy during the night, which was so unlike him. He'd woken Callie before dawn. She'd taken his temperature, which was normal, and had tried everything to soothe his whining. And when he'd said mama, and looked pleadingly at her with those big blue eyes of his, she'd almost stayed at home. But she couldn't allow a fourteen-month-old child to dictate her actions. Especially not when she and that spoiled little boy depended upon her job for their livelihood.

Callie's quick steps clicked her sensible two-inch heels along the corridor in the office suite of Lonigan's Imports

and Exports, which comprised the entire twentieth floor
of an impressive skyscraper in the heart of the Square
Mile. The relatively new building, constructed in the mid
eighties, blended into the landscape in and around the Bar-
bican Center and the nearby Tower Bridge over the Pool
of London. As she hurried toward her office, she nodded
and spoke to various employees. She'd been employed
here only two and a half months, but she already knew
everyone by first and last names and could recite each
person's individual title and duties. Of course, acquiring
that knowledge had been part of her job as Burke
Lonigan's personal assistant.

"Good morning, Ms. Severin," her secretary, Juliette
Davenport, said in greeting. "Would you care for some
tea and scones?"

"Yes, please, thank you. I didn't have time for breakfast." Callie pushed open the door to her office, then
paused and asked, "By the way, has Mr. Lonigan arrived?"

"No, but he did telephone and leave you a message.
He said to proceed with the McMaster's shipment and that
he'd be in by noon."

"Oh. Yes, I'll take care of it."

She couldn't help wondering if Burke had spent the
night with a friend last night, as Enid had, and that was
the reason he would be late coming into the office this
morning.

Callie dropped her briefcase on top of her desk, plopped
down in her leather swivel chair and punched several keys
on her computer to bring up the McMaster's file. The facts
and figures blurred before her eyes as her mind filled with
thoughts of Burke and another woman. Some tall, leggy
brunette or some luscious blonde.

She had found out a great deal about Burke Lonigan in

the past few months, and one of the few things she didn't like about him was his penchant for womanizing. As part of the London social set, he was seen frequently in public, each time with a different attractive lady on his arm. She didn't blame the ladies. After all, Burke was a very handsome, quite charming and excessively wealthy man, not to mention a fantastic lover.

Just the thought of the night she'd spent with him suffused Callie's body with heat and flushed her cheeks. That night almost two years ago had changed her life forever. For Burke Lonigan had given her more than a sweet memory. He had given her a child.

When she had told Enid she was pregnant, her cousin had assumed the baby belonged to Laurence, but Callie had quickly corrected that misconception. Enid had been the one who'd found out who Burke Lonigan was and how he could be contacted, but Callie had refused to go to the man and tell him he was going to become a father. She didn't blame Burke for what had happened that night. She blamed only herself. She'd been sober and in her right mind. He hadn't. Truth be told, she had felt certain that Burke wouldn't even remember her. And she had been right, of course, much to her own dismay.

After endless needling by Enid, Callie had gone to Burke's house a few months after Seamus was born. While she'd been hesitating on the pavement, trying to garner enough courage to ring the bell, a chauffeured Rolls had pulled up and Burke had emerged. He'd looked right at her, smiled, nodded and walked past her—without recognizing her. After that, she hadn't attempted to approach him again. Not until a few months ago, when she had applied for the job as Burke's PA. Even after working with her for over two months, the man still didn't have a clue that they had shared a night of passion.

Although she'd put on a few pounds, had cut her waist-length hair to shoulder length and wore the curly mass in a neat bun while at work, she really hadn't changed all that much, had she? An eye infection had temporarily ended her use of contact lenses about six months ago, but a pair of small, gold-rimmed specs couldn't possibly make her look that different. After all, she wore them only for reading and working at the computer.

Callie had come to the conclusion that Burke simply didn't remember that night. For whatever reason, he had blocked the memory from his mind. Perhaps because he'd been plastered after downing so much Scotch and had acted rather emotional for a man who, she had learned, was never emotional. Perhaps he associated that night with the agony he'd suffered not only from losing his father, but from having been denied the right to say a proper goodbye. Whatever the reason, he seemed to have no recollection of her whatsoever.

She had learned that Burke was a tough, shrewd, in-control businessman who managed an import-export business that was worth over five hundred million pounds. Although, as Burke's PA, she was privy to Lonigan's records, she suspected that all of his assets hadn't been acquired through legitimate means. Rumors abounded about Burke being an illegal arms dealer. She tried to tell herself that the rumors weren't true, but her intuition told her that they were.

"Here's your tea and scones." Juliette set the pastry, cup and saucer on the desk. "Are you all right? You look knackered."

Despite the fact that she had lived in London for several years and her mother had been a U.K. citizen, some British words still seemed strange to Callie, whereas she had adapted others into her everyday speech. Although hav-

ing grown up all over Europe as the daughter of a diplomat, from the age of twelve her education had been
acquired in the States, so she often found her vocabulary
to be a mixture of American and British English. Oddly
enough, the same held true for Burke. He had been born
in London and had lived here for the past fifteen years,
but he had been brought up and educated in the States, as
she had.

"I'm fine," Callie said. "Please, don't worry about
me."

Callie smiled pleasantly at the freckled-faced young
woman, who was a whiz at her secretarial duties. A talk-
ative, carrot-topped redhead, Juliette often chatted endlessly. Deliberately, Callie didn't instigate further conversation this morning, as she often did. She was too out of
sorts after her early morning with Seamus and was worrying about where Burke might have spent his night.

She hadn't come to work for Burke to renew their romance, an inner voice reminded her. Ha! Referring to their
former relationship as a romance was indeed a laugh.
There had never been a romance. Only one sexual encounter. A night Burke couldn't even remember! She
hadn't sought the job as Burke's PA because she harbored
any silly romantic notions about the man. Instead, she'd
taken the job in order to get to know the father of her
child, so that she could make a well-thought-out, rational
decision about whether or not she should tell Burke about
his son. Someday Seamus was bound to ask about the man
who had fathered him.

Although she found herself liking Burke more and more
with each passing day, she also could not ignore the rumors about the mysteries surrounding his wealth and fabulous lifestyle. If her child's father really was an illegal
arms dealer and his import-export business was a conve-

nient—albeit highly profitable—front, she could never risk letting Burke know he was Seamus's father.

Perhaps taking this job had been a mistake, but she had thought it the best possible way to get to know Burke. And she'd been right.

In ten weeks, she had been at his side five days a week as well as several nights and even an occasional Saturday. Although their relationship remained a professional one, she knew that he was aware of her as a woman. This past week, when she had worked a couple of hours overtime, Burke had ordered dinner delivered to his office and they had enjoyed a lively chat and a delicious meal. But when he'd helped her on with her coat, just as she was leaving, an electrifying current passed between them. Burke had almost kissed her. He would have kissed her if she hadn't turned her head and stepped out of his reach. She had wanted that kiss—wanted it very much. But she didn't dare allow herself to become involved with Burke. She had to know everything there was to know about him before she risked bringing him into her private life and introducing him to her son.

His son, too, an aggravating inner voice reminded her.

Callie sipped her tea and returned her attention to the McMaster's file. Time passed quickly when she focused on business and forgot about personal matters.

With her teacup empty, scones polished off and three hours of solid work behind her, Callie leaned back in her chair and stretched. Barely stifling a yawn, she covered her mouth with her hand and closed her eyes. She found that five-minute rest breaks often refreshed her.

A knock sounded at her closed office door. Juliette opened the door just a crack and peeped at Callie. "Mr. Lonigan is in his office now, Callie. He looks knackered, as if he's been up all night."

So, Burke looked exhausted, did he? Worn out by another paramour, no doubt!

"He wants to see you immediately," Juliette said. "His exact words were, 'Tell her to come in here and be quick about it.' He asked me to order lunch and have it delivered. Seems you're in for a long afternoon."

"Tell Mr. Lonigan that I'll be in shortly."

As soon as Juliette closed the door, Callie lifted the telephone receiver and rang Seamus's minder. Before Burke demanded her undivided attention, she thought it best to make sure her son was all right.

Mrs. Goodhope answered quickly, her voice ever so pleasant. Callie asked about Seamus and was told that the lad was asleep.

"I might have to work late this evening, but if I do, I'll ask Enid to look after Seamus," Callie said.

"Enid isn't here," Mrs. Goodhope said. "But don't you worry none, dearie. I can stay over a couple of hours. Our Seamus is a good little nipper. And he's talked my ears off this morning."

"Has he?"

"Oh, yes. Can't understand anything he says, except wa-wa for water, bla for banana and of course, mama and dada."

"He's been saying dada?" Callie's heart sank. Seamus had been saying dada for quite some time now and he was smart enough, even at fourteen months, to associate the word with all males. He often heard other children in the park calling their fathers daddy. And on the children's programs she allowed him to watch, the little ones always had mamas and daddies. How long would it be before Seamus wanted to know where his dada was? A year? Two years?

"Give Seamus a kiss from his mother and tell him I'll

be home to read him a bedtime story and tuck him in
tonight.''

One of the stipulations she'd made perfectly clear concerning her position as Burke's PA was that unless she
had to travel with him, she would be home each night in
time to put her son to bed. Burke had agreed, had even
commended her on being a good parent, but he'd never
questioned her about her child or the fact that she was an
unmarried woman. She hadn't lied on her job application.
She would never lie about Seamus.

*And what will you do if Burke ever asks you about your
son's father?* her inner voice taunted.

If and when that time came, she would know what to
do, what to say. Wouldn't she?

Burke drank coffee from a Royal Doulton cup. He had
picked up the habit of drinking coffee from his military
stepfather, Gene Harmon, who had been a colonel in the
United States Army. Gene had introduced him to some
high-ranking government officials when, as a young college freshman, Burke had shown an interest in the FBI
and the CIA. Little had Gene known that those entrees
would bring Burke to the attention of an organization that
would mold and shape him into the man he was today.
As an operative for the top-secret SPEAR agency, his life
was only partially his own. Lonigan's Imports and Exports had been funded by SPEAR, and even though
Burke's expertise helped maintain the company's extraor-
dinary success, his job required far more from him than
simply acting the part of a rich London businessman.

When SPEAR had sent him to London fifteen years
ago, he'd understood why, of all the top young agents, he
had been the one chosen for this position. He was, after

all, London born, with a father who still resided there. No one would question why he'd returned to the U.K. to live.

SPEAR's head honcho, a man known only as Jonah, had telephoned Burke late last night, both using cellular phones that possessed special scrambling security frequencies. Burke had been up until dawn putting into action a preliminary plan for his latest assignment. Making use of all his contacts, he had sent out word that a certain arms shipment, very much wanted by a man named Simon, had by circuitous route made its way into Burke Lonigan's control. Being known the world over by certain people as an illegal arms dealer placed Burke in the perfect position to carry out his latest job for the agency.

Now, all he had to do was wait. Wait for the notorious Simon to make the next move. Every top SPEAR agent had been called into the war against this man—a traitor determined to bring down the entire agency. Burke and his comrades were united in an effort to eliminate the lethal threat Simon posed to the agency. But until it was time for Burke's next move in this strategic game with the enemy, it would be business as usual for Lonigan's Imports and Exports.

A soft knock sounded on the outer door. Burke lifted his head just in time to lock gazes with his personal assistant. The lovely, elusive and very-disturbing-to-a-man's-libido Callie Severin breezed into his office, a tentative smile on her face.

"Good morning, Mr. Lonigan. Or should I say good afternoon?" Callie sat in the chair across from Burke's desk, crossed her ankles and folded her hands in her lap.

Had he heard just a hint of censure in her voice? Burke wondered. What had her in a snit? "It is noon, isn't it?" He chuckled pleasantly. "Are you upset with me for some reason?"

"No, of course not. Why should I be? What you do in your personal life is none of my concern."

"My personal life?" He grinned broadly. "Ah, I see. You assume my tardiness is due to my having spent the night in some fair damsel's boudoir, making mad passionate love until dawn."

He liked the way Callie blushed. Few women blushed these days. But then she had the complexion for it. Pale and creamy, without a hint of a freckle despite her dark auburn hair and smoky gray eyes.

"As I said, it's none of my—"

"None of your concern." He finished her sentence.

She nodded.

"I've ordered in a meal for us," he told her. "I'm afraid I must impose on you to help me get an important dinner party planned and then I must ask an enormous favor of you."

"Doing my job is not imposing on me," she said. "And please, ask your favor."

"I'll need a hostess for this affair. Naturally I'll pay for your dress and provide the right jewelry and—"

"Isn't there someone else more suited than I am to serve as your hostess?" she asked, nervously rubbing her hands together. "I'm sure Lady Ashley or Mrs. Odum-Hyde would—"

"Lady Ashley is in Paris visiting her sister, and Mrs. Odum-Hyde has landed herself a Brussels diamond broker and is now wearing a ring the size of an apple."

Callie giggled. Burke liked her giggle, too. Girlish, yet throaty and seductive. If he were totally honest with himself, he'd have to admit that he liked everything about Callie. She was more than competent at her job. Actually she was the best PA he'd ever had.

But something about her bothered him. Not that he

didn't trust her. He did. Implicitly. Her background check had given him every reason to think highly of her—as a PA and as a person. A master's degree from the Owen Graduate School of Management at Vanderbilt University and glowing recommendations from her previous employers had been the reasons he'd hired her. That and the fact he had immediately liked her when he'd interviewed her. She'd been nervous, but charming.

She was a bright, hardworking young lady with an impeccable work record. He knew she was unmarried and yet was the mother of a small child. If he remembered correctly, the child was almost two. Although he had never questioned her about anything remotely personal, he couldn't help wondering about her child's father. What sort of man could have walked away from a woman such as Callie and deserted his own child?

Not much of a man, Burke thought.

I've never been with a real man, only a self-centered boy. The words echoed inside Burke's mind, but he had no idea who had said them or when. Had some woman he had bedded spoken those words? If so, why couldn't he remember the woman or the incident? Could it have been that night two years ago? He vaguely remembered drowning his sorrows at the Princess Inn after he'd been told his father had died and the family had turned him away. And occasionally, through the fog of his subconscious, he could almost make out the face of the woman who had gone home with him that night.

"Is something wrong?" Callie asked.

"What? No, nothing's wrong. Why do you ask?"

"You had a most peculiar look on your face, as if you were in pain."

"You can alleviate any pain I might be experiencing if you agree to act as my hostess next week."

"Of course, I'd be delighted to act as your hostess."

"Good, then that's settled."

When he rose from his desk chair, Callie stood. She was only a wisp of a girl—no, not a girl, he thought. A woman. She was twenty-seven and a mother. Hardly a girl. Size wise, she was just shy of being petite. Short, small-boned, fragile. Round in all the right places, with a slender waist. Not skinny like so many of the young women were today.

His stepfather had often told his mother, "I like a woman with some flesh on her bones." Mary Kate Lonigan Harmon had been a plump, black-haired beauty, who had passed her striking black Irish looks on to her only son and to her two daughters, Kathleen and Fiona, who had been fathered by Gene Harmon.

And like his stepfather, Burke preferred a woman with some flesh on her bones. Callie fit the description quite nicely. Although he had more sophisticated, more elegant ladies at his disposal, Burke fancied Callie and had since the first day she walked into his office. He couldn't understand why he was so attracted to her, more so than to any woman he'd ever met.

Knowing better than to mix business with pleasure, he had never become personally involved with any of his employees and usually listened to his common sense. Besides being too old for Callie—a good fifteen years too old—he was a man living a secret life as an agent for SPEAR, which existed in a shadow world of espionage and danger. He had spent most of his adult life in cloak-and-dagger activities, using his cover as an illegal arms dealer to the benefit of whatever the agency required at any given moment.

He couldn't deny that in many ways he lived the good life. A magnificent home in London. A flat in Paris. A villa in Italy. An apartment in New York. Lonigan's Imports and Exports afforded him the lifestyle most men only dreamed of having. Expensive clothes purchased on Savile Row. A chauffeured Rolls and a Porsche. And beautiful ladies vying for his attention.

But something was missing in his life. He felt that deep aloneness more and more with each passing year. Was that the reason he couldn't get Callie Severin out of his mind? Why he found himself fantasizing about her frequently? Did he think one specific woman could fill that void and give meaning to his life on a personal level?

"Mr. Lonigan, you aren't listening to me," Callie said. "Your mind seems to be a million miles away today. Are you sure there isn't something bothering you?"

Dragging his mind away from errant thoughts to concentrate on the present moment, Burke said, "No, no. Nothing's wrong. Just mentally going over the guest list I have in mind. I'll want you to handle the invitations. We'll keep this rather intimate. No more than fifty guests. All business associates."

Smiling warmly, Callie nodded. "Would you like for us to make the list now?" But what she actually wanted to ask was, *Which business associates? The import-export business or the illegal arms business?*

Really now, Callie, she cautioned herself. *You have no proof that Burke is involved in the illegal arms trade. But you also have no proof that he isn't,* her nagging inner voice warned. Remember the old American adage, "Where there's smoke, there's fire." Why would so many persistent rumors abound about Burke's notorious secret life if there was no truth to the rumors?

"Why don't you leave the list to me," he said. "You attend to the caterer, the florists, the musicians and the printer and whatever else needs attending to. I'll be sure you have the list ready later today, since this affair is to take place Saturday night.''

"Saturday night!" He certainly wasn't allowing them much time to coordinate an elegant party, even one for fifty. "Oh, all right. Now, I'll need a few details, so we should get started on the plans immediately.''

"That's one of the things I like about you, Callie. You're highly efficient.''

"One of the things you like about me? Are there more?'' Any fool could see that she was flirting with her boss. She'd been saying and doing things like that since the first day of her employment. And she couldn't seem to stop herself. As much as she tried to deny her feelings, she was as drawn to Burke now as she'd been that night Seamus had been conceived.

Burke scraped the underside of her chin with his curled index finger, tilting her head upward and aligning her gaze with his. "There are many, many more things I like about you, Callie. Too many to name. Everything from your sweet smile to your sharp mind.''

When Burke grinned at her, she went weak in the knees. This must stop, she told herself. She couldn't continue letting his sexy smiles and dreamy gazes make her heart flutter. And she couldn't allow her feelings for this man to get out of control. She had to remember that she couldn't do anything foolish because she had a child to think about. An affair with Burke, no matter how appealing, would affect not only her life, but Seamus's life, too.

She couldn't allow Burke Lonigan to know that he had a son—not until she was certain that he was the type of man she wanted to introduce into Seamus's life as his father.

"Now who's woolgathering, Ms. Severin?''

Callie stepped backward, putting some distance between them. "We really should get to work, Mr. Lonigan."

"Why won't you call me Burke?" he asked, walking toward her. "I've asked you several times to stop calling me Mr. Lonigan."

As he drew near, Callie eased back farther and farther until her hips encountered the paneled wall behind her. When Burke reached her, he spread his big hands, palms open, on either side of her. She sucked in her breath as he lowered his head. His warm breath mingled with hers. His lips hovered ever so close.

"I want to hear you say my name," he told her.

She had refused to use his given name because when they'd made love that night, she had sighed his name, whispered his name and cried out his name. Referring to him aloud by his name seemed far too intimate. The name on her lips would conjure up anew the heated passion they had shared.

"Come on," he cajoled, his lips almost touching hers. "Say my name."

"I—I prefer to call you Mr. Lonigan." She couldn't allow him to kiss her. A kiss would take their relationship out of the strictly business area and into something far more personal. She wasn't ready for that—not yet. Maybe not ever. She laughed nervously. "After all, as my employer, I owe you a certain amount of respect, don't you think?"

"I respect you, Callie." His lips brushed hers ever so lightly. "And I'm beginning to think of you as much more than just my assistant." Although only mere inches separated their bodies and he kept his hands in place on the wall, he lifted his head. "If I'm making unwanted advances, please, tell me now and I'll back off."

Tell him! her mind screamed. *Tell him that you aren't*

interested. "I—I…well, you see…I am interested. Oh, dear. What I mean is that I think you're terribly attractive and I find you…. But we shouldn't. We really shouldn't."

"Shouldn't what?" Burke's heated gaze forced her to confront him directly.

"Shouldn't become more than employer and employee," she said.

"Something tells me that we've already moved beyond that point, my darling."

She gasped. "Why did you call me that?"

"Call you what?"

"My darling. Why did you—"

"Because you look like a darling to me."

"Is that your standard endearment for your lady friends, Mr. Lonigan?"

"As a matter of fact, it isn't." Lifting one hand from the wall, he eased it behind her head and pulled her to him. "My favorite pet name for the ladies is *love.*"

"You've never called anyone else *my darling?*" Callie held her breath, waiting for his reply.

"Not that I recall."

"Oh, Burke…"

Then he kissed her.

Chapter 2

Burke's lips covered hers with a tender urgency. Soft, yet demanding. She closed her eyes and savored the feel of his mouth on hers. How many long, lonely nights had she dreamed of this moment? How often had she shuddered with desire at the memory of the hours she had spent in this man's bed? The rational part of her mind warned her of danger. Burke Lonigan was a man of mystery, perhaps a man with a deadly secret life. She shouldn't become involved in an affair with a man who might well be an international criminal.

As Burke deepened the kiss, his tongue seeking entrance, he leaned forward until his body pressed hers against the wall. A shiver of recognition rippled along her nerve endings. This is the way she had felt the night she had given herself to a stranger and he had given her his child.

Resist him, her mind screamed. *Don't do this!* But her body refused to listen. She melted against him, loving the feel of his hard chest pressed into her breasts and his lips devouring her. Of their own volition, her arms lifted up and around his neck, drawing him even closer. When her mouth opened invitingly, Burke delved within to explore and pillage. A gentle humming rose in her throat and turned into a soft moan when it reached her lips. He captured that moan with his mouth, diffusing it into fragments of minuscule sounds.

Callie's nipples peaked. Her femininity clenched and unclenched. Heaven help her, she wanted Burke. Now. This very moment. Here. Up against the wall.

Don't do this! You'll be sorry if you do! her conscience warned. *Don't forget you have more to consider than yourself—you have Seamus. Whatever happens between you and Burke will ultimately affect your child.*

Callie forced herself to end the kiss. When she did, Burke groaned and rubbed himself against her in a doesn't-this-feel-good way that elicited a whimper from her. In order to avoid him instigating another kiss, she turned her head, eased her arms from around his neck and gave him an insistent shove.

Burke lifted his head and stared into her beguiling gray eyes. He couldn't remember the last time he had ached so to make love to a woman. Since the first moment he'd seen Callie Severin, he'd been attracted to her, but he never mixed business with pleasure. A cardinal rule that he had just broken.

Undoubtedly she had the same reservations as he and that's why she'd ended their kiss. He knew damn well that she wanted him every bit as much as he wanted her. His instincts had been telling him for weeks now that Callie felt the same sexual tension that he did. But she was his employee, the best PA he'd ever had. An affair that might end on a sour note could wreck their perfect working relationship.

Burke lifted his hands from the wall and stepped backward, placing a couple of feet between them, but he kept his gaze riveted to hers. She smiled weakly. Burke swallowed hard. Just the sight of her did crazy things to his libido. Callie possessed a fragile beauty, an old-fashioned loveliness that drew him to her. Her curly auburn hair couldn't be confined within the neat bun at the base of her neck. Flyaway tendrils curled about her ears and forehead. Her flawless peaches-and-cream complexion complemented her dark fiery hair and her cool, storm-cloud gray eyes.

His gaze traveled to her lips and lingered. Her mouth, devoid of lipstick, was full and slightly swollen from his kiss. He wanted to kiss her again. Wanted to pull her into his arms. Wanted to strip her naked and make mad, passionate love to her.

Burke shut his eyes, hoping that by blotting out Callie's pretty face and luscious body, he could control his desire for her. *She's just a lovely lady, like so many others,* he told himself. *There's nothing special about her.*

Ah, but that wasn't true. There was something special about Callie. He couldn't explain what it was about her that made her unique, different from the other women he'd known.

But there had been one other woman—a woman he could barely remember—who haunted his dreams. A faceless memory. A soft voice. A sweet body. And a scent of flowers. His mind alternated between wanting to remember and trying to forget.

"Mr. Lonigan...Burke?"

His eyelids opened to reveal his brilliant blue eyes. Callie sucked in a deep breath. How was it possible that one night with this man had spoiled her for any other man? She compared every male that entered her life with the indomitable Burke Lonigan, a man of strength and courage and an unconquerable spirit. An expert lover. Passionate. Considerate. Powerful.

"If you keep looking at me that way, I'll have no choice but to kiss you again," he said.

"Oh, I—I didn't realize…I'm sorry that—" She averted her gaze.

Tucking his fist under her chin, he lifted her face so that her gaze met his. "We have a problem, don't we, Callie?"

"Yes, sir, we do."

He caressed her cheek with his fingertips, then withdrew his hand. "I've never become involved with an employee. Keeping my business life and my personal life separate has been a cardinal rule. One that I've never broken. Until you."

Callie's mouth rounded on a silent sigh. "I was engaged to my boss and the relationship turned out badly. I swore I wouldn't become involved with my employer ever again. And I haven't. Not until… What are we going to do about this?"

Burke wondered if her former employer was the father of her child. Had her boss been a married man as his own father had been? Had he refused to acknowledge his son as Burke's father had done?

"I'm not sure how we proceed," Burke admitted. "I've never been in this position before, so I have no frame of reference. But I do know one thing—I want us to become lovers."

Callie gasped audibly. "You do?"

"Yes, I do. And unless I miss my guess, you want the same thing, don't you?"

Tell him that he's wrong, that you do not want to have an affair, her inner voice cautioned. "I know your reputation with women, Mr.—er, Burke. You've had countless affairs. The women in your life are all very beautiful and rich and sophisticated. You've dated countesses and models and movie stars and—"

"And not one of them was as tempting as you are."

The heat of his stare warmed Callie to her bones. His desire was so strong that it vibrated with energy and curled about her like an invisible band.

"If—and I'm saying if—we become lovers and the affair ends, what then?" she asked. "There's no way I could continue working for you, seeing you every day and knowing you were dating other women."

"I realize an affair would be a complication in your life and in mine." Burke shrugged. "I suppose we have to decide which is more important to us—continuing our working relationship or becoming lovers. I risk losing the best PA I've ever had."

"I need this job," she told him. "I have a child to support, and positions like the one I have here at Lonigan's Imports and Exports aren't easy to come by, you know."

"If, when our affair ends, you choose not to remain with Lonigan's, then I'll make sure you find a job with equal pay and benefits."

"Mm."

"Callie, I never make promises that I can't keep," he said. "And who knows, by the time we grow tired of each other, we might find that we're perfectly capable of being only friends."

"Is that how all your affairs end?" she asked. "You and the lady become only friends?"

"Are you saying that you haven't remained friends with your ex-lovers?" Burke grinned broadly.

"I'm afraid my experience doesn't equal yours. I've had two lovers. My former fiancé, who is definitely not a friend, and my son's father."

"I don't mean to pry into your personal life, but I've wondered about your child's father. Does he take any responsibility for his son? Does he give you any type of financial support?"

Okay, you asked for this, Callie thought. *You deliberately put yourself in this position. So what are you going to do now? Lie?*

"No. He—he doesn't. But I've never asked anything of him. I'm afraid it's an awkward situation and I don't know how to—"

"Is he married?"

"Mercy, no! I'd never become involved with a married man."

"Then if he isn't married, why haven't you demanded that he take responsibility for his son? No man should father a child and then abandon him."

Callie understood Burke's vehement reaction because she knew his history with his biological father. Burke Lonigan was the type of man who would take responsibility. But she had never given him the opportunity. Dear God, how would he feel and what would he think of her when she told him. No, not when, if. *If* she told him.

"I'm not sure that my son's father is someone I want to be a part of his life. I'm uncertain about his ability to be a suitable father."

"You didn't tell this man about his child?" Burke's eyes narrowed into slits, his expression accusatory.

"As I said before, it's an awkward situation and rather complicated. I'd prefer not to discuss it anymore."

Burke grasped her shoulder. "Is this man the reason you're reluctant to have an affair with me? Did you love him? Did he hurt you terribly?"

How could she answer his questions? she wondered. Not with the complete truth. With lies, perhaps. Or maybe with half-truths. She wasn't ready to be totally honest with Burke Lonigan. Not yet. Maybe not ever.

"I can't talk about this with you."

Burke glared at her speculatively. "Are you still in love with your child's father? Is that the problem? You're sexually attracted to me, but you love another man?"

Callie couldn't restrain the bubble of laughter that formed in her throat and escaped from her lips. "I'm sorry."

"What's so funny?" he asked. "I fail to find any humor in what I asked you."

"Do you always find it so difficult to accept a refusal from a woman? Do you always cross-examine her and try to find hidden motives for her rejection?"

"A refusal?" His eyebrows lifted in mock surprise. "I don't think I heard you refuse."

"Burke, I like you. I like working with you. And yes, I'm very attracted to you. But I can't just have an affair with you. I'm not, as my father would say, footloose and fancy-free. I'm a mother and my first responsibility is to my child."

"Then you're saying that you don't want us to become lovers?"

We've already been lovers, she wanted to shout. *For one glorious, wildly passionate night, we were lovers.* "I'm saying that I do not want to rush into a relationship that might end up hurting me and creating problems in my life."

"Fair enough," he said. "You take all the time you

need, but you won't fault me if I do everything in my power to persuade you.''

"You really don't know how to take no for an answer, do you? What have you done in the past when a lady refused you?''

With a cocky grin, Burke shrugged. "It's never happened. Would you believe me if I told you that you're the first?''

Callie's giggle turned into amused laughter. She nodded. "Yes, I'd believe you. You're quite an irresistible man.''

He tugged her against him. With his lips only a hairbreadth away from hers, he said, "But you're resisting me and you know that I find that resistance challenging. You want me to work for my reward, don't you? That's what this is all about.''

Callie pulled away from him, walked past him and halted at the door. "Maybe you're right. The worthwhile things in life are usually more difficult to acquire.''

When Callie opened the door, Burke called after her, "Wait!''

She glanced over her shoulder. "Yes?''

"This isn't over. Not by a long shot.''

After a short walk from the High Street Kensington subway station, Callie rummaged in the side pocket of her shoulder bag to find her key. Her home was located on a quiet street with little traffic. After Seamus was born, Enid had insisted that they needed a larger place to live and had promptly acquired a three-bedroom town house in central London. Callie wasn't sure what she would have done without her cousin, who was not only her dearest friend, but also Seamus's godmother. During the months she hadn't worked after Seamus's birth, Enid had generously supported them.

"What's the good of having a sizable trust fund if I can't spend it on something as worthwhile as a new mother and her baby?" Enid had asked.

Just as Callie started to unlock the latch, the door swung open. Enid stood there with a screaming Seamus on her hip.

"Thank God, you didn't work late tonight." Enid thrust Seamus into Callie's arms. "He must be teething or something. He's been wailing like that for half an hour. I rubbed that nasty-tasting gel on his gums, but that didn't seem to help."

"What's the matter, sweetheart?" Callie dropped her bag onto the floor in the living room, which, along with the dining room and kitchen, comprised the ground floor of the three-story house. "Have you been a bad boy for Aunt Enid?"

"Oh, he's never a bad boy," Enid said. "He's just very loud when he's in a bad mood."

Holding Seamus on her hip, Callie eased one arm through the sleeve of her coat, switched her baby to the other hip and finished removing it. After draping the tan wool coat on the back of the sofa, she sat in the rocking chair by the door that opened onto the courtyard their home shared with four other houses. A fish pond and fountain decorated the terrace.

As Callie rocked, talking nonsensical words to Seamus, he quieted and cuddled against her. She smoothed the damp strands of his curly black hair, as silky and dark as his father's. When he gazed at her with Burke's brilliant blue eyes and said, "Hi, Mama," she kissed both of his cheeks and hugged him to her.

"I fed Seamus about an hour ago," Enid said. "He seemed hungry and ate quite well."

"Thank you." Callie glanced at her cousin and realized she was dressed for the evening. "Are you going out?"

"Some of us are going on a pub crawl," Enid said. "We're meeting at Riki Tik in about an hour. If the night turns out as I hope, I won't be home till morning." Enid's little-girl giggle was in direct contrast to her very adult body. "Some night you should ask Mrs. Goodhope to stay so you can go with us. It's time you—"

"Burke asked me to have an affair with him."

"What!"

"Today. He kissed me, told me that he wanted us to become lovers and—"

"Did he say that he remembers you?" With her eyes wide and her hands waving excitedly, Enid rushed toward Callie. "Does he or does he not admit that he remembers the night you two first met?"

Callie shook her head. "He doesn't remember. And I've told you that I truly believe he has no recollection of it. For some reason he has blotted out that night. Maybe because of the association with his father's death. Or maybe because he allowed a woman to see him weak and vulnerable."

"I have my doubts about his convenient loss of memory," Enid said. "If he was so plastered that he has no memory of that night, I don't see how he was able to perform. Heavy drinking usually leaves a man not fully charged."

"Maybe other men."

"Oh, please! You act as if no man on earth could compare to Burke Lonigan as a lover." Enid huffed. "And what did you have to compare him to anyway? Laurence Wynthrope! That nancy boy!"

"Laurence might not have been the most masculine man in the world, but he wasn't—"

"Admit it—he was a lousy lover and a real bastard. But at least he didn't leave you pregnant. Which is exactly what Burke Lonigan did."

Seamus let out a loud yelp. Callie soothed him with a few silly words that soon had him laughing. She cast a sharp glance at her cousin.

"We've discussed this a hundred times and I've told you repeatedly that what happened wasn't Burke's fault. It was mine. I was sober and—"

"So tell the man what he doesn't remember and introduce him to his son."

"I can't do that. Not yet."

"Oh, dear. Do you really think those rumors about him being an illegal arms dealer are true?" Enid asked.

"I have no proof one way or the other, but if Burke is a criminal, then how can I allow him to become a part of Seamus's life?"

"So, what did you say to him when he told you that he wanted to be your lover?"

"I said that I wasn't ready for an affair."

"And he accepted your refusal?"

"He accepted the fact that getting me into bed won't be as easy as he'd hoped it would be."

"At least not this time," Enid said smugly.

Burke poured himself a snifter of brandy, then sat in the leather wing chair in front of the roaring fire in the living room. He had lived the good life for many years now, enjoying the trappings of wealth, privilege and power afforded him by his disguise as a legitimate businessman.

Recently Burke had begun to wonder if this was all

there would ever be to his life. He was forty-two, no longer a young buck eager for danger and excitement. Occasionally the thought of retiring crossed his mind, but then he'd ask himself a critical question. Retire and do what? He had become a SPEAR agent shortly after college graduation and had never once regretted that decision. So why was he suddenly so disillusioned by it all?

Because he was getting old? Because he didn't want to wake up at fifty and still be alone? There were at least a dozen suitable women who would gladly become Mrs. Lonigan. But not a one of those lovely ladies was the woman with whom he wanted to spend the rest of his life.

What about Callie Severin? an inner voice asked.

"Yes, what about Callie Severin?" he repeated.

The chemistry between them was undeniable. Every time they were together, sparks ignited. And the fact that she was being coy with him, making him wait for her favors, made him want her all the more. But was her reluctance genuine or just a game she played to whet his appetite? If he made love to her, would that satisfy him?

Burke swirled the brandy in the glass, then lifted it to his lips and sipped the aged liquor. He closed his eyes and relaxed. Unbidden memories floated through his mind. A faceless woman. The musty scent of two bodies mating mingled with the heady scent of flowers. A lush, loving body lying beneath him. A sweet, soft voice whispering his name.

He became aroused. For nearly two years *she* had haunted him. He had tried—unsuccessfully—to forget her and their time together. He'd been a complete mess that night. Plastered. Self-pitying. Pathetic. And desperately in need of comfort.

She had comforted him. Loved him selflessly. Given herself to him with abandon. He could remember the feel of her, the scent of her and even the taste of her. But his mind refused to remember her face. Or her name, if he'd ever known her name.

He had never been as weak and vulnerable, as completely at the mercy of another human being as he had with her. He hated the thought that he'd opened himself up and put himself at risk with a stranger, a woman who could have easily ripped his tattered emotions to shreds. He had allowed her to see his weakness, to view the hurt and angry little boy inside him.

Somewhere out there was a woman who knew him inside and out. Every inch of his body. Every beat of his heart. Down to the very depths of his soul.

She had touched something within him and he within her. Two strangers giving solace. A man and a woman who had sought only physical union and had somehow connected on a deeper level.

Did he love this woman whose face he couldn't remember? Whose memory was a beautiful, faded blur? He didn't know. Wasn't sure. He doubted he could even begin to put into words the way he felt about her. But what did it matter? She had vanished from his life as quickly as she had entered it. And since that night, loneliness akin to none he'd ever known had been an integral part of his life.

His loneliness had nothing to do with being alone. He could easily surround himself with people and fill his empty bed with his pick of eager women. And he had, on occasion. But the loneliness remained. He wanted that gut-wrenching desolation to come to an end. And he thought Callie Severin might well be the woman to accomplish that deed. He knew one thing for certain—she was the only other woman who had ever tempted him beyond reason.

Chapter 3

Callie stood at Burke's side smiling warmly as they greeted his guests. Acting as his hostess for this affair reminded her of the occasions when she had served as her father's hostess at embassies around the world. Everyone had thought it adorable for Arthur Severin to allow his teenage daughter to play at being a grown-up. However, on none of those occasions had she worn a designer gown or diamonds worth a small fortune. Burke had insisted on the dress, a pale pink silk that clung to her curves yet somehow managed to achieve a demure appearance. She wore diamond and pearl studs in her ears and a diamond bracelet. A large diamond-and-pearl heart-shaped pendant rested just above the crevice between her breasts.

When a pause came in welcoming guests, Burke leaned down and whispered, "You look ravishing tonight. I like your hair worn down about your shoulders. I wish you'd wear it that way at the office." He chuckled. "On second thought, you'd better not."

"Thank you. I think."

Before their conversation could progress further, another couple arrived. While she smiled and made idle chit-chat, Callie's mind began to wander. During the past week, since Burke had suggested they become lovers and she had declined, he hadn't actively pursued her. And yet she had been aware of his subtle looks, his innuendos and the way he often allowed their hands to accidently touch. And at least once a day he somehow managed to maneuver her into a position where their bodies brushed against each other.

It had become quite obvious that Burke Lonigan wasn't going to take no for an answer. Callie glanced at him and her stomach tightened. *Look at him,* an inner voice said. *No woman in her right mind would reject that man.*

He was handsome, glamorous, ultra masculine and extremely wealthy. Wearing a stylish Armani tuxedo and an air of supreme confidence, he epitomized the sophisticated millionaire. Unless they knew his background, no one would ever think he'd been born the illegitimate son of an Irish housemaid. He wore the mantle of a gentleman easily, with only a hint of the wild Irishman lurking in his persona.

Every time she looked at Burke, she was reminded of how very much Seamus resembled him. No doubt, when her son was a grown man, he would be his father's double. The only feature he had inherited from her was his mouth—his smile was identical to hers.

Burke leaned close and whispered, "Woolgathering, my darling?"

"What?" She realized that she hadn't responded to a question Sir Thomas Warfield had asked. "I'm so sorry, Sir Thomas, I'm afraid I was thinking about my son."

"Didn't know you had a child, Ms. Severin." The

portly, middle-aged banker raised an eyebrow when he spoke.

Although having children out of wedlock was generally more accepted these days, there were still those who frowned on the practice. Sir Thomas and most of Burke's guests would be appalled that his PA was an unwed mother. She glanced at Burke, silently asking him how she should respond.

"The little nipper is almost two, isn't he?" Burke slipped his arm around her waist. "Callie's quite a devoted mother. I greatly admire women who are good mothers and put their children's needs first, don't you, Sir Thomas?"

Pasting a weak smile on his pale face, Sir Thomas nodded. "Indeed. Indeed."

Within five minutes all the guests had arrived and Burke took Callie's hand in his and led her into the living room. Before he released her, he brought her hand to his lips and kissed it.

"The circumstances of your son's birth are no one's business but yours," Burke told her. "You don't owe anyone an explanation, especially not a pompous jerk like Thomas Warfield."

"If he's such a pompous jerk, why did you invite him to your party?"

"This isn't a gathering of friends. You should know that. These people are business acquaintances. Nothing more."

"Yes, of course." In the two and a half months she had been working for Burke, she had come to realize that the man had hundreds of friendly acquaintances, but few friends. Actually, she wasn't sure he had any friends. And she found that odd. Burke's personality most certainly leaned more toward his being an extrovert than an introvert, yet he seemed adept at keeping others at arm's length.

"We should mix and mingle a bit," Burke suggested. "Just be your beautiful, charming self and you'll have them all eating out of the palm of your hand."

"I'm afraid you overestimate my charm."

Burke gazed into her eyes. Butterflies danced in her stomach.

"You *underestimate* your charm," he said.

Blushing profusely, Callie smiled. "You're such a flatterer, Mr. Lonigan."

Suddenly a tall, willowy blonde draped her arm through Burke's as she rubbed herself against him. Callie recognized the woman instantly. And why shouldn't she? Hayley Martin's picture graced the covers of countless magazines. She was this year's most popular supermodel. At six feet tall in her three-inch heels, the waif-thin beauty stood shoulder-to-shoulder with Burke.

"I'm a tad upset with you, love. You've been neglecting me terribly." Hayley pursed her collagen-fat lips into a sultry pout.

"I've been back from Paris for weeks now and you haven't rung me even once."

When Burke kissed Hayley's cheek, Callie felt an unpleasant stirring of jealousy in her heart. *Don't show him that you care,* her inner voice cautioned. *Don't let him see that you're upset.* After all, she was well aware of Burke's womanizing reputation. And she'd known about his affair with Hayley Martin. The affair had been the hot topic at Lonigan's Imports and Exports when Callie had first gone to work there.

Hayley glowered at Callie, but kept her syrupy-sweet smile firmly in place. "Burke, love, you should have let me know that you needed a hostess for tonight. I could have saved your little PA the trouble of working over-time." Leaning forward so that she stared Callie right in the eye, Hayley laughed. "He's such an ogre, isn't he? Must be simply awful being his assistant. If he's as de-manding at the office as he is in bed—"

"That's enough!" Burke grabbed Hayley's arm and jerked her against him. His eyes narrowed into angry slits.

"And he's so forceful." Hayley sighed. "I just love the beast in him."

"Please, excuse us." Burke glanced pleadingly at Callie, then dragged Hayley across the room and into a private corner.

"People shouldn't air their dirty laundry in public," an American voice said.

Callie turned her head to the left to see who had spoken to her and came face to face with a plump, platinum-haired woman of indiscernible age. "I beg your pardon?"

"Hayley Martin is an idiot," the woman said. "She's been furious with Burke ever since he ended their affair. She knows he's found himself another playmate, but she hasn't been able to discover the lady's identity. Not until tonight."

"If you're implying that I—"

"I'm not implying, dear girl, I'm stating a fact. Anyone with eyes can plainly see that Burke's taken with you. What is it that the Brits say? Oh, yes, he fancies you."

"I'm afraid you're mistaken. I'm Mr. Lonigan's PA, not his latest paramour."

"Perhaps I should introduce myself. I'm Marilyn Far-ris."

Callie gulped. "*The* Marilyn Farris?"

"I plead guilty."

"The gown I'm wearing tonight is one of your de-signs."

Marilyn smiled, revealing a set of perfect teeth, snow-white against her red lips. "When Burke called to order something special for you, I knew instantly that you were more than his assistant. He's never purchased clothes for any of his women. You're the first."

Callie's face flushed with warmth. "I—I don't know what to say."

"You're different. I'll give you that. Pretty, but not glamorous. And you're not a model or an actress or a countess." Marilyn playfully slapped Callie on the arm. "He's a rogue, you know. But a devastatingly charming one. You mustn't let him break your heart."

"I can assure you that I know about Mr. Lonigan's reputation and I have no intention of—"

"You could be the one," Marilyn said, speaking as if she hadn't interrupted.

"The one what?"

"The one who brings the big man to his knees, of course." Marilyn inspected Callie from head to toe. "You're not his type at all, but it's obvious he's smitten. I don't think I've ever seen him being so—" Marilyn waved her hand in the air "—so obvious. Usually the women chase him, but this time, he's the one doing the chasing, isn't he?"

"Ms. Farris, I—"

"I think I'll start on your trousseau. I'm sure Burke will want me to dress you for the wedding and the honeymoon." Marilyn stepped back a couple of feet and inspected Callie again, more thoroughly this time. "Classic, but understated. Burke was right in his assessment. No frills and certainly nothing radical and funky."

"Ms. Farris, I assure you that you've misunderstood—"

Burke sauntered beside Callie and draped his arm

around her waist. "What is it that Marilyn has misunderstood?"

"Did you take out the trash, darling?" Marilyn's
Cheshire cat grin displayed a set of soft dimples in her
cheeks.

"Leland took care of it," Burke said, referring to his
chauffeur-butler.

"Good. Good. And as for any misunderstanding—there
is none. I was telling Ms. Severin how much I'd like to
design some other clothes for her. She's absolutely lovely,
Burke. A real little gem."

"Designing some more things for Callie sounds like an
excellent idea," Burke agreed.

Callie jerked free, said, "Pardon me," and fled. She
had no intention of standing there listening to Burke and
Marilyn Farris discuss her as if she were Burke's mistress.
Was that what all these people thought? she wondered.
That he had simply gone from Hayley Martin's bed to
hers?

Callie rushed upstairs, wanting to find her purse and
her wrap so she could leave. She was hardly dressed to
ride on the tube, but she had no intention of wasting
money on a taxi. When Leland had picked her up earlier
this evening, Burke had met her on the staircase and taken
her purse and wrap to his bedroom.

Her hand hovered over the doorknob. She wasn't sure
she was prepared to go inside and face the past. She had
spent several fantasy hours in Burke's bedroom, hours she
had never been able to forget. Garnering her courage, she
opened the door and walked inside. Two bedside lamps
burned brightly, illuminating the elegant room. There on
the bed—the huge four-poster antique—lay her wrap and
her purse. She stood staring at the bed as memories invaded her thoughts.

Hot, wanton kisses. Lingering touches that had brought her to the brink of ecstasy again and again. Earthy, erotic words whispered in the dark. Perspiration-dampened bodies coming together in unbearable pleasure.

A child conceived in the throes of passion.

"You'll create more of a stir by leaving abruptly than you will if you stay," Burke said from where he hovered in the doorway.

Simultaneously gasping and whirling, Callie gazed at Burke, praying that her expression didn't reveal any of her thoughts. Delicious, sexual thoughts about him. "Everyone here thinks I'm your latest mistress."

Burke grinned, and she wanted to slap that cocky smile off his face. What gave a man that kind of self-confidence? she wondered. He was so damn sure of himself and his ability to get whatever he wanted.

"Who told you…ah, Marilyn Farris, the old busybody. Well, she was snooping, seeing if you'd reveal your innermost thoughts and feelings to her."

"Do you know what she said to me?"

"No, but do tell me."

"She said that she was going to start work on my trousseau. Have you ever heard anything so ridiculous?"

"Mm." Burke rubbed his chin. "Then she assumes you're my fiancée and not my mistress. And we know both assumptions are incorrect, don't we?"

"Yes, we do. And I'd very much like all those people down there to know—"

"Would you like me to make an announcement? Ladies and gentleman, Callie Severin is not my fiancée and she's not my mistress, despite my desire for us to become lovers. How does that sound?"

"It sounds ridiculous!"

"Hm, I suppose you're right." Burke entered the room,

sashaying leisurely toward Callie. "Come back down-stairs and follow through with your duties as my hostess. You don't really care what these people think. You're upset with me for putting you in this position. And for that I do apologize. I must admit that I knew certain guests would speculate about our relationship."

"And you don't care, do you?" Callie debated whether to leave or stay. Burke was right. If she left people were bound to think the worst. A lovers' quarrel. A jealous rage over Hayley Martin's appearance at the party.

Before Callie could reply, Burke's cellular phone rang. He retrieved the small, compact telephone from his inside coat pocket, flipped the lid and placed the receiver to his ear.

"Lonigan here."

Callie noticed Burke's frown and his hushed tone as he spoke. Who had called him? she wondered. Some woman? Or an unsavory business associate?

Burke held the phone away from his ear as he spoke to her. "Callie, please go back downstairs and see to my guests. This is a very important call and I need to take it in private."

She nodded and headed for the door. He called her name. She stopped and glanced over her shoulder.

"When the party is over, I'll personally see you home."

"That isn't necessary. You can get me a cab or just have Leland drive me to Kensington."

"No arguments. I'll see you home myself."

She slipped out of the room, closing the door behind her. But instead of going downstairs immediately, she leaned her head against the door and listened, hoping she could overhear Burke's part of the conversation. If Burke Lonigan was involved in the illegal arms trade, she had a

right to know, didn't she? She needed to find out everything she could about her child's father before she made
a decision that would affect Seamus for the rest of his
life.

The music, laughter and conversations from below
drifted up to the second story, creating a distraction. She
pressed her ear closer to the door. She heard the muffled
sound of Burke's voice, but couldn't make out what he
was saying.

Then she heard Burke say "Jonah" and a few minutes
later she thought he said something about "Russian-
made" and "waiting for him to contact me." If only the
door wasn't so thick. If only the noise from downstairs
wasn't so loud.

"May I help you, Ms. Severin?" a male voice asked.

Callie gasped and jumped away from the door. Leland
Perkins looked down his sharp nose at her, an expression
of suspicion on his craggy face. How had such a big man
crept up on her so silently? Burke's chauffeur-butler stood
at least six-two and had the build of a wrestler. Quite often
she had wondered if Leland's job description shouldn't be
amended to chauffeur, butler and bodyguard.

"No, thank you, Leland." Callie tried to keep her ner-
vousness out of her voice. "Mr. Lonigan is on the telephone—his cellular phone—and I was just going back
downstairs."

"Yes, ma'am." Leland almost clicked his heels as he
stood at attention.

Callie would bet money that Leland Perkins had some
type of military background. His stance, appearance and
demeanor screamed soldier. She wished she knew more
about Leland and his relationship with Burke. If Burke
really was involved in illegal dealings, that would explain
why he needed a bodyguard.

Stop assuming the worst, that irritating inner voice scolded. *As a multimillionaire businessman, Burke has every reason to need a bodyguard.* Wealthy people were routinely kidnapped, weren't they? And Burke Lonigan was a well-known figure in and around London.

Callie resumed her duties as hostess, but deliberately avoided Marilyn Farris during the next half-hour. She'd begun worrying about Burke when he finally put in an appearance. Their gazes met and locked as he smiled at her from across the room.

You could ask him about the rumors, she told herself. *Tell him that you've heard his import and export business is just a front for his illegal arms deals. Oh, yes, by all means ask the man if he's a criminal. He'll either laugh in your face or fire you on the spot. Don't do anything stupid. Bide your time and sooner or later you'll discover the truth about Seamus's father. But in the meantime, you have to protect yourself and your son. Burke mustn't learn the truth. Not yet. Maybe not ever.*

Burke asked Leland to wait, so Callie assumed Burke would walk her to the door, say good-night and leave. A fine for parking on a prohibited street, which meant almost every street in central London, was the equivalent of forty-five U.S. dollars. But to a man as wealthy as Burke that would be pocket change.

When they reached the front door, Callie turned, smiled and said, "Thank you for seeing me home."

"Aren't you going to invite me in for a drink?" Burke asked teasingly.

"It's quite late and I'm sure Enid is already asleep and—"

The door swung open. There stood Enid in jeans and an oversize shirt, with her waist-length sable hair hanging over her shoulder in a loose ponytail. "Come on in. It's freezing out there."

At that precise moment, Callie could have strangled her cousin. She knew exactly what Enid was doing—getting a closer look at Burke Lonigan. She wanted to check him out.

When the three of them entered, Burke closed the door behind them and quickly scanned the interior.

"Here, let me have your coat, Mr. Lonigan." Enid practically ripped the wool overcoat off his back. "I've put on the kettle, so we can have tea. Please, go on into the living room and make yourself at home."

"Thank you, Ms...."

"Ludlow, but you must call me Enid. I'm Callie's cousin."

After Burke bestowed his most devastating smile on Enid and wandered into the living room, Callie grabbed Enid and dragged her into the corner.

"What do you think you're doing?" Callie demanded.

"My God, you didn't tell me he was *that* handsome," Enid said. "How can you keep your hands off him? If I'd ever had him in my bed, I'd never have let him out."

"Will you please lower your voice!"

"Why are you so nervous? Seamus has been sleeping for the past three hours. He's well hidden upstairs in his bed, so—"

"I didn't want Burke to come inside with me. And he wouldn't have if you hadn't opened the door on us."

"I couldn't get a proper look at him through the window," Enid admitted. "You didn't exaggerate when you said how much Seamus resembles his father. If he ever sees Seamus, he'll know the truth immediately."

"He's not going to see Seamus unless I decide to tell him that he's Seamus's father."

"And how long is it going to take you to decide what to do?"

"I'm not sure. As long as it takes for me to be certain that Burke will be a good father to his son. And whether or not he's some sort of criminal—"

"Ladies, is there a problem?" Burke called from the living room.

Callie shed her coat, flung it at Enid and said, "Sorry. Enid had a bit of news about a friend." She glowered at her cousin and whispered, "Get that tea ready, and as soon as Burke's had a cup, he's leaving. And don't you dare try to prolong his visit!"

The moment Callie entered the living room she noticed Seamus's framed picture atop the mantel. Her heartbeat accelerated. *Oh, no! Please don't let Burke see that photograph.* Callie waltzed in, a wide smile on her face. "Won't you sit down?"

Burke sat on the sofa and glanced around the room. "This is a very nice place. Rather expensive, isn't it?"

"Oh, yes, quite. Actually, it's Enid's house. She inherited a rather sizable trust fund." Callie maneuvered her way behind the sofa and to the mantel. She ran her hand across the smooth wooden surface and in the process eased the framed photograph facedown. "I want to thank you again. Despite our little disagreement, I enjoyed acting as your hostess. And the dress and jewelry—oh, my." Callie's hand covered the heart-shaped pendant. "I should have removed these and given them back to you before we left your house. I simply forgot."

"Keep them," Burke said.

Callie gasped and shook her head.

"Keep them until Monday." He revised his statement. "You can bring them with you when you come to work."

"Oh, but what if I were to lose them or what if they were stolen or—"

"They're insured," he told her. "Good lord, woman, will you sit down? You're fluttering around like a crazed butterfly. What ever is the matter with you?"

A nervous smile curved her mouth in an upward slant. Nervously, she licked her bottom lip, then realized Burke was watching her intensely. The desire in his eyes was unmistakable.

"Tea's ready." Enid entered the living room, a silver serving tray in her hands.

At that precise moment a loud, piercing wail alerted one and all that Seamus was awake and quite unhappy. Callie froze to the spot. No, please, God, no!

"I'll get him," Enid said.

"No!"

Both Enid and Burke stared quizzically at Callie.

"I'll see about him. You two go ahead and have your tea." Callie halted as she exited the room, looked directly at Enid and said, "Don't bore Mr. Lonigan with any family stories."

Enid smiled wickedly. Callie's heart sank. Seamus's sweet little voice called to her. "Mama...Mama..."

The moment Callie disappeared up the stairs, her cousin set the silver tray on the antique serving cart by the window. "Milk? Sugar? Lemon?"

"No, thank you," Burke replied.

He studied Callie's tall, rawboned cousin. The girl looked as if she belonged in the country. Riding horses. Frolicking with the dogs. She was a big, hard-looking female. Not unattractive, but definitely no beauty. Her dark brown eyes studied him as she handed him his cup of tea.

"I've been accused of being blunt, Mr. Lonigan," Enid said. "And with good cause. So let me get right to it."

"By all means." Burke sipped the tea, which was quite good.

"Callie has had her heart broken twice and I don't want to see it happen again." Enid poured herself a cup of tea, added sugar and then sat in the chair directly across from the sofa. "There have been only two men in her life, her fiancé and Se—her son's father. She isn't the type for affairs. If that's all you're planning to offer her, then my advice to you is to bug off."

"Callie's a grown woman," Burke said. "Don't you think she's capable of making her own decisions?"

"As a general rule." Enid nodded. "But with you, Mr. Rich and Sophisticated, she's out of her league. You know it and I know it. There are other pretty little fish in the sea, so why bother reeling in a sweet mermaid who deserves marriage and a happily ever after?"

"You care about Callie a great deal, don't you?"

"She's the closest thing I have to a sister. She was an only child and so was I." Enid set her cup on the arm of her chair, leaned forward and focused her gaze on Burke. "What Callie needs is a good man—for herself and for her child. You really aren't husband and father material, are you, Mr. Lonigan?"

Burke smiled sadly. Cousin Enid had him dead to right. What could he say? He couldn't deny her accusation. "Quite right. I'd probably make a lousy husband and I don't know the first thing about children."

But I could learn, the loneliness in his soul cried. *With the right woman, I could be faithful. And even though I've never been around children, I'd be willing to try my best to get along with Callie's son.*

"If you have any real feelings for Callie, do the right

thing and don't pursue her. You must know how easily you could break her heart."

"I would never force—"

Enid's laugher was like the woman herself—large, robust and earthy. "Seduction is just a gentle form of force. And you could easily seduce her. I'm asking you—no, I'm telling you to leave—" Enid paused when she and Burke heard Callie's footsteps coming down the staircase.

"I changed his nappy and sang him a song and he went back to sleep instantly," Callie said.

Burke rose to his feet. "I should be going."

"Oh?" Callie glanced from Burke to Enid.

"It's late and Leland is waiting and... Thank you, Callie, for your assistance tonight." He walked over to meet her where she stood in the foyer.

She went with him, opened the front door and waited in the doorway when he crossed the threshold. He looked into her expressive gray eyes and saw confusion.

He stroked her cheek with the back of his hand. "I'll see you at the office Monday."

"Yes. Of course."

"Thank you again."

"You're welcome."

Damn! He knew that Enid was right. Despite the fact that she was a twenty-seven-year-old unwed mother, Callie *was* an innocent. And as a general rule, he didn't dally with innocents. He'd been wrong to pursue a personal relationship with a girl who wanted a husband for herself and a father for her son. He knew better than to seduce women who confused sex with love. Those types, despite what they said, always expected more—a rose-covered cottage and a picket fence. Burke Lonigan really wasn't the home and hearth type and he, better than anyone, knew that fact. At least he should.

But God, how he wanted Callie! Without thought of the consequences, he reached out and pulled her into his arms. Before she had time to protest, he covered her lips with his. He quickly deepened and intensified the kiss, consuming her with his desire. When he finally ended the sensuous plundering and lifted his lips from hers, Callie was breathless. She stared at him, adoration in her eyes. *Don't look at me that way,* he wanted to tell her, but remained silent. She didn't realize it, but this had been their goodbye kiss.

"Good night, Callie."

"Good night."

She stood in the doorway and watched him until he reached the Rolls. Leland opened the back door for him. When Burke got in, he glanced at the house. Callie waved and smiled. He nodded.

When Leland slid behind the wheel, Burke said, "Drive over to Notting Hill."

"Sir?"

"You know where Ms. Martin's flat is."

"Are you sure you want to—"

"What I want and what I'm going to do are two different things, Leland. Now shut the hell up and drive!"

Chapter 4

Despite the chill in the air, Callie strolled with Seamus through Hyde Park as she did almost every Sunday when it wasn't raining. From her home she could walk entirely in the park to Oxford Street. The central park of London buzzed with activity. People milled about, walking, bicycling and roller-skating. In warmer weather residents often sunbathed and picnicked or enjoyed boating and fishing. Like a breath of country air in the middle of the city, the park provided a bucolic setting. Trees, flowers, lakes and wildlife. And Callie occasionally stopped at one of the cafés for tea and biscuits.

Today's outing had begun like any other, only with the early November weather, she had bundled up Seamus and worn her heavier coat. But she liked the cool, crisp air that reddened her cheeks and invigorated her spirit. After the odd way her evening with Burke had ended last night, she certainly needed the fresh air to clear her head. She'd slept fitfully after a brief argument with Enid. Her cousin had gone beyond the bounds of friendship and family ties when she'd warned Burke off.

Whether or not she had an affair with her employer and whether or not she ever chose to tell him that he was Seamus's father was her decision to make, not Enid's. Oh, she understood why Enid had rushed in, as she was prone to do, and had persuaded Burke that he was dealing with a fragile flower whose heart could easily be broken. Her cousin had always played her protector. Perhaps because Enid was four years older and perhaps because she considered herself more worldly-wise and experienced when it came to love affairs.

Enid had slept late this morning and when Callie and Seamus returned from church, she was gone. She'd left a succinct note. *Off to Bristol with Freddy and Kipp. Will ring you midweek.* So like Enid to run away to avoid confrontation!

A sharp wind swirled leaves across the pavement and swayed the tree branches. Callie stopped, tightened the scarf around her neck and checked the blanket wrapped around Seamus. She smiled warmly and gave her sleeping toddler a kiss on the check.

Suddenly she felt it again—that odd sensation someone was watching her. When she'd left home, she had sensed someone was following her, but after scanning the area and seeing no one suspicious, she'd felt silly. Who would be following her?

But there it was again—that niggling worry, that unsubstantiated concern. Trying to be very subtle in her perusal of the people around her, Callie kept her smile in place and gave a friendly nod to another young mother she often saw in the park. Several of the faces were familiar. Men, women and children she'd seen on numerous occasions. None of the strangers appeared threatening. And no one seemed unusually interested in her.

What's the matter with you? an inner voice scolded. *You're imagining things. You're perfectly safe. No one intends to harm you or Seamus. Relax and enjoy this beautiful afternoon.*

He rubbed the back of his hand across the scars on his forehead and down across the heavy beard that covered his face. He stayed a good distance away from Callie Severin and her child, but remained close enough to study her. She was a pretty little thing, nothing like the type of woman he thought a man such as Burke Lonigan would choose for a mistress. But word had it that Lonigan's new PA was more than an employee. All of London knew that she'd served as his hostess last night, and that fact was a telltale sign of their relationship. It was a known fact that usually Lonigan's latest paramour served as his hostess. But if this sweet young thing was indeed Lonigan's latest lover, why had he paid a late-night visit to Hayley Martin?

Whenever he did business with a man, he made sure he learned everything possible about that man. But with someone as complicated and mysterious as Burke Lonigan, he'd found unearthing more than superficial information difficult.

It always paid to be careful. And knowing a man's weaknesses gave him an edge that could prove useful. Was Callie Severin one of Lonigan's weaknesses? Perhaps his only weakness? Or was she nothing more than a temporary dalliance, easily replaced?

He had arrived in London three days ago, but he hadn't rushed into a meeting with Lonigan, despite his desire to strike a deal with the notorious arms dealer. Word was that Lonigan had in his possession the shipment of weapons that had disappeared in the Sinai—his weapons! And he intended to have what was his, no matter what.

For the right price, Lonigan would make a deal. His reputation as a shrewd businessman with unrivaled contacts in the underground made Lonigan dangerous. That's why providing himself with an insurance policy was the smart thing to do before they met face-to-face. Knowledge was power. And he suspected that in brokering a deal with Lonigan, he'd need all the power he could acquire.

He knew where Callie Severin lived. Knew that her roommate had left, with suitcase in hand, around noon. And he knew that Ms. Severin had a child she seemed to dote on. What he didn't know was what this woman and child meant to Burke Lonigan. Everything? Or nothing? He intended to find out.

Burke lounged in the library, a copy of Dick Francis's latest novel lying open, spine up, on the arm of the tan leather chair in which he reclined. After a restless night, he'd finally fallen asleep around dawn, then stayed in bed until noon. After leaving Callie abruptly last night, he'd begun having second thoughts before he reached Hayley's flat in Notting Hill. Why should he allow Enid's warnings about breaking Callie's heart to stop him from pursuing an affair? *Because Callie isn't like the other women you've known,* his conscience reminded him. *You realized that fact from the very beginning and chose to ignore it. She's a sweet young woman who was abandoned by her child's father, as your own mother was abandoned.* Callie needed a man like Gene Harmon, a man willing to marry her and be a father to another man's son. But he wasn't that man. Or was he?

Burke stood and stretched, then pulled down his cashmere sweater, which had ridden above his waist. He hated

Sunday afternoons alone. The house was too quiet. On days like today, the walls seemed to close in on him. Even with Leland about somewhere, probably puttering in his herb garden in the tiny greenhouse out back, Burke felt the loneliness of his solitary life more today than ever before. And he could blame Callie Severin for his morose attitude.

Damn the woman! Damn her for making him want her. Damn her for refusing him. And damn her for being the type of girl who wanted to get married.

Stalking about the library like a caged animal, Burke forked his fingers through his hair and cursed. What the hell was wrong with him? More important—what had been wrong with him late last night when he'd paid that impromptu visit to Hayley Martin? She'd been surprised to see him and had tried to slam the door in his face. But once he'd apologized for his earlier behavior, she'd welcomed him with open arms.

"That little bit of sweetness turned out to be a real bore, didn't she, love?" Hayley had taunted. "You found out rather quickly that she couldn't satisfy you the way I can."

He had kissed Hayley with all the passion he felt for Callie. One woman was as good as another, he'd told himself. If you can't have the one you want, want the one you can have.

But he hadn't been able to go through with it and had called a halt to their encounter. Hayley hadn't been the woman he wanted and he couldn't bring himself to use her. In retrospect he asked himself if he'd walked away because of Callie. He wasn't sure. Maybe. But then again, although Callie had been the woman on his mind when he'd arrived at Hayley's, she hadn't been the one he'd been thinking of when he'd pushed Hayley away.

You fool! You bloody fool! he berated himself. *You were thinking about her, weren't you?* The mysterious woman whose face he couldn't remember. The loving, caring woman who had held him in her arms and comforted him on the most miserable night of his life. With Hayley offering herself to him, it had been *her* body he'd felt, *her* scent he'd smelled, *her* taste on his lips.

God help him, he was in love with an illusion!

In love? Hell, he wasn't in love with anyone. Not Callie. And not his mystery lady. Enamored. Infatuated. Bewitched. Yes, most definitely. But not in love.

Enamored with Callie? Or with the other one? Infatuated by Callie's luscious body? Or infatuated by a vague memory of perfection? Bewitched by Callie's sweetness? Or bewitched by a phantom with whom he'd shared indescribable sexual pleasure?

A knock on the door snatched Burke from his fanciful thoughts. Thank God something had distracted him. More thinking like that and he was apt to go around the bend.

"Yes?"

The door opened; Leland Perkins stood at the threshold. "Would you care for afternoon tea, sir?"

"No, thank you, Leland," Burke replied. "But please, go ahead and have your tea. I might go out for a bit. Take myself a walk and clear the cobwebs from my mind."

"Given the present situation, sir, wouldn't it be advisable for me to accompany you?"

Burke grinned. "The present situation being that somewhere out there a man known only as Simon is being fed information about a certain shipment of Russian-made weapons that miraculously are now in my possession?"

"Yes, sir."

Burke walked toward the door, stopping as he approached his trusted companion and fellow SPEAR agent.

"Don't you think I'm capable of taking care of myself?" Burke asked, halfway joking.

"I know you are, sir. But it is my duty to act as your bodyguard. Your position within the organization is essential. I am expendable. You are not."

"Don't kid yourself, Leland. We're all expendable. Even the great Jonah."

"Perhaps. What I should have said is that I would be easily replaced, whereas you would not."

Burke clamped his hand on Leland's thick shoulder. "Leland, you're much more valuable than you'll ever realize. Enjoy your tea. If I decide to take a walk, I'm sure I'll be quite safe."

"Very well, sir."

When Leland turned to leave, Burke again squeezed his shoulder before releasing him. "Do you ever think about retiring from the agency?"

"No, sir."

"You're older than I am," Burke said. "Are you telling me that thoughts of retiring have never crossed your mind?"

"Of course, I've considered the possibility," Leland admitted. "But what would I do with my life? I've been with SPEAR since I was a lad of twenty-two. A good twenty-five years. I'm an old bachelor, no children and no family to speak of, except a few distant cousins in York."

"Mm. We've both spent our lives within SPEAR's circle, haven't we, old man? But there are times when I... Well, I suppose I'm not cut out to be a family man, am I?"

"I wouldn't know, sir. Could it be that Ms. Severin and her child have put such thoughts in your head?"

Laughing heartily, Burke patted Leland on the back. "I'm afraid I'm suffering from a case of unrequited lust."

"Yes, sir. I thought as much."

Burke's cellular phone rang. He spied the compact instrument where he'd tossed it on the oak side table by his chair.

"Even on a Sunday afternoon!" Burke took his time retrieving the phone.

The moment he answered, a familiar voice said, "Someone is asking a lot of questions about you. About your business and about your private life."

"Simon?"

"That's our guess," Jonah said. "And if it is Simon, then he's preparing to make contact. Today. Tomorrow. We can't be certain when, but it will be soon. He's anxious to get his hands on that shipment of weapons."

"I'll be ready for him, whenever he sets up a meeting."

"Don't be surprised if he doesn't call first. He's known for doing the unexpected."

"I'll keep that in mind."

"There's something else you should keep in mind," Jonah told him.

"What's that?"

"Simon will use whatever means necessary to get the upper hand. And that could mean danger to anyone who gets in his way. I understand there's a new lady in your life."

"There's always a new lady in my life," Burke said.

"If we know about Callie Severin, then there's a good chance that Simon knows about her."

"Possibly," Burke said. "But Leland doesn't report my every move to Simon the way he does to you."

"Touché. But don't underestimate the enemy."

"I never have."

* * *

Burke hadn't come into the office at all Monday. And he hadn't bothered ringing her or even sending a message through Juliette. The staff had speculated about what he was doing, and the consensus seemed to be that he was with some new lady friend.

Callie had hated the sympathetic glances and whispered comments behind her back. She realized they were all talking about her and the fact she had served as Burke's hostess on Saturday night, but had apparently been dumped shortly thereafter. It seemed that everyone—except she—knew that being Burke Lonigan's hostess meant that you were his latest lover. How could she have been so stupid?

She glanced at the necklace, bracelet and earrings cupped in her hand. She'd brought them with her yesterday to return to Burke, then stuffed them in her purse and taken them home with her. And here it was after ten-thirty on Tuesday and her employer hadn't put in an appearance.

Callie summoned Juliette, who stuck her head in and asked, "Something you need, Callie?"

"Yes." She laid the jewelry atop her desk. "I'm going to put these items in the company safe and I need you to witness the transaction."

"Certainly."

Callie picked up the jewelry, exited her office and entered Burke's. Juliette followed directly behind her. Lonigan's Imports and Exports had two safes in the office suites. Both were in Burke's private office. One was his personal safe and the other was the company safe. She and several of the executive officers had the combination to the company safe. Only Mr. Lonigan knew the combination to his personal safe.

"They're quite lovely, aren't they?" Juliette commented as she gazed at the jewelry while Callie worked the combination to the safe.

"Yes, they're beautiful."

"I imagine they looked splendid on you Saturday night." Juliette gasped as if she'd suddenly realized that she had broached a taboo subject. "I'm sorry, Callie, I forgot—"

"It's quite all right. Really." The lock clicked. Callie opened the safe's door, deposited the jewelry inside and promptly shut the door.

"You won't be leaving the company, will you?" Juliette asked.

"Of course not. Why should I?"

"No reason. But some of us were wondering…that is, we weren't gossiping, just being curious. Won't you find it difficult to work with Mr. Lonigan after…well, after what happened?"

"What do you and the others think happened?" Callie asked.

"Oh, dear, I'm afraid I've upset you. Pardon me for—"

"Mr. Lonigan and I have not had an affair. We are not lovers."

"You aren't?"

"No. I can assure you that I didn't know it was customary for his mistress to host his parties. If I'd known, I would have declined his invitation."

"Dear me." Juliette sighed. "What an embarrassment for you."

"Yes, indeed, but one can easily survive embarrassment, can't one?" Tilting her chin, Callie held her head high. "Now, let's get back to work. It seems Mr. Lonigan isn't going to favor us with his presence again today, so—"

"What's this about my not favoring you with my presence today?" Burke asked as he entered his private office.

Juliette jumped and squealed with shock. Callie gasped silently. Burke blew into the office like a whirlwind, apparently energized and enthusiastic. Perfectly attired in his charcoal gray pinstripe suit, pale gray shirt and crimson silk tie, he smiled warmly at Juliette.

"I'd like my coffee in ten minutes," he told her, then turned to Callie, effectively dismissing the secretary. "I apologize for not contacting you yesterday and leaving you to handle everything around here, but I had a personal situation that needed my immediate attention."

"You don't owe me an explanation, Mr. Lonigan."

Callie made a move to walk around Burke so she could exit his office, but he reached out and placed a restraining hand on her arm.

"We need to talk, don't we, Callie?"

"That's not necessary."

"Ah, but I think it is." He ran his hand down her arm and manacled her wrist. "I'm not very good at dealing with messy personal situations."

"Was the personal emergency you had to handle yesterday a messy one?" she asked sarcastically.

He tugged on her wrist, encouraging her to follow him to the sofa. When she refused to look at him, he jerked her down on the sofa as he sat. "Yesterday's problem consisted of an unpleasant meeting with my half brother and two half sisters. We've been trying to come to an agreement about my late father's estate and I'm afraid that after two years of haggling, we've resolved nothing. I've allowed them to drag things out this long in the hopes we wouldn't have to go to court."

"I'm so sorry," Callie said, her tone softening. "Did you resolve the problems?"

"Not hardly." Burke grimaced as if the very thought of his half siblings angered him. "Despite the fact that my father's will plainly states that I'm to be given an equal share, his legitimate children are determined to see that I get nothing." He glanced at Callie. "Yes, that's right. I'm a bastard."

"No, you're not!" she said vehemently. "You're no more a bastard than my little Se—than my son is. I hate that term. I hate that people still use it to refer to a person's parent's marital status when they were born. It's so unfair."

Callie couldn't stop the tears from gathering in her eyes or several droplets from trickling down her cheeks. Burke wiped away the teardrops with his fingertips. He and Callie stared at each other for one long, breathless moment.

"Don't cry for me, sweet Callie."

"I'm afraid I get very emotional when it comes to this issue. What happened between your parents is their doing—their fault—not yours."

"And what about you, Callie? Who do you blame because your son has no father?"

"I blame myself," she replied, boldly facing Burke.

"Not the man? Not your child's father?"

"No, I—I can't blame him."

"Why the devil not?" Burke's voice boomed. "The son of a bitch got you pregnant and deserted you, didn't he?"

"Not exactly. He didn't know I was carrying his child."

"Yes, of course. So you've said. What I don't understand is why you didn't tell the man."

"Please, Burke...Mr. Lonigan, my circumstances were entirely different with my son's father than your mother's situation was with your father, so I don't think you should compare the two.''

''How do you know what my mother's circumstances with my biological father were?''

Oh, goodness gracious, she'd done it now! How indeed would she be privy to something so personal? ''Uh, er, I don't know. I'm simply assuming. Forgive me.''

''Hell!'' Burke shot to his feet, then raked his fingers through his thick hair. ''I didn't intend to come in here today and discuss this problem with you or with anyone. What is it about you, Callie Severin, that makes me want to pour out my heart to you?''

''I really have no idea, sir.''

''Dammit, don't call me sir. And don't call me Mr. Lonigan. I thought you'd agreed to call me Burke.''

''Yes, of course, but that was…that was before what happened Saturday night. Before Enid scared you off.''

Burke laughed, but the humor wasn't genuine and the laughter died before it reached his eyes. ''Ah, yes, the formidable Enid. Everyone should have an Enid in their lives. Someone to slay dragons for them and keep lecherous men from taking advantage of them.''

''Is that what Enid accused you of doing?'' Callie's lips curved into a hint of a grin.

''Something like that,'' Burke admitted. ''She's certain that I'll use and abuse you and then toss you out like yesterday's trash.''

''And would you?''

Burke laughed again, and this time it was genuine. ''I like you, Callie. I like you and I respect you. And I want you. I want you now more than ever.''

Her eyes rounded and her mouth formed a shocked oval.

"Does that surprise you? That I'm honest enough to admit that I still want you desperately?"

"I thought that after you ran off Saturday night, you probably went straight to another woman. Am I wrong?"

"What makes you think that I—"

"You were randy Saturday night. You wanted a woman. I may not be terribly experienced, but I'm not a complete innocent when it comes to men. If you'd thought I would come around in a day or two, you might have waited, but when you left, you'd given up on me, hadn't you?"

"I'd given up on *us*."

"You should have asked me how I felt instead of allowing Enid to convince you that I wasn't the type of woman for a temporary affair."

"I knew before Enid made a point of telling me," Burke said. "I just wanted you so much that I chose to ignore your refusal. I thought I could persuade you. And I probably could have. Enid pointed out that if I did seduce you, I'd break your heart, and since two other men had already done that quite effectively, you deserved better treatment. I agree with her, Callie. You deserve better. You deserve a man who's willing to marry you and be a father to your son."

"And you aren't that man, are you, Burke?"

She saw the confusion in his eyes, that momentary flicker of uncertainty, and a spark of hope ignited in her heart.

"No, my darling, I'm probably not that man. But I almost wish that I were."

"Almost." The newborn hope within her died instantly.

"I apologize for putting you in the middle of some rather unpleasant gossip, but once everyone sees that we're continuing our highly compatible working relationship, the rumors will die down.''

"Yes, I'm sure you're right." Callie stood and faced Burke. "Will you need me for anything else right now?''

Burke smiled wickedly, and she knew what he was thinking. He most certainly still wanted her. The truth was there in his eyes, in the expression on his face as well as the hardness of his body. And heaven help her, she still wanted him.

"Not right now. But pull up everything you have on the Argentina deal and we'll discuss how to expedite the shipments to Buenos Aires after I've had my morning coffee.''

"Yes, sir." Callie headed for the door.

"By the way…''

Callie glanced over her shoulder. "Yes?''

"I went straight from your house Saturday night to Notting Hill to see Hayley Martin.''

Heat flushed Callie's face. She nodded. *Let me get out of his office before I start crying,* she pleaded silently.

When she started to open the door, Burke called after her. "Nothing happened. Odd thing, I couldn't make love to her because she wasn't the woman I wanted.''

Chapter 5

"Thank you for staying late this evening." With Seamus securely on her hip, Callie walked Mrs. Goodhope to the door. "I appreciate your giving Seamus his bath, too."

"No trouble at all, my dear. I think of Seamus as one of my grandchildren, now, don't I?" She tickled Seamus under the chin. "He's a splendid little fellow."

The motherly minder was all warm smiles and gentle hugs. Callie often remarked to Enid how fortunate she'd been to have found someone so ideally suited to the care of young children.

The moment Callie started to close the door, Enid bounded around the corner and ran up the pavement. "Hold up," she called, then raced up the steps and into the house. "Close that door. It's freezing out tonight."

"And where have you been?" Callie demanded. "You were due home two hours ago. Mrs. Goodhope had to stay over."

"I thought you had to work late tonight." Enid stripped out of her coat and hung it in the closet just off the foyer. "What are you doing home?"

"Mrs. Goodhope rang me an hour ago to tell me you were still out." Callie shifted Seamus's fat little body from one hip to the other. "I couldn't ask her to stay longer, not knowing for certain how late I might be tonight. And neither of us had any idea whether you'd show up or not."

"Don't be upset with me." Enid gave Callie her pitiful puppy-dog pout. "I was posing for Leonardo and lost track of time." She tapped Seamus playfully on the nose. "Tell your mummy not to be mean to Auntie Enid."

Seamus giggled, that sweet toddler laugh that quickly diffused the tension between his mother and aunt.

"I'll read him his bedtime story and then I must get back to the office," Callie said. "Burke was very understanding about my leaving, but he really needs my help. We have a major deal pending and we simply have to have all the details ironed out tonight."

"Mm. I had wondered, when you rang earlier today to say you'd be working late, exactly what that work entailed." Enid followed Callie to the second story, which consisted of two bedrooms and a bath. "You've been absolutely horrid to me since Saturday night and you haven't told me a thing that transpired between you and Burke since then."

"Not that it's any of your business, but Burke and I have agreed that it's best if we keep our relationship strictly business." Callie eased opened the door to Seamus's room, carried him in and laid him in his bed.

She and Enid had painted the walls of the room a light yellow, brought Callie's baby furniture out of storage and decorated the nursery with Winnie-the-Pooh items, everything from coverlet to wallpaper border.

"What will it be tonight?" Callie asked her son as she removed a handful of small books from the seat of the yellow rocking chair.

"Bad Wuff," Seamus said. At fourteen months he had a remarkable vocabulary, although as yet he hadn't comprised a complete sentence and his pronunciation was often not precise.

"All right." Callie picked up her son's favorite fairy tale, *The Three Little Pigs*. The book had been in a box filled with gifts from her father on Seamus's first birthday.

"Give Auntie Enid a night kiss, lovie."

Seamus wrapped his arms around Enid's neck and planted a wet kiss on her cheek. "Wuv you."

Enid smiled and returned the kiss. "I love you, too, you little angel."

Callie sat in the rocker, scooted it close to Seamus's bed and opened the book. "Once upon a time there were three little pigs…"

By the time she had gotten to the part where the big bad wolf was huffing and blowing in an effort to destroy the brick house, Seamus was fast asleep. Callie closed the book and laid it in her lap. Sighing contentedly as she watched her son sleeping so peacefully, she thought about how she had always longed for a home and a family. Two parents. Brothers and sisters. Roots. A house to live in for a lifetime.

Since she'd grown up in various countries throughout Europe, traveling with her diplomat father and social butterfly mother, in her formative years she'd spent as much time with a nanny as she had her parents. And then, when her mother had died suddenly in a car crash when she was twelve, her father had sent her to the United States to attend boarding school and to spend weekends and holidays with his sister, a corporate lawyer. Aunt Nelda didn't have a maternal bone in her body and had made Callie feel like an unwanted intruder in her life. However, Callie's summer vacations in England with Enid and Enid's parents had been the high point of each year. During those glorious summers, she and Enid had formed a strong and lasting bond of sisterhood.

As a girl and later as a young woman, Callie had dreamed of falling in love, marrying and raising a brood of children. She had fancied herself living in the country, with woods and orchards and a stream for swimming and fishing. A big, old house with fireplaces, large, airy rooms and a huge family kitchen. Horses to ride. Dogs to pet. An idyllic storybook life.

When she'd fallen in love with Laurence, she'd foolishly thought all her silly little dreams would come true. They'd discussed the possibility of buying a place in Sussex or Kent, once they'd saved up enough money. But Laurence had been a skillful liar. She'd placed her trust in the wrong man.

Then along came Burke Lonigan. The most irresistible man on earth. And what had she done? She'd had sex with a stranger and gotten herself pregnant, that's what she'd done. She realized now that her feelings for Laurence Wynthrope paled in comparison to the way she felt about Burke. She'd spent one night with the man and been unable to forget him.

Callie's gaze rested on Seamus. *Perhaps the fact that your son is a little replica of the man might have something to do with the fact that you couldn't forget him,* she reminded herself.

Glancing at her watch, Callie grimaced. She needed to

get to the office. Burke had told her to take a cab, if she found that she could return to work tonight.

She leaned over, kissed Seamus's forehead and drew the covers to his neck. "I want to tell your father about you, sweetheart. Really I do. But I'm afraid telling him might be a big mistake. You see, I'm not all together certain that your father is an honorable man. He could very well be involved in some illegal dealings and we wouldn't want that kind of man in our lives, would we?"

Callie picked up the baby monitor and carried it with her to the third story, which Enid occupied. A large bedroom and bath to the left and a small den to the right. Callie entered the den where Enid was watching television. She set the monitor on an end table.

"It could be midnight before I return," Callie said.

"I am sorry about being late." Enid shrugged. "You know how forgetful I am when I'm, er, posing. I'll pay Mrs. Goodhope for the extra time she had to stay."

"I'm not worried about the money, Enid. My position with Lonigan's Imports and Exports pays quite well. What upset me was inconveniencing Mrs. Goodhope as well as Burke."

"Ah, Burke."

"Don't start up with me again. The subject of Burke Lonigan is off-limits."

"One question?" Enid's eyes rounded and her lips curved ever so slightly in a beseeching half-smile.

"What?" Callie tilted her head.

"If you decide not to tell Burke that he's Seamus's father, are you going to continue working for him?"

Leave it to Enid to cut right to the chase and ask the question that Callie had been trying to avoid. She had so hoped that once she became acquainted with Burke, she'd discover he was a man longing for a wife and children.

And she'd been so sure that the wicked rumors about him being an arms dealer were unfounded. Now, she realized she'd been wrong. Burke appeared to have little interest in changing his playboy ways. And the longer she worked for him, the more certain she became that he was hiding something, that he did indeed have a secret life.

Burke removed his silk tie, rolled it up and stuffed it into his pocket, then removed his coat and hung it over the back of his chair. Callie had just called to tell him she was taking a cab to the office. Good, he thought. Working together, they'd be able to sew up the loose ends of the Argentina deal.

When she had rushed home, he had thought about Callie. About their relationship. About how dissatisfied he was with the agreement they'd reached yesterday. He tried to tell himself that they were both better off to maintain a business relationship and forget about becoming personally involved. The only problem with that kind of reasoning was that they were already personally involved.

He wanted her. And she wanted him.

There had been numerous women in Burke's life. Not as many as people believed, but more than enough to fuel the rumors about him being a playboy. He supposed he'd become spoiled by how easily he was able to charm any lovely lady he wanted. When he'd been younger, any pretty girl would do. Now his vague, haunting memories of one particular woman plagued him. Why, for pity's sake, couldn't he remember that woman? He could feel her body, smell her feminine scent, taste the sweetness of her skin and even hear her cries of completion. But he could not see her face. Couldn't recall one single feature. Didn't know if she'd been a blonde or a brunette or a redhead.

What he remembered all too vividly was her unselfish, comforting, loving aura. She'd been a temptress and a caretaker. A passionate lover and a sympathetic friend. A seductress. An angel. A Madonna.

And that was why he fancied Callie Severin. She possessed similar qualities. He knew instinctively that if any woman could free him from the tormenting memories of that night, Callie could. You fought fire with fire, didn't you? Preventive medication for serious illnesses often possessed a mild strain of the disease itself. And that's what Callie could be for him. Not necessarily a preventive, but a cure.

Alone in the suite of offices that comprised the twentieth floor, Burke tensed when he heard a faint noise. His instincts warned him that he wasn't alone any longer. And Callie hadn't had time to return from Kensington. Checking his watch, he reassured himself that it wasn't time for the maid service's arrival. So, who was in the office suite with him?

Without taking time to go over every possible scenario, Burke removed his key chain from his pocket, chose a specific key and unlocked the bottom drawer of his desk. He flipped the lid on a metal box and removed the 800 Cougar Beretta from its bed, then picked up his coat and slid the pistol into the pocket. After slipping into the coat, he made his way across the room and into the open reception area between his office and Callie's. He kept one hand free and the other nestled inside the pocket, resting on the high powered 9mm.

The hallway that led to the elevators was illuminated by recessed lighting that remained dimmed from the time the employees left in the late afternoon until they returned at nine in the morning. But the view was clear. Not a soul in sight. Like a wide painted line, light from Burke's office spread across the floor in front of and behind him. He eased quietly toward the corridor. Then he heard the sound again. Someone walking. Softly. Almost silently.

How had anyone gotten past the guard downstairs? Burke wondered. But he knew if the intruder was who he thought it was, slipping past a guard and bypassing security codes would have been an easy task.

As if from out of nowhere, a tall shadowy figure in a dark trench coat appeared directly in front of Burke. Instantly tightening his grip on the pistol in his pocket, he prepared to defend himself, if necessary. He looked at the trespasser, who stood a good three inches taller than he.

"Lonigan?" the deep voice asked.

"Yes, I'm Lonigan," Burke replied. "Who are you?"

"My name is unimportant. Only my business should concern you."

"Office hours are from nine to five-thirty, Mr...."

The man harrumphed harshly. "I understand you conduct a different sort of business...after hours."

"And where would you have heard such a rumor?"

"From Haroun al Rachid."

Burke's lips spread in a cocky, self-assured smile. With his free hand he gestured a cordial welcome as he said, "Please, come into my office, Mr...."

"Call me Simon."

The voice possessed a vague familiarity and yet had no accent that Burke could identify. So this was Simon. The man who had been able to elude SPEAR time and again.

"Please, come into my office...Simon," Burke said.

"After you," Simon replied

Burke felt uneasy turning his back on a man of Simon's reputation. An enemy perfectly capable of shooting a person in the back. But Simon wasn't here to murder the one man who might be able to restore to him his shipment of

Russian-made weapons. In a show of supreme confidence, Burke returned to his office. He felt the other man's presence as Simon followed him.

Burke veered slowly, changing directions, then halted and came face-to-face with the notorious Simon. Although a heavy beard covered most of the man's face, it wasn't completely able to camouflage the severe scars. Burn scars, from the look of them, Burke surmised. Taking a casual survey, he noted that his visitor was at least six-three, rock solid and somewhere in his fifties.

"Won't you sit down?" Burke invited.

Simon glanced at the two chairs across from Burke's desk. That was when Burke realized the man had a glass eye. His left eye.

Simon took a seat. Burke eased his hip down on the edge of his desk, removed his hand from his pocket and crossed his arms over his chest.

"What can I do for you?" Burke glanced at his watch. If she'd had no trouble getting a cab, Callie would be at the office shortly. Damn, that was the last thing he needed. To have Callie interrupt when he was negotiating a deal with Simon.

"A shipment of weapons, belonging to me, was lost somewhere in the Sinai," Simon explained.

"How unfortunate."

"It has come to my attention that—somehow—those weapons have found their way into your control."

"Hm." Burke rubbed his chin. "Is that what your informants have told you?"

"Have I been misinformed?" Simon glowered at Burke with his good eye. A murky brown eye, the color of muddy water. His glass eye was clearer and a shade darker.

"It so happens that quite recently a shipment of Russian-made weapons did—by circuitous route—come into my hands.''

''My weapons!'' Simon's mouth tightened. His jaw clenched.

''I'm afraid not, old man. Not unless you're willing to pay for them.''

''Name your price, Lonigan.''

Burke thought he heard the elevator. God, no! Not yet. He couldn't let Simon and Callie come into contact with each other. Maybe he'd imagined the sound. He sure as hell hoped so.

''Meet me tomorrow,'' Burke said, hoping he could get rid of Simon quickly. ''We can arrange a suitable time and place to—''

''Not tomorrow. Tonight. I won't leave here until we've reached an agreement.''

Callie hummed a silly tune that she'd recently heard on one of Seamus's BBC programs as she waited for the elevator to reach the twentieth floor. She'd had the driver stop at the bakery a block from her house, where the proprietor was a friend of Enid's. Callie lifted the sack to her nose and sniffed the delicious aroma of cinnamon and raisin pastries. She and Burke had skipped dinner, so she thought freshly baked pastries would go nicely with the coffee Burke liked so well.

The elevator doors opened. Callie exited. As she walked down the dimly lit corridor toward the reception area, a odd sensation hit her in the belly. Something wasn't quite right. She couldn't figure out what was wrong, but her instincts warned her of danger.

Oh, don't be silly, Callie, she scolded herself. You've been seeing things lately, allowing your imagination to run away with you. Sunday, in the park, you thought someone was watching you. And last evening when you got off the tube, you thought someone followed you home. But you didn't see anyone suspicious either time. And now here you are thinking that you're in danger in the safety of the Lonigan's Imports and Exports suite of offices.

When she reached the reception area she noticed that Burke's door stood slightly ajar and not wide open as she had left it. That doesn't mean anything, she told herself. *You're being ridiculous.*

Then she heard the voice. Not Burke's voice. Another man's deep, hard voice. Callie slipped to the door, stopped and listened.

"You've heard my offer, Lonigan. It's a generous one, so don't tell me that you expect more. I want that shipment delivered tomorrow night. When you produce the weapons, you will receive payment in full."

Oh, my God! Callie rammed her fist into her mouth to stifle a gasp. There was no doubt in her mind what she had overheard. Burke was in his office, right this minute, brokering an arms deal with someone. The rumors were true! Seamus's father was an arms dealer. She had read about them, heard about them, these men who provided illegal weapons to the highest bidder, regardless of their political agendas. But in her heart of hearts, she had believed that Burke wasn't capable of such blatant disregard for the mayhem illegal weapons created around the world.

Why had Burke set up an appointment with this man knowing she would be returning tonight? she wondered. She had rung him before she'd left her house. Was it possible that he thought, as his PA, she would become involved in his secret criminal life? Or had this particular business associate shown up without an appointment?

What should she do? *Leave,* an inner voice warned. *Walk back to the elevators. Take a cab and go home. Call*

*Burke and tell him...tell him what? That Seamus is run-
ning a slight fever and you don't want to leave him. Yes,
that sounds reasonable. Go. Go, now!*

When she whirled around, she bumped into the edge of
the receptionist's desk. The staple gun, which had been
sitting precariously on the edge of the desk, fell and hit
the floor with a resounding thud. Damn! Had they heard?
She held her breath.

Run! Run like hell, her instincts urged. But before she
could move, the door to Burke's office swung open wide
and someone grabbed her from behind. She squealed with
fear when the big hand clutched the back of her neck and
turned her to meet the most frightening face she'd ever
seen. A face from a nightmare.

Callie screamed.

"Let her go!" Burke clamped his hand on the monster's shoulder.

The man released her and shoved her toward Burke. "I
thought your assistant had left for the evening. How unfortunate for her that she returned."

"Callie, are you all right?" Burke slipped his arm
around her, pulled her to his side and ran the back of his
hand across her cheek.

Trembling from head to toe, she managed to nod.

"Get rid of her, Lonigan."

"What?" Callie and Burke spoke simultaneously.

"No doubt your snoopy little assistant heard our conversation," the man said. "And she's seen my face. If she
didn't know before about your other business, she does
now. She's a liability, and I expect you to dispose of her."

Burke kissed Callie. A forceful, lingering kiss on the
lips. Callie clung to his arm, seeking support for her shaky
legs.

"I'm sorry about this, my darling," Burke said. "Simon, here, seems to be an overly cautious man."

"Yes—" Callie cleared her throat. "Yes, he does, doesn't he?"

Burke smiled at the man he'd called Simon. "I'm afraid your suggestion to eliminate Callie is out of the question. I assure you that she's totally trustworthy. She's privy to all my business dealings. You see, Ms. Severin is more than my personal assistant. She is my fiancée."

"Your fiancée?" Simon raised a skeptical eyebrow.

"Yes, my fiancée. The woman I'm going to marry."

Simon studied Callie for a couple of minutes, then said threateningly, "If you're lying to me, Lonigan, you and Ms. Severin are both as good as dead."

Chapter 6

Burke held Callie close, so close he felt the tiny quivers pulsating through her body. He realized how frightened she was—and with good reason. Any fool could see that Simon was a dangerous man. Damn, he'd never intended for Callie to become a part of this scenario. But now that she was, he intended to protect her at any cost.

"Why would I lie to you?" Burke asked.

"To save this bitch's life." Simon glared menacingly at Callie.

"Kindly refrain from speaking about my fiancée in such crude terms," Burke warned. "Callie is a lady and unaccustomed to being insulted by the likes of you."

Callie grasped Burke's hand tightly, but self-assurance and warmth were in the smile that spread across her face. "I've heard worse, darling. You mustn't be rude to your guest." She turned that dazzling smile of hers on Simon. "I'm so sorry that I overreacted, but I wasn't expecting to be grabbed from behind by a perfect stranger. You startled me, sir. I had no idea that Burke had arranged one of his secret meetings tonight.''

''What do you know about his secret meetings?'' Simon asked, suspicion written plainly on his face.

''She knows that I use Lonigan's Imports and Exports as a front for my real business,'' Burke said, fearing that he had damned himself in Callie's eyes. What would this sweet girl think of him if she believed him to be a ruthless arms dealer?

''If you two are engaged, why hasn't there been an announcement?'' Simon asked, then pointed to Callie's left hand. ''And why isn't she wearing a ring?''

''We haven't made the announcement yet,'' Burke said. ''I only proposed this past weekend. And as for the ring…I'm having a special one made for her.''

''I don't buy this little tale.'' Simon sneered. ''And I hate being lied to—by anyone.''

Burke casually slipped his hand into the pocket of his coat. His fingertips brushed the Beretta. God, he hoped he didn't have to use the gun. ''What's wrong? Don't you think someone as nice and sweet as Callie would be interested in a wicked old playboy like me?''

Simon reached into his trench coat and removed the weapon Burke had known he'd been hiding there. A pistol Burke recognized as a Walther P-88 Compact, 9mm, with a fifteen-round capacity. If Burke was an expert at anything, other than the import-export business, it was weapons. In his line of work, he had gained an astounding amount of knowledge.

Feeling Callie tense when she saw the gun Simon held, Burke squeezed her hand so tightly that she winced. *Don't give us away, my darling,* he silently pleaded. *Play this game with me. Our lives could depend on it.*

"When are you getting married?" Simon asked, the gun aimed directly at Callie.

"Put that damn thing away," Burke ordered. "You're upsetting Callie. She's not accustomed to—"

"When are you getting married?" Simon made no move to withdraw his weapon.

"This coming weekend," Burke said, realizing that things were quickly getting out of hand.

"Why so soon?" Simon asked skeptically.

"It's not so soon," Callie said, glancing from Simon's ugly face to Burke. She smiled nervously. "You see, I've been in love with Burke for quite some time and...well, we had a brief affair a couple of years ago, but we went our separate ways. Until recently. When I came to work for Burke, we figured out that we've both been in love with each other all this time."

Burke stared at Callie, momentarily amazed at how quickly she'd thought up such a convincing lie. And she'd told the fabrication with enough conviction to make a nonbeliever believe. "I'm a damn lucky man." Burke wrapped his arm around Callie's shoulder. "Not only am I getting a wife but a son in this deal."

"Ah, yes, the child." Simon grinned, the expression an ugly parody of a genuine smile. "I watched you with him in the park Sunday."

"You!" Callie took a step forward, but Burke restrained her.

"You've been following Callie? Why?" Burke asked.

"Curiosity," Simon said. "I've been checking you out for several days. I always like to have an edge. And I thought perhaps Ms. Severin might be your Achilles' heel. Seems I was right, wasn't I?"

Damn the man! Burke knew he was caught in a trap of his own making. If he said no, that Callie wasn't important to him, he would prove himself a liar and Simon wouldn't hesitate to try to kill them both. But if he said yes, then he did indeed give Simon a weapon to use against him, to insure the arms deal.

"So which is it, Lonigan? Is she or isn't she?"

"I am!" Callie broke loose of Burke's hold and dared to face the ghoulish and arrogant Simon. "I'm the woman he loves. And…and the mother of his child."

Burke caught himself before he questioned her statement with a resounding, "What?"

"The boy is Burke's son?" Simon's lips twitched.

Amusement? Burke wondered. God, what sort of game was Callie playing? Didn't she realize that she was simply giving this man more power over them?

"Yes," Callie admitted. "My son, Seamus, is Burke's son. The result of our affair nearly two years ago and named for Burke's father."

Simon did smile then. Burke wasn't sure if that was a good or a bad sign. When Simon returned his pistol to its sheath beneath the trench coat, Burke surmised that Callie's lie had worked a minor miracle. It seemed that Simon had bought her fabricated love story.

"I tend to believe you, Ms. Severin," Simon told her. "But I'd prefer some type of proof."

"I have proof…in my shoulder bag," Callie said. "May I remove my wallet from my bag?"

"Unzip the bag," Simon instructed. "I'll remove the wallet."

"Very well." Callie opened the bag and held it toward Simon.

He grabbed inside the large leather purse, then pulled out the wallet. "What now?"

"I have pictures of my son in the wallet. Take a good look at him and tell me he isn't Burke's son."

My God! Burke thought. Callie's taking an enormous risk. What if Simon doesn't see any resemblance? After all, it was hardly likely that the child, fathered by another man, would bear a striking resemblance to him.

Simon flipped open the wallet, then turned it sideways to view the photographs within their plastic folders. He stared intently at what Burke assumed was Callie's son. He glanced at Burke and then at the picture.

Without saying a word, Simon dropped the wallet into Callie's purse. "All right. I believe you." He turned to Burke. "Tomorrow. Noon. I'll call and tell you where to meet me. We'll finalize our transactions then."

"Yes. Fine." Burke held out his hand to Simon.

Simon ignored the offered hand. "If anything goes wrong with this deal, then something might go wrong with your woman or your child. Accidents happen all the time, don't they."

"I understand," Burke replied. "I assure you that nothing will go wrong."

Simon glanced from Callie to Burke, then turned to leave. Before he reached the far side of the reception area, he stopped and, without looking back, said, "I'll expect to hear the news of your wedding this weekend. I prefer to wait until your marriage is a fait accompli before we swap guns and money." Simon walked out of the office, down the corridor and to the lift.

The minute the elevator doors closed and the lift began its descent, Callie collapsed into the nearest chair. Burke rushed over and knelt on one knee in front of her.

"Are you all right?" he asked.

"I—I think so. Ask me again after my heart starts beating and my body stops shaking."

"Oh, my darling, I'm so sorry that I got you involved in—"

"That man—Simon—he actually would have killed us, wouldn't he?"

"He would have tried." Burke lifted the Beretta from his pocket just enough to show Callie that he, too, was armed.

She gasped when she saw the weapon, which Burke hastily returned to his pocket. "That reassures me," she said sarcastically. "I could have been caught in the cross-fire."

Burke ran his hands up and down her arms, partly as a comforting gesture and partly to convince himself that she was indeed all right. "If I'd known Simon would show up here at the office tonight, I'd never have asked you to return. Mistakenly I had thought the man would arrange for us to meet elsewhere or simply show up at my home. My, er, other business transactions usually take place far away from these offices."

"Then it's true, isn't it?" Callie looked at him, her eyes pleading for him to tell her that it had all been some horrific mistake. "You really are an arms dealer, aren't you? You deal in black-market military weapons. I didn't want to believe it, but—"

Burke grabbed her shoulders. "Things are not always what they seem."

"What do you mean by that?"

Damn! Damn Simon! Damn Jonah! Damn SPEAR! And damn his code of honor that prevented him from revealing the truth to Callie. The confusion and the re-vulsion in her eyes tore at his guts like a falcon's talons. If there was anyone on earth he wanted to think highly of him, it was Callie Severin. And the odd thing was— he didn't know why.

"What I mean is that I need for you to trust me, Callie."

She glanced at her lap, avoiding eye contact.

"Look at me," he said.

She did. Hesitantly.

"We've gotten ourselves into a bit of a pickle," he told her. "Through no fault of yours. But I'm afraid we have no choice but to follow through with the marriage this weekend. It will take some hurried maneuvering, but I think we can pull it off."

"I can't marry you!" She glared at him, her eyes round with shock and her pale cheeks tinted with just a hint of color.

"Callie, I thought you understood that neither of us has a choice." Burke came up off his knees, then sat beside her. When he tried to take her hands, she jerked away from him.

"We were playacting," she said. "That's all it was."

"Yes, we were playacting," Burke agreed. "And we're going to have to continue the ruse. At least for a while. It's the only way we can keep you safe."

"We're going to continue pretending we're engaged until the arms deal is complete?"

"Yes, and for a bit longer." If only he could be honest with Callie. He wanted to tell her that he wasn't an evil man, simply a complicated one.

"How much longer?" she asked.

"We'll marry this weekend, just as I told Simon. And in four or five months, I'll arrange for a divorce."

"Four or five months!"

"There are things I can't explain to you." He tried again to grasp her hands, and again she pulled away from him. "Please, trust me. You played along beautifully. I thought you understood what was at stake. Making Simon believe that I'm your son's father—in telling him that you

named the boy in honor of his grandfather—was a stroke
of genius.''

"Yes, he did believe me, didn't he?"

"By the way, how did you know my father's name was
Seamus? And how could you be so sure that Simon would
see a resemblance between your son and me?"

"I think you must have mentioned your father's name.
I really don't recall exactly how I knew. And as for the
resemblance between you and my little Seamus—his father had your black Irish looks, which my son inherited.
Seamus's black hair and blue eyes were enough to convince your Mr. Simon."

Something wasn't quite right with Callie's explanation,
but Burke couldn't put his finger on exactly what. He was
fairly sure he'd never mentioned his biological father's
name to Callie, but how else could she have known? And
as for her son possessing eye and hair color similar to
his—well, he supposed that could account for why Simon
had seen a resemblance.

"I'll take you home now, Callie." Burke grabbed her
hands, refusing to allow her to withdraw, then lifted her
to her feet. "You'll tell Enid that I've asked you to marry
me and you've accepted. You mustn't tell her anything
about what conspired here tonight. It's best if she believes
this is a love match. Do you think you can lie to your
cousin?"

"I won't like lying to Enid, but yes, I can and will
make her believe that we're marrying because we love
each other. I wouldn't want to put her in any danger because of what's going on with Simon."

"Come along." Burke took her hand in his. "You've
had a nerve-racking experience. You need some rest. And
don't worry about Simon showing up and causing you

any problems. I'll arrange for someone to keep an eye on your house.''

Callie shivered. ''Yes. Thank you. Just the thought that he...that Simon was following me in the park Sunday afternoon—''

Burke halted. ''Everything is going to be all right. As long as we follow through with the marriage and keep up the pretense for a while, no one will harm you or your son.''

''Your son,'' Callie said softly.

''Yes, that's right. We'll have to let others think that your little Seamus is my child.''

Tears glazed Callie's eyes, and Burke wondered what had prompted them. Aftershock? Concern about her child's safety? Or something to do with the boy's real father? If he asked her, what would she tell him?

As they walked to the lift, Burke said quite casually, ''Is there any chance Seamus's real father will show up and create problems for us?''

Although Callie didn't slow her stride, Burke sensed the hesitation, the momentary pause, before she punched the down button for the lift. ''I've told you before that Seamus's real father doesn't know he exists.''

''You're getting married this weekend?'' Enid's voice possessed an edge of total disbelief. ''You and Burke Lonigan are getting married.''

''Yes,'' Callie said as she made her way upstairs to Seamus's bedroom. She desperately wanted to see her child, to reassure herself that he was safe.

Dear God, what have I done? What deadly world had she entered tonight? By seeking out Burke Lonigan, by accepting a position as his PA, she had inadvertently put herself and her son in harm's way. The man who had fathered her child was a criminal. All those dark whispers, all those ugly rumors were true!

"I told you that Seamus has been sleeping like an angel ever since you left," Enid said, as she followed Callie into the child's room.

Callie hovered over Seamus's bed. Reaching out, she lifted a stray lock of curly black hair off his forehead. A lone tear escaped and ran down her cheek.

"What's wrong?" Enid asked. "Why are you crying?"

"Nothing's wrong," Callie said. "It's just that I love Seamus so much and I want what's best for him."

"You told Burke that he's Seamus's father, didn't you?"

"In a way."

"In a way? I don't understand. Either you told the man he was Seamus's father or you didn't."

"I did," Callie said. "But—"

"He's not convinced you're telling the truth! After you told me that the two of you were getting married, I wondered why he hadn't come in with you, why he wasn't in a hurry to see his son. This isn't a good way to begin a marriage, you know."

"Don't worry about it, Enid. Really. Everything will work out…in time."

"I'm totally confused. The man isn't convinced that Seamus is his child and yet you're going to marry him. Are you saying he wants you whether or not—"

"He will accept Seamus as his child because—" the lie hung in Callie's throat "—because he loves me."

"None of this makes sense to me." Frowning, Enid studied Callie's face. "Why the rush to marry? You aren't pregnant again, are you?"

"No, I'm not pregnant. And I do wish you'd stop asking me so many questions."

Callie hadn't realized that she'd raised her voice until Seamus opened his eyes and gazed sleepily at her. "Mama?"

"Oh, love, I didn't mean to wake you."

Seamus held up his fat little arms to her. She lifted him out of bed and cuddled him close. *I swear that I'll protect you, that somehow I'll find a way to keep you safe. From Burke's enemies. And from Burke himself.*

"I've made the arrangements, sir." Leland Perkins stood by Burke's desk in the library. "There will be someone guarding the house at all times and someone keeping watch over Ms. Severin."

"I've gotten myself into a real mess, Leland." Burke lifted his glass of Scotch and took a large gulp, then groaned when the liquid hit his stomach like a ball of fire.

"Yes, sir, it appears that you have."

"I never figured that Simon would risk coming to my office. The man has brass. He's a cocky bastard. He must think, even with that ugly mug of his so easily recognizable, he's too clever to be caught."

"I've found that overconfidence usually leads to downfall."

"Quite right. And in Simon's case, I hope that proves true."

"Yes, sir."

Burke cocked his head to look at Leland. "You've been unusually reticent on the subject of my marriage to Ms. Severin."

"What would you have me say, sir?"

"I'd like for you to tell me that there's another solution to our problem. I'm afraid Ms. Severin is as reluctant to marry me as I am to marry her. But we're both trapped by the lies we told Simon."

"A marriage in name only, sir. For a short duration. Not so terrible a price to pay for insuring the success of your assignment, not to mention the safety of the lady and her son."

"Her son. Yes, the child." Burke swirled the whiskey in the glass, then lifted it to his mouth and downed the remainder. Hot coals in his belly to dull his senses. "I'll play daddy to the lad. That's part of the charade. She told Simon that the boy was mine. A consequence of an affair we supposedly had nearly two years ago. Simon took one look at a picture of the boy and believed her."

"Does the child resemble you, sir?"

"Does he—how the hell should I know?"

"Didn't you see the picture?"

"No, I didn't."

"Hm."

"I'm not the type to be a husband and father, am I, Leland?"

"I wouldn't know, sir."

Burke grinned. "Go on to bed, man. It's past midnight and we've a busy day ahead of us tomorrow."

"As you wish, sir." Leland nodded, pivoted and made a dignified exit.

Where had SPEAR found Leland Perkins? Burke wondered, and not for the first time. A gentleman through and through and quite good at his performance as the devoted servant. But there was much more to the man than met the eye. Burke would stake his life on it.

Leland had been in his employ for nearly eight years and he knew nothing of the man's personal history. SPEAR employees tended to be secretive, seldom making friends with one another even when they were assigned to work together. Leland had been given the assignment as Burke's backup, his man of all seasons, capable of serving him as well as protecting him. The man who had held that position before Leland, a rather burly Scotsman named Fergus, had lost his life saving Burke. In the twelve years he and Fergus had worked together, they'd formed a bond, if not friendship. Burke had deliberately tried to keep his relationship with Leland as detached as possible, but despite his best efforts, he had taken a liking to the man.

Burke poured himself another Scotch. Did you see the picture? he heard Leland ask. Did you see the picture?

Why hadn't he asked Callie for a look at the picture? The child wasn't his and they both knew it, so why had he been so reluctant to take a look at her little boy?

Because Callie's son was the result of her love for another man. Her coupling with someone with his own black Irish looks. How could he see the boy and not think of the father?

Burke had seldom experienced the ugly emotion, jealousy. In the first few months of his mother's marriage to Gene Harmon, he'd been jealous of his stepfather. But he'd soon grown fond of the man who had treated him like a son. And years later, when he'd met his biological father, he'd been jealous of the man's legitimate children, his half brother and half sisters. But he couldn't recall a time in his life when he'd been jealous over a woman.

A strange unbidden thought entered Burke's mind. A flash of memory. *You need me tonight, my darling, as much as I need you.* The voice was muted, barely more than a whisper. His voice echoing from the past.

Who was she? And where was she now? And if he couldn't get her out of his mind, why the hell couldn't he remember her face? Why couldn't he put an identity to the woman who haunted him?

And why did he keep confusing his mystery lady with

Callie? No, he didn't confuse the two. How could he? What kept confusing him was his emotions. What he'd felt that night with this other woman had been unlike anything he'd ever known—hadn't it? And now he had similar feelings for Callie. A raw hunger. An ache that wouldn't go away.

Out there somewhere was another woman—a woman who could have gotten pregnant that night. He was fairly certain he hadn't used any type of protection. The next morning, he'd found no evidence that he had. Ironic, wasn't it, that he was going to marry Callie and claim another man's child as his own, when just possibly some unknown man had married his mystery lady and claimed Burke's child.

Damn it! Burke shot to his feet, tossed his glass of Scotch into the fireplace and cursed loudly. Shards of crystal sprayed across the burning logs.

He couldn't forget his mystery lady, even though he had no memory of her physical appearance, not simply because she had bewitched him, but because on a subconscious level, Burke had feared that he had repeated his father's mistake and gotten some innocent girl pregnant.

Well, he might not ever know the truth—whether he had fathered a child—and there wasn't much chance he could ever claim the child, if one existed. But he could protect Callie and her little Seamus. He could be to Seamus, if only on a temporary basis, what Gene Harmon had been to him.

Burke picked up his mobile phone and punched one button. Listening to it ring, he waited and then hung up. A few minutes later his phone rang.

''What's the word?'' the caller asked.

''Jonah, our man made contact. Unexpectedly, tonight. In my office.''

"Bold move on his part, coming to your office."

"He's a cocky bastard," Burke said.

"Is the deal set?"

"No, but it should be by noon tomorrow." Burke cleared his throat. "There was a minor complication."

"How minor?"

"My PA returned to the office and overheard part of my conversation with Simon!"

"Damn! What happened? Is Ms. Severin all right?"

"Ms. Severin is fine. Come this weekend, Ms. Severin will become Mrs. Lonigan. We persuaded Simon that she was also my fiancée."

"Will she keep her mouth shut or—"

"She'll play along," Burke assured his superior. "She has a child to protect. She won't do anything to put him in danger."

"I expect you to handle the situation with Ms. Severin. Do whatever you have to do. Just don't blow this operation," Jonah said. "As soon as the deal with Simon is set, let me know and we'll put things into motion."

Chapter 7

Callie stared at the ring on her finger. Three one-carat diamonds flanked the center setting—a four-carat marquise-cut emerald. The matching wedding band Burke had purchased had one-carat diamonds and emeralds alternating across the platinum circle. She had repeatedly tried to tell him the rings were much too extravagant, but he had ignored her protests. As a matter of fact, Burke had pretty much disregarded any comments or suggestions she'd made this morning while he'd hurried her around London. First Leland had taken them from Callie's house to the jewelers, where Burke had purchased the rings, then they had applied for the superintendent registrar's certificate and license. One clear day would have to pass before the registrar could issue the certificate and license, but after that they would be free to marry. Burke had informed her that the ceremony would take place Saturday, in the registrar's office.

Afterward, Burke had taken her to Marilyn's, the exclusive shop on Regent Street where Marilyn Farris's latest designs were sold. He'd kissed her quite passionately before he'd left, promising to return in time for them to share a late lunch. Although she'd enjoyed the kiss immensely, Callie suspected the show of affection had been an act for the satisfied Marilyn, who had kept saying, "I knew I'd be preparing your trousseau," as if she'd correctly guessed the exact moment of some history-altering event.

Callie sipped tea and watched the models as they displayed the outfits that Marilyn insisted were essential for her honeymoon. The very thought of a honeymoon with Burke was almost more than she could bear. Surely he didn't expect to whisk her off somewhere for a week or two. And if he thought they were going to share a bed—well, he'd better think again! This would be a brief, in-name-only arrangement. A pretense to keep her and Seamus safe from the wrath of one of Burke's sinister business associates.

With everything happening so fast, she'd had little time to figure out a way to keep father and son apart. It would never do for Burke to realize that Seamus was his child. She wondered if it were possible that Burke could look at Seamus and not see the striking resemblance between the two of them. Surely Burke wouldn't want to be bothered playing daddy to her little one. He didn't strike her as the paternal type. Maybe she could keep Seamus hidden from Burke. But for how long? Days? Weeks? Indefinitely?

"Callie, you aren't paying the least bit of attention to these lovely frocks of mine," Marilyn scolded.

"Sorry, Marilyn. I'll try to pay closer attention."

"No need to apologize. If I were marrying Burke Lonigan on Saturday, I'd be thinking of nothing else but the man himself."

"Yes. Quite right. Burke is something to think about, isn't he?"

"Mm. Indeed." Marilyn dismissed the models with a wave of her hand. "You can always come back tomorrow and finish choosing the items for your trousseau. I do wish I had time to design some things just for you. It would have been such a delight."

"Thank you, but with the wedding on Saturday—"

Marilyn leaned over and, with a conspiratorial grin on her face, said, "Why the hurried wedding? There's not a little one on the way, is there?"

Callie bestowed her most gracious smile on the nosy designer. "I can assure you that isn't the case. In fact...I can be perfectly frank with you, can't I?"

Like a cat anticipating a bowl of fresh cream, Marilyn licked her lips. "Most certainly. I can be a very trustworthy friend."

Without a doubt Marilyn Farris was the queen of gossip in and around London. Her own mother wouldn't have trusted her with a secret. "Burke and I have decided to wait until our wedding night."

Marilyn's eyes grew large and round as realization dawned on her. "My dear girl, how very clever of you. Making him wait. No wonder he's totally bewitched by you."

Marilyn clapped her hands, and a rather prissy young man came running to do her bidding. "Dudley, we aren't going to bother with more items for the trousseau today. Ms. Severin will return tomorrow for that. But it's essential that we find the perfect wedding dress for her. I'd like you to—"

"A suit," Callie said. "Not a dress."

"A suit?"

"Burke and I are marrying at the registrar's office. I want a suit. Something in a beige or a cream or even a pale yellow."

"Not white? I'd have thought, under the circumstances—"

"Marilyn, I'm not a virgin bride. Besides, with my coloring, I look ghastly in white."

"You're quite right, of course." Marilyn patted her on the arm. "Wait here. I'll choose several suits personally and have the girls model them for you."

"Thank you."

Callie checked her watch. Burke had left her here over three hours ago. What was taking him so long? She knew that he'd set up a meeting with that horrible man named Simon. While she was viewing Marilyn Farris's latest fashions, Burke was brokering an illegal arms deal. A shiver raced up her spine. She was going to marry a criminal. And not just any criminal. A multimillionaire global arms dealer.

Marilyn returned, waving her arms like a bird ready to take flight. "Are you sure you don't want some champagne?"

"No, thank you, the tea is fine."

"Very well. Now, take a look at these. I've chosen five divine suits for you to view. Any one of which would be perfect for a morning wedding."

Callie tried to keep her mind on the outfits as, one by one, the models displayed five absolutely stunning suits. But with the reality of her soon-to-be marriage bombarding her incessantly, she found it difficult to concentrate on choosing the right apparel. She had more important concerns than picking out something to wear on her wedding day. Things like keeping Burke from finding out that he was Seamus's father. And making sure that she didn't succumb to Burke's hard-to-resist machismo. She couldn't risk falling in love with him. If that happened, she'd be lost. And so would Seamus. They'd both be trapped in Burke's life—and the secret part of his life that had put them all in danger. She didn't want a global arms dealer to be her child's father.

But he already is, an inner voice taunted. *No matter what you do, you can't change the fact that Burke Lonigan is Seamus's biological father.*

Neither of them ever have to know! For Seamus's sake, she had to find a way to protect him from the truth.

Burke relaxed in the back seat of the Rolls as he replaced his cellular phone in his coat pocket. The deal with Simon had been made. Jonah had been informed and the wheels set into motion. Saturday, while Burke Lonigan married Callie Severin, the SPEAR operation to capture Simon would move forward, and by the time the newlyweds arrived in Italy, the exchange would have taken place. And if everything went as planned, Simon would be snared in SPEAR's trap.

"Leland, I think perhaps you should stay with Enid Ludlow and young Seamus while Callie and I are in Italy. I know we'd planned to send someone else, but I'd feel better if you took this assignment yourself."

"Yes, sir. Have you informed Ms. Severin that a bodyguard for her cousin and son will be necessary?"

"I'll tell her before we leave for Italy," Burke said. "A honeymoon, even a brief weekend at my villa, will be expected, by everyone in London as well as by Simon and his associates. Until Simon is captured or he no longer suspects me of betrayal, we must do everything possible to make this marriage appear on the up-and-up."

"If Simon is captured, then you and Ms. Severin should be able to end the marriage rather quickly, shouldn't you?"

"Not too quickly. It would look rather odd if we didn't stay married at least six months. After several weeks, we can start a few rumors that there is trouble in paradise."

"What will you do about keeping Ms. Severin on as your PA?" Leland asked.

"Hm. That poses a problem. She's quite good at her job, but it would be impossible for us to work together afterward. I'll arrange another position for her, something with equal pay and benefits."

"We're here, sir."

Leland pulled the Rolls up in front of Marilyn's, but before he stopped the car, a man rushed toward the vehicle. Leland unlocked the door, and the man jumped into the front seat.

"We've got a problem," the man said. "I had to call in backup."

"What sort of problem?" Leland asked.

"What the hell's going on, Quigley?" Burke reached over the seat and clamped his hand on the man's shoulder. "Is Callie all right?"

"No harm has come to Ms. Severin," Quigley said. "MacDougal is with her. I thought it best to have someone right at her side. Seems there's a couple of nasty fellows following her. One's posted at the back of the boutique and the other's just across the street. I know these two, Mr. Lonigan. They're both common criminals who'd cut their dear old mum's throat for fifty quid."

"Damn!" Burke released his tight grip on Quigley's shoulder. "Simon hired them, no doubt. As much to warn me not to let anything go wrong as to keep tabs on Callie." Burke slapped his right fist into the palm of his left hand. "What did you tell her when you stationed MacDougal at her side?"

"I told her the truth." Quigley glanced over his shoulder, his gaze locking with Burke's. "That MacDougal and I worked for you. I showed her my identification. That silly woman who owns the boutique kept trying to eavesdrop on our conversation, so I told her that we'd been sent to help Ms. Severin with her packages."

"I doubt Marilyn believes you." Burke slid across the seat, opened the door and got out, but stopped abruptly and stuck his head back into the Rolls. "Until this deal is completed, I want full protection not only for Callie, but for Enid Ludlow, Mrs. Daisy Goodhope and most importantly, Seamus Severin. There's no way to predict the actions of a man like Simon. He might decide to escalate his warnings into something a bit more deadly."

"That'll run up quite a tab, Mr. Lonigan." Quigley shook his head as if he'd added up the sum and was amazed by the amount. "Three shifts for four people."

"What the hell do I care what it costs," Burke bellowed, then slammed the door and marched toward the entrance to Marilyn's.

Fury boiled inside him, threatening to explode. He'd dealt with scum like Simon more times than he cared to consider. But in the past, no one else had been involved. No good friends. No special woman. And certainly never a child. Callie's child. God help Simon if he did anything to harm Callie, her child or anyone she cared about.

Burke hated the feeling of helplessness that consumed him. He could handle the danger involved with being a SPEAR agent. In truth, there had been a time when he'd thrived on it. But things were different now. He'd screwed up royally by not expecting the unexpected from Simon. Why had he assumed the mysterious, notorious Simon wouldn't pay him a late-night visit at his office? Because no one in their right mind would do something so stupid. Or so arrogant? That was what Burke hadn't counted on. That the man would be arrogant enough to think that no one could outsmart him and thus capture him.

As he entered the boutique, Burke saw MacDougal, a tall, lanky Scotsman in a dark suit, who held two boxes in one hand and kept his other hand at his side. His gun hand, Burke surmised. Callie stood next to him, a couple of small bags draped over her arm. The moment she saw Burke, she lifted her hand and waved. No smile. Just a wide-eyed questioning stare. He deliberately forced himself to slow his pace, not to race to her side and frighten her more than she was quite obviously already frightened. Marilyn Farris hurried along behind, a curious look in her eyes.

"Afternoon, sir," MacDougal said.

"Take Ms. Severin's packages out to the Rolls and report in to Quigley," Burke ordered the bodyguard, then focused his attention on Callie. "Are you all right, my darling?"

"Yes, I'm fine." Callie smiled weakly.

"Burke, love." Marilyn Farris kissed the air on each side of Burke's cheeks. "She chose her wedding suit and a few other small items, but she must return tomorrow and make decisions on the rest of her trousseau."

"That can be arranged," Burke said. "Thank you, Marilyn. And if Callie and I host a reception after our honeymoon, your name will head the list of guests."

Marilyn beamed, her large, red mouth spreading to form an ear-to-ear smile. "Of course, you must have a reception. It will partially make up for denying everyone the joy of attending a huge wedding."

"Are you ready to go?" Burke asked Callie.

Callie nodded, then endured Marilyn's kissing-the-air ritual before she clasped Burke's arm. "I want to go home and check on Seamus."

"Your son is all right," Burke assured her, as he led her toward the boutique entrance. "There's a man guarding your house and within the hour Seamus and Mrs. Goodhope will have bodyguards, as will Enid…if we can find her."

"Oh, Burke."

"Shh." He led her out of the boutique and into the bright sunlit street. "As soon as this deal with Simon goes through—"

"How can you be involved in something so terrible, with people capable of murder… What kind of man are you, Burke Lonigan?"

Not the kind of man you think I am, he wanted to say. *I'm one of the good guys, my darling.* For nearly a century and a half, good men had dedicated their lives to an organization that got the job done when all else had failed. With tentacles that reached into domestic and foreign affairs as well as private business, SPEAR tried to safeguard the world from evil.

"Get in the car," Burke ordered. "This isn't a discussion I want to have in the middle of Regent Street."

Leland opened the door for Callie, who obediently slid inside, her actions robotic. Burke turned to MacDougal and Quigley, who stood beside the Rolls. "Follow us."

Once inside the car, Burke spread his arm across the seat behind Callie. She scooted away from him, as far as she could get on the other side of the Rolls. Slumping her shoulders, crossing her arms and holding her knees tightly together, Callie knotted herself into an agitated ball of rage.

"Don't make this any harder than it already is," Burke

said. He also wanted to kiss her until she was breathless and begging him to make love to her. But more than anything he wanted to be able to tell her that he wasn't a ruthless international criminal.

"I really don't think I can eat a bite," she told him. "I'd prefer skipping lunch and going straight home."

"Your son is safe," he reiterated, then took a deep breath. "And you have to eat. We have reservations at Bracewells. We're a newly engaged couple and it's essential that we be seen having a celebration lunch. After all, I want to show off my bride-to-be and she wants to show off her ring, doesn't she?"

Burke grabbed Callie's wrist, which she tried to snatch away from him. But he held fast and forced her to open her fist so that he could examine her ring. She glowered at him. He smiled at her.

"I've already apologized to you, Callie. I've told you how much I regret that you inadvertently became a part of the darker side of my life. But what's done is done. Neither of us can change what happened. What we're doing now is considered damage control."

"How long will we have to live this charade?" She stared at her manacled wrist.

He released her immediately. "Six months, at most."

"Six months!"

"I have a reputation to uphold," he told her. "After the danger from Simon has passed, I'd prefer we didn't end the marriage immediately. What would people think if Burke Lonigan couldn't hold on to his bride for more than a few weeks?"

"You could tell people that I was at fault, that I didn't live up to your expectations." Callie looked at him pleadingly. "Now that I know what kind of man you are, I couldn't bear being your wife, even in name only, for longer than necessary.''

''I see.'' Burke's halfhearted smile disappeared, replaced by a sullen frown. ''All right then. Let's follow through with the marriage and afterward, we'll take it one day at a time. Will that suit you?''

''Yes,'' she said. ''It will have to suit me since it's the best you can offer.''

''I don't suppose it would do any good to ask you to have a little faith in me, would it?''

Callie scanned Burke's face as if she were searching for the truth. ''I'd very much like to have a little faith in you, Burke, but I'm afraid you've done nothing to warrant it.''

''Quite right. Best that we leave things the way they are.''

Callie really couldn't bear it. She simply couldn't! Enduring her fittings at Marilyn's had been difficult enough without anything being added to the embarrassment of putting on a show for the city's most notorious gossipmonger. And having other diners at Bracewells staring at them and whispering behind their backs had been dreadful.

But nothing could compare to the surprise party given by the staff of Lonigan's Imports and Exports.

The moment Burke and Callie stepped out of the lift onto the twentieth floor, the well-wishers surrounded them. Juliette Davenport led the pack of smiling faces. Champagne corks popped. Classical music droned loudly from the corner where a string quartet played. Three waiters in white coats served canapés of lobster, foie gras and caviar.

''Smile, my darling.'' Burke clutched her arm tightly

and dragged her to his side. "These people think you're a happy bride-to-be."

Callie wanted to scream and run as fast as she could. Her dreams about Burke Lonigan had turned into a nightmare. One from which she couldn't escape. She was trapped.

God, give me strength, she prayed silently. *I have to do this. For Seamus's sake. I have to go through with this marriage. But as soon as Burke releases me from our arrangement, I'll take Seamus and leave the country. I'll go to America. I can never allow a man like Burke to become a permanent part of Seamus's life.*

Juliette grabbed Callie's hand. "I just knew there was something going on between the two of you. You could have given a girl a clue, you know, instead of denying that you fancied Mr. Lonigan." Juliette lifted Callie's left hand, and her eyes bugged at the sight of the ring. "Give us a look at that. Good God!"

"Why did you two keep your romance a secret?" Herbert Garvey, Lonigan's accountant, asked.

"It—" Callie cleared her throat. "It all happened so suddenly."

"I swept her off her feet." Burke proceeded to demonstrate by scooping Callie into his arms.

Loud guffaws and tinkling giggles spread through the crowd. Several of the women sighed and swooned just a bit.

Smiling ever so sweetly, Callie spoke under her breath. "Put me down. Now!"

Burke eased her onto her feet but kept a tight hold about her waist. "Don't try to escape, my darling. People wouldn't understand why you would want to run away from the man you love."

"When's the big day?" Juliette asked.

"Saturday," Burke replied.

"Not this Saturday," several voices protested.

"I'm not taking any chances that Callie will change her mind," Burke said. "If she hears too many stories about my sordid life, she may think she's made a bad deal and—"

"Nonsense," Juliette said and all the ladies nodded. "You know the old saying, a man wants to be a woman's first love and a woman wants to be a man's last love."

"Am I your first true love?" Burke asked teasingly, but Callie noted the tension in his voice and the threatening look in those crystal blue eyes.

"Yes, you are," she said softly.

"Hey, old man, after that sort of confession, you'd best tell the lady what she wants to hear," Herbert Garvey advised.

Burke pivoted Callie so that they faced each other. He cupped her face with his hands and gazed into her eyes. "If I am your first true love, then, my darling, I promise that you will indeed be my last love."

The kiss took her unawares. His lips mated with hers in the most tender yet passionate of kisses. Of their own volition, her arms lifted to drape around his neck. When Burke pulled her closer so that their bodies aligned perfectly, she moaned with pleasure. Instantly, he deepened the kiss and in seconds the world disappeared, leaving the two of them cocooned within a sweet moment out of time.

When Burke ended the kiss as abruptly as he'd begun it, Callie staggered slightly and opened her eyes. Everyone stood quietly, as if in hushed awe, their gazes riveted to the engaged couple. A heated blush stained Callie's cheeks.

"Wow!" Juliette exclaimed.

Callie heard a collective sigh from all the ladies. She

The Silhouette Reader Service™ — Here's how it works:

If offer card is missing write to: Silhouette Reader Service, 3010 Walden Ave., P.O. Box 1867, Buffalo NY 14240-1867

NO POSTAGE
NECESSARY
IF MAILED
IN THE
UNITED STATES

BUSINESS REPLY MAIL

FIRST-CLASS MAIL   PERMIT NO. 717   BUFFALO, NY

POSTAGE WILL BE PAID BY ADDRESSEE

SILHOUETTE READER SERVICE

3010 WALDEN AVE

PO BOX 1867

BUFFALO NY 14240-9952

knew that they envied her and longed to be in her shoes. No woman alive could resist Burke Lonigan. He possessed an abundance of animal magnetism, bold black Irish good looks and a hypnotic charm.

Nausea churned in Callie's stomach, but she knew she didn't dare excuse herself. If she was sick, everyone would assume she was pregnant. No doubt that would be the speculation regardless. Why else would Burke be marrying her in such a hurry? But she could hardly tell them the truth, could she? That some lunatic with whom Burke did his underhanded business threatened to kill her. She wanted to scream at the top of her lungs, *You people have no idea what kind of man you're working for, do you? He's a criminal who makes millions off the suffering of others. He sells weapons to anyone for the right price. Even terrorists!*

How could she have ever thought herself in love with this man? A tormenting voice inside her replied, *Because he's the most exciting man you've ever known. An incredible lover. And Seamus's father. Deny it all you'd like, but despite what you now know about Burke Lonigan, you still want him.*

No, I don't! she cried silently. *Yes, you do.* Her heart wept.

Chapter 8

If this were a real marriage, I'd be the luckiest man in the world, Burke thought. Callie was beautiful. Her dark red hair had been piled atop her head with a band of tiny flowers circling the loose bun. She wore a simple silk suit of pale yellow, with shoes dyed to match. Her only items of jewelry, except for her engagement ring, were a strand of pearls and small pearl ear studs, which had belonged to her mother. Or so Enid had told him.

When he had suggested having young Seamus at the ceremony, Callie had adamantly opposed the idea.

"I'd prefer that Seamus doesn't become attached to you in any way, that for the duration of our marriage, you have very little contact with my son," Callie had said. "Since we'll be married only a brief time, I'm afraid it will confuse him if he becomes accustomed to you and then one day you're no longer a part of our lives."

Since Seamus was her son, he felt it only reasonable that she be the one to set the rules that governed the child.

She was right, of course. Better for the child if they didn't become accustomed to each other.

Poor Callie. Burke wished there was some other way to protect her, her son and the supersensitive deal with Simon. But there wasn't. Despite her elegant attire and the bouquet of cream roses she held—courtesy of Enid—Callie looked more like a condemned woman than a blushing bride. But then she had made it abundantly clear that she considered this marriage a prison term, something to be endured. He shouldn't care what she thought of him, but he did. Other women were fascinated by the rumors of his dark secret life and found him all the more appealing because of it. But not Callie. Knowing that he was an arms dealer had drastically altered her opinion of him. And heaven help him, he didn't want her to think badly of him. If only he could tell her the truth. But without permission from Jonah, no operative could reveal his association with SPEAR, not even to close friends, family and loved ones.

Is that how you think of Callie? an inner voice asked. *Do you consider her a loved one?* She *was* going to become his wife, even if the marriage was an elaborate hoax to curb Simon's suspicions. He would have liked the two of them to continue as friends and perhaps become lovers. The physical attraction between them had been apparent to him and to her from the first day they'd met. He had naturally assumed that, sooner or later, they'd indulge in a brief affair. But considering the way Callie felt about him now, he'd be lucky if she would let him shake her hand.

"Are we ready?" With a cordial smile on his face, the registrar, a portly, bald man in his late fifties, motioned them into his small office. "You've brought two witnesses, I see.'' He glanced from Leland's somber face to Enid, who offered him a weak smile.

"Quite ready,'' Burke replied.

"Very well. Will the bride and groom step forward and stand right here?'' The registrar showed them where to stand for the ceremony.

Burke turned to Leland and asked if he had the ring. Leland, dressed in his best navy blue suit, nodded and held up his pinky, showing that he had the band secured on the tip of his finger. *Let's get this over with,* Burke thought. *Let's finalize this farce.* Waiting outside were a couple of bodyguards he had hired for Callie and Enid as a precaution. He had no doubt that Simon had sent at least one representative to make sure the marriage took place.

Following the registrar's instructions, Burke took Callie's hand. "I do solemnly declare that I do not know of any lawful impediment why I, Burke Padriac Lonigan, may not be joined in matrimony to Caledonia Elaine Severin.''

After Callie swore to the same, they exchanged rings. Burke glanced at the thin platinum band on his finger, and an odd sensation knotted his stomach.

Repeating the vows, Burke said, "I call upon these persons here present to witness that I, Burke Padriac Lonigan, do take thee, Caledonia Elaine Severin, to be my lawful wedded wife.''

Callie swallowed hard, then lifted her gaze and looked directly at Burke. *You've come this far,* she told herself. *You can't back out now. Do what you have to do.*

"I call upon these persons here present to witness that I—I—'' Her voice cracked. Burke squeezed her hand and gave her a reassuring smile. She knew he was trying to convey that everything would be all right. But she knew better. Nothing would ever be all right again.

"I, Caledonia Elaine Severin, do take thee, Burke Padriac Lonigan, to be my lawful wedded husband."

This was not the wedding day she'd dreamed about all her life. There was no church filled with friends, relatives and well-wishing acquaintances. She didn't wear a bridal gown of white lace and satin. No long veil trailed behind her as her father walked her down the aisle.

"I'll need you to check the entry in the register," the registrar said. "And then both bride and groom must sign, as well as the two witnesses."

The entire event had taken less than ten minutes. A mockery of a union that was supposed to last a lifetime. And silly girl that she was, Callie had always believed that when she married, it would be forever. She'd never thought she would enter into a marriage that was doomed to end within a few months.

"I'll get the car, sir," Leland said when the foursome exited the building.

Burke nodded, then turned to Callie. "My plane is ready for takeoff whenever we arrive at the airport. No rush. So when we stop by for your bags, feel free to take as much time with Seamus as you'd like."

Avoiding eye contact, Callie glanced across the street where double-decker red buses filled with tourists and numerous black cabs mingled with other Saturday traffic. Not a cloud in the sky, only sunshine on her wedding day. She wished it had rained. The weather would have better suited her gloomy mood.

"Is it really necessary that we fly off to Italy for the weekend?" Callie asked. "I'd rather not leave Seamus. With things the way they are—"

"I've already explained to you that at least a brief honeymoon is expected and until—" he glanced at Enid. "I suppose she's told you everything, hasn't she? So there's no need to pretend.'' Burke snorted. Damn situation to be in! ''Callie, I promise you that your son will be guarded by Leland Perkins, the best bodyguard in the business. And backup guards will be nearby at all times. Until the situation with Simon is taken care of, we must act like happy newlyweds.''

''I'm not sure that I'm that good an actress.''

Burke laid his hand in the center of her back, but she jerked away quickly. ''Dammit, I'm not going to hurt you.''

''Sorry.'' She took a quick peek at him and noted the tension in his face. He wasn't pleased with her. Too bad. She wasn't pleased with him, either!

''If you'd rather not be separated from your son, then bring him along. I suppose it's not unheard of to take a child on one's honeymoon.''

Now what? Callie asked herself. What possible excuse could she give him for not taking Seamus with them? She could hardly say that she'd rather he not get a good look at her son because he might see the striking resemblance between her child and himself. The longer she could put off their meeting, the better. And if she were lucky, Burke wouldn't insist on ever being around her son.

''Can you truly promise me that Seamus will be safe while I'm away?'' she asked.

''Yes. I honestly don't think that Simon will try to harm any of us as long as he believes we haven't duped him or I haven't double-crossed him.''

''You—you don't intend to double-cross him, do you?''

''The less you—'' he glanced at a glowering Enid ''—and Enid know about my dealings with Simon, the better.''

''If you deliberately put us in danger, I'll find a way to

rip your heart out, Burke Lonigan," Enid warned. "You've caused nothing but trouble for Callie. From the very beginning, you—"

Callie jabbed her irate cousin in the ribs and gave her a will-you-please-shut-up look. "There's Leland with the car."

"So it is."

Leland hopped out and opened the back door. Callie and Enid got into the Rolls.

Burke stuck his head into the car and said, "Leland will drive you to Kensington and bring you along to my house later."

"Where are you going?" Callie asked.

"Some last-minute loose ends to tie up," he said, then slammed the door.

Within minutes Leland had merged the Rolls into the traffic. Burke snorted. He wanted a stiff drink. But he needed to keep a clear head. He could always get plastered tonight, once they were in Italy. After all, what else would there be to do on his wedding night?

Half an hour later, Burke unlocked the door to his private office at Lonigan's Imports and Exports. He'd been followed by one of the bodyguards Leland had hired, as well as someone he felt certain was reporting to Simon. Leland's man followed him into the elevator, exchanged an acknowledging nod and then, once on the twentieth floor, stood guard outside Lonigan's Imports and Exports. Simon's man undoubtedly had waited downstairs.

Burke unlocked his office and flipped on a light, then closed the door behind him. After removing his cellular phone, he sat down behind his desk, made contact and waited for Jonah to call from his secure phone. The mysterious head honcho of SPEAR was a perfect stranger to Burke. He'd been following the man's orders for years and yet the two had never met face-to-face. Burke felt certain that only a select few had ever made personal contact with the boss.

The moment the phone rang and he heard the familiar voice, Burke said, "The wedding went as planned. We leave shortly for a weekend honeymoon on the Amalfi Coast. Leland will personally guard Callie's child."

"If we pull this deal off, we should have Simon in custody by the time you return," Jonah said. "But until you hear from me, consider yourself, Ms. Severin and the child still in danger."

"And what happens if something goes wrong? If Simon thinks I've betrayed him, he'll come after me, my wife and her child. I don't want that to happen, Jonah. Do you understand?"

"No matter how things go down, I'll see to it that your hands are clean and that Simon doesn't hold you responsible."

"I'll expect you to keep that promise."

The connection ended and Burke groaned. He knew that Jonah was a man of his word. He'd never lied to Burke. If he said he'd protect Burke, that's exactly what Jonah would do. All Burke had to do was wait—wait for Simon to be captured.

In the meantime, he had a reluctant bride to deal with and a phony two-day honeymoon to endure. How the hell was he going to spend forty-eight hours in paradise with Callie and not make love to her?

"I can't thank you enough for staying with Seamus today, Mrs. Goodhope." Callie gave the motherly minder a hug as she slipped an extra ten quid into her coat pocket.

"Oh, Callie, lovie, it was my pleasure." She held

Callie's hand and smiled. "Aren't you just the prettiest bride ever."

Callie walked Mrs. Goodhope outside, then hurried in and went straight to where Seamus sat on the living room floor playing with his wooden building blocks.

"You'll be a good boy for Auntie Enid, won't you darling?" She gathered Seamus into her arms, eased onto the sofa and placed her son in her lap. "Mama will miss you, but I'll be gone only until Monday. And if you miss me terribly, Auntie Enid can ring me and we can talk on the telephone." She glanced at Enid, who stood with Leland in the foyer. "You have the number at the villa, don't you?"

"I have all the information. Don't worry about Seamus and me." Enid entered the living room, came over to the sofa and sat. She ruffled Seamus's black curls and winked at him.

The child laughed, and during the process of trying to imitate Enid's wink, he opened and closed both eyes rapidly.

"Oh, you little angel, you!" Enid held out her arms and Seamus went happily to his auntie. Enid glanced at Callie. "Might as well get this over with while I've got his attention and he's quite content."

"I don't want to leave him. I can't bear the thought that he could be in danger and I'll be hundreds of miles away."

As if on cue, the doorbell rang. Leland responded immediately. The man called Quigley, whom she'd met earlier in the week, entered the house and spoke in quiet tones with Leland.

"Is something wrong?" Callie asked.

"No, ma'am. Nothing's wrong," Leland assured her.

"Quigley's here to stay with Ms. Ludlow and young Seamus until I return."

"Oh."

"I'm not rushing you, Ms. Sev—that is, Mrs. Lonigan," Leland said. "Take all the time you need to settle things here."

"Things are as settled as they're going to be." Callie kissed Seamus on both cheeks, then stood. "My bags are upstairs. I'm afraid there are two rather large ones. Marilyn Farris sent them over, already packed with my trousseau. Undoubtedly she thought I'd be away for more than a couple of days."

"I'll get your bags, ma'am, if you'll tell me which room upstairs."

"Callie, aren't you going to change clothes before you leave?"

"No, I don't see any reason to change."

Enid stood, lifted Seamus onto her hip, then picked up the bridal bouquet, which Callie had tossed onto a side table when they'd returned home. "What shall I do with this? Will you want it—"

"Throw it into the trash," Callie said sharply.

"Mama?" Seamus seemed to have picked up on Callie's uneasiness.

"It's all right, my little love," Callie told her son. "Why don't you go in the kitchen with Aunt Enid for milk and biscuits?"

The minute Enid took Seamus for his afternoon treat, Callie led Leland Perkins upstairs. The two large leather suitcases were just inside her bedroom door.

When Leland went to lift the luggage, Callie laid her hand on his arm. "How long have you worked for Mr. Lonigan?"

"Eight years, ma'am."

"And have you always known about…about his other business?"

"I'm not at liberty to say, ma'am."

"I see." Callie jerked her hand away, as if touching him had contaminated her.

"No, ma'am, you don't see," Leland said. "Not really. I can't say why, but you should have more faith in Mr. Lonigan. I realize it won't be easy to trust him, given the circumstances, but I know for a fact that he's a good man."

Callie searched Leland's eyes, wanting to see deception, but all she saw was a set of dark brown eyes that seemed to be pleading for her understanding. "How can I possibly have faith in a man who is a notorious arms dealer? I had thought…had hoped that the rumors weren't true."

"There are truths and then there are truths, ma'am."

"What are you trying to say? You're speaking in riddles."

"Sorry, ma'am." Leland lifted the suitcases. "I've already said more than I should have."

When Leland walked into the hall, Callie followed. "Do you truly believe that Mr. Lonigan is a good man?"

Without slowing his steps or glancing at her, he replied, "Yes, ma'am. He's one of the best men I've ever known."

"We're taking your private plane?" Callie sat inside the luxurious Lonigan's Imports and Exports jet.

"Why should we travel like the tourists?"

"Why, indeed."

"It isn't my wealth you disapprove of, is it, my darling," Burke said. "If you thought I'd made my millions in the import-export business, you wouldn't wrinkle up your nose in disdain. But you assume that all this—'' he spread his arms ''—is ill-gotten gains. You believe I earned it through illegal means, don't you?''

She glared at him, refusing to allow herself to admit that she found him unbearably attractive. He had changed into casual brown slacks and a beige cashmere sweater. She, on the other hand, wore her yellow silk wedding suit beneath her woollen coat.

''Didn't you get all of this through your illegal business dealings?''

''Would you believe me if I said no? If I told you that not one penny of my money was earned by—''

''I'd rather you not lie to me,'' she said.

''Very well, I won't waste my breath trying to persuade you to trust me.''

He turned and went into the cockpit. Callie heard him speaking to the pilot, but she couldn't make out the words. The interior of the plane was tastefully decorated, but then she had expected nothing less. Burke's home in Belgravia was sheer perfection, and his suite of offices in the city had no rival.

She stood, eased out of her heavy coat, laid it aside and took a seat on the tan leather lounger. If only Burke were a good man, an honest man. She sighed. *If only this marriage was real and we loved each other and were planning a future together—the three of us. Burke and Seamus and I. If only I were looking forward to a real honeymoon, anticipating a wedding night in Burke's arms.* But that wouldn't happen. It couldn't. She didn't dare allow herself to indulge in even the briefest of affairs with Burke. If she did, he might walk away unscathed, untouched by their relationship, but she understood herself only too well. Despite knowing what kind of man Burke Lonigan was, if she became his lover, she would fall in love with him. If the truth were told, she was halfway in love with the man already.

And you're a fool! she told herself. *A bloody fool!*

Burke returned, carrying a silver bucket that held a magnum of champagne in one hand and two crystal flutes in the other hand. "If you're hungry, there's—"

"I couldn't eat a bite," she said, and hated herself for snapping at him. Her belligerent attitude wasn't helping the situation. Burke hadn't wanted this marriage any more than she had, but he was making the best of a bad situation. The least she could do was try to help him. "I'm sorry, I didn't mean to sound so... I promise I shall do better."

"You have every right to be upset and angry." Burke placed the champagne and glasses on the table, then sat beside her, leaving several feet of space between them. "Once this is all over, I promise that I'll arrange for you to get a good position at another company. And if you'll let me, I'd like to set up a trust fund for Seamus." When she opened her mouth to protest, he held up a restraining hand. "I know you wouldn't accept money from me, but a trust fund for Seamus wouldn't be money for you. It would be security for your son's future. I feel as if I owe you that much."

Now why had Burke made such a generous offer? Why, when she was convinced he was evil personified, did he do something so incredibly nice? *He's one of the best men I've ever known.* She heard Leland Perkins's declaration replaying itself in her mind. But how was it possible for someone who dealt in illegal weapons to be a good man? *You should have more faith in Mr. Lonigan.* Again Leland's words haunted her.

Don't do this to yourself, the sane part of her mind warned. *Why should you believe Leland? The man is a*

*loyal employee, someone who is probably involved in
Burke's illegal dealings.*

"I don't know what to say." Callie averted her gaze,
glancing at her folded hands resting in her lap.

"Please, just say that you'll consider my offer."

"All right. I'll consider your offer."

"Good." Burke smiled, then reached over and lifted
the champagne from the silver bucket.

Callie tried not to look at him while he opened the
champagne, but her hungry gaze studied him from the top
of his silky black hair, down his broad shoulders to his
slender waist and hips. While he was busy pouring the
bubbly into the flutes, she drank her fill of her incredibly
handsome husband. Without warning, the memories of
that long-ago night surfaced. She had never known anything like the passion she had experienced in Burke's
arms. Together they had shared a wondrous night. Bodies
mated. Hearts exchanged sweet intimacies. Souls touched
ever so briefly. She had given him comfort and understanding and all the passionate love within her. And he
had taken all that she offered and in return exposed the
most vulnerable, tormented part of himself. And he had
made love to her with incomparable expertise and an
earth-shattering tenderness that she would never forget.
Not as long as she lived.

How could that man be evil? How was it possible that
he could be the monster who made a profit from ungodly
savagery that promoted war and terrorism? Somehow she
simply could not relate one with the other. Dear God, was
it possible that Leland was right? Was there more to
Burke Lonigan's secret life than she knew? If so, what
could it be?

"Champagne?" Burke handed her a filled flute, the ef-
fervescent bubbles foaming to the brim of the glass.

She accepted the flute and in the process their hands accidently brushed. Their gazes met and held for just a second, but long enough for her to see the longing in Burke's eyes. She knew that at least his desire was real.

But she suspected that if she had seen the truth in his eyes, he had seen the same in hers. That meant he knew she wanted him, despite all her noble protests.

Burke lifted his glass, his gaze still focused on Callie's face.

"Here's to you…and me…and to both of us getting what we want."

Warmth suffused her body as a flush crept up her neck and stained her cheeks pink. With only a slight hesitation, she lifted her glass and said, "To wishes coming true." And just before her lips touched the rim of the crystal flute, she made her silent wish.

I wish that Burke were the kind of man that I would be proud to introduce to Seamus as his father. And…and if he were that kind of man, I wish that he would love me.

Simon entered the smoky pub in East London. He pulled the brim of his hat over his forehead and turned up the collar of his trench coat. With his good eye, he scanned the bar area and met the gaze of the man he'd come to see. He nodded, motioning for the guy to come to him.

Larson brought a couple of mugs of beer with him as he headed toward the booth Simon had chosen.

"Here we are," Larson said.

Simon took the mug, but didn't bother with polite conversation. Not with the likes of Mick Larson, whom he'd hired to oversee the job of keeping tabs on Burke Lonigan and his fiancée. He saved his good manners for people and occasions that deserved them.

"Lonigan and his woman boarded that private jet of his and it took off for Italy this afternoon," Larson said. "Still got a man keeping tabs on the cousin and the laddie. Seems Lonigan's man, Perkins, is staying at the Kensington town house with them."

"Good. That means Lonigan didn't take my threats lightly." Simon took a hefty swig of the dark beer, then wiped his mouth with the back of his hand. "I'll let you know when to call off your men. As soon as my business is completed, I'll be in touch." Simon reached into his coat pocket and pulled out a sealed envelope. "Here's the amount we agreed on. Once this is over, I'll see that you get a bonus."

Larson grabbed the payment, lifted his mug and slid out of the booth. Simon remained at the pub long enough to finish his beer, then slipped onto the foggy East London street. With Burke Lonigan, true to his word, married and away on his honeymoon, Simon was ready to proceed with the arms deal. Lonigan had made the arrangements several days ago. All that was required now was a simple phone call to tell Lonigan's associates that the time was right.

Within twenty-four hours, the shipment of weapons would finally be in his possession. The corners of Simon's mouth lifted in a satisfied smile.

Chapter 9

From the airport in Naples, a chauffeured limousine took them to Burke's villa on the Amalfi coast. They arrived just before twilight. The lingering sunlight washed the world with transparent gold—the sky, the earth, the atmosphere glimmered with an aureate sheen. Callie hadn't been in Italy for years and she'd almost forgotten what a magnificent country it was. Beautiful in the way only ancient countries that honored their history could be.

Callie's family wasn't rich, only moderately wealthy. What her American relatives referred to as upper middle class. But Burke was rich. Super rich. With a private jet. A home in Belgravia. A villa in Italy. And apartments in Paris and New York. Her husband lived in a world that most people only dreamed of and never saw except in movies and magazines.

Just as they rounded a bend in the narrow road the Villa Bella Di Vista came into view. Callie gasped. She hadn't meant to voice her surprise, but the sight of the elegant, incredibly magnificent villa situated on the cliffs above the sea took her breath away. She had heard that this was the most romantic of all the Italian coastlines, and now she believed it. Words could never express the magnificence of the villa, the grounds and the panoramic view.

"Do you approve?" Burke asked.

Callie glanced at him to see if he was joking, but the look on his face was somber. "It's beautiful."

When the chauffeur opened the limousine door, Burke emerged and held out his hand to assist Callie. "Then you do like it?"

"Like it? I love it." Callie pivoted slowly as if her body were on an axis. "I don't think I've ever seen anything so breathtaking."

"Good. It would seem I made the right choice for our honeymoon."

Callie tensed momentarily at the mention of their honeymoon. But when Burke turned immediately to issue instructions to the chauffeur concerning their luggage, she walked toward the white columned portico entrance to the palatial villa.

Burke came up behind her, slid his arm around her waist and diverted her attention from the house to the grounds. "Would you like a tour of the gardens before it gets dark?"

A shiver of sexual awareness rippled along her nerve endings. Just the gentle touch of his arm around her ignited unwanted urges within her. But she didn't pull away. Somehow it would seem foolish to overreact to such an innocent act.

"I'd very much like to see the grounds," she told him.

The villa was surrounded by large gardens that led to a terrace with a breathtaking view. Balconies hung over the cliffs and miniature gardens descended to the sea. A large swimming pool, situated on the terrace, caught Callie's eye.

"It's heated," Burke said. "We could take a swim later tonight, if you'd like."

When she wiggled away from his loose hold, he didn't try to reclaim the physical connection. "I'm tired. We've had a long day."

"Yes, of course. And you're probably hungry, too." With a welcoming sweep of his hand, he invited her into his villa. "I gave instructions for dinner to be ready for us when we arrived."

"Do you have servants here?" she asked as she followed him toward the house.

"Yes, a husband and wife, who look after the house and grounds. But they left several hours ago, as instructed, so we could have our privacy."

"Because you want them to think this is a real honeymoon."

"Yes."

Callie noted the odd expression on Burke's face and couldn't help wondering if he felt as awkward as she did. But how was that possible? Could the suave, sophisticated Burke Lonigan ever feel ill at ease? Perhaps. After all, he'd never gone on a pretend honeymoon before, had he?

The chauffeur met them on the steps leading to the portico. Burke spoke to him in Italian, thanking him in one sentence and dismissing him in the other. Callie's mother had been fluent in Italian, but her own knowledge was rudimentary at best. She understood a word now and then during the conversation.

The chauffeur smiled at Callie and then said to Burke, *"Il vostro bride e molto bello."*

Burke draped his arm around Callie's shoulders and

drew her to his side. "He's right. My bride is very beautiful."

"Vi auguro molta felicità," the chauffeur said in parting, then got in the limousine and drove away.

"What was that last thing he said?" Callie asked, as Burke opened the double doors leading from the portico to the grand foyer.

"He wished us much happiness."

Callie took a deep breath as she entered the house, but found she hadn't been prepared for such splendor. A marble staircase led up to the second floor. White and light and airy and yet elegant and filled with priceless antiques.

"What do you want first?" he asked. "We can eat or you can go upstairs to the bedrooms and…relax."

"I think I'd like to go upstairs, freshen up and change clothes."

"This way." Burke led her up the curved marble staircase. "There are three bedrooms. I took the liberty of having your luggage placed in this one—" he opened the doors to a large, magnificent room with pale gold walls, polished wooden floors and a massive canopy bed of rich, dark mahogany "—but if you'd prefer one of the other—"

"No, this one is wonderful." Callie floated across the room and opened the French doors that led onto a balcony that overlooked the sea. She sucked in her breath. If only this really were her honeymoon, she would think herself in heaven. She turned to Burke. He stood in the doorway, the width of the room separating them. "Your villa is…well, it's fabulous."

"Thank you." Burke nodded toward a closed door to his left. "The bathroom is through there. Each bedroom has its own private bath. After you've freshened up and changed clothes, we can eat dinner."

"If you're hungry, please go ahead and have dinner without me."

"I'll wait," he said. "You'll find me in the study downstairs."

"All right. Thank you."

Burke closed the door behind him, leaving her alone. Callie whirled about the room and then collapsed on the antique bed. A canopy of gold satin met her uplifted gaze. Glancing across the room, she noticed what she felt certain was a priceless antique tapestry hanging on the wall. Although she'd never lived in squalor, being surrounded by such opulent luxury overwhelmed her. In the embassies around the world, she had been a visitor, but here she was the mistress, if only temporarily.

Cautioning herself not to allow Burke's great wealth to seduce her, Callie jumped off the bed, straightened the satin spread and searched for her luggage. She found both suitcases stationed beside a nine-foot mahogany armoire decorated with intricate carvings. She lifted one suitcase onto the chaise longue by the windows, then opened it and began rummaging through the contents.

My God! The entire suitcase was filled with lingerie. Expensive, beautiful underwear and negligees. White and pale yellow. Soft pastels and rich jewel tones. She chose cream satin underwear, then stuffed the other contents into the case, set it on the floor and lifted its mate. She breathed a sigh of relief when she opened the second case and found it filled with usable clothing. After sorting through the items, she chose a pair of cinnamon-colored satin slacks and an oversize beige blouse. Designer clothes. The possessions of a rich man's wife.

She could not allow herself to become accustomed to living this way. As soon as she and Seamus were no longer in danger from Simon, she would insist on ending this farce of a marriage. And then she'd take Seamus and go far away.

Your son is entitled to all the privileges that come with his father's wealth, a nagging inner voice reminded her. But what price would her child have to pay for the trappings of wealth and privilege, when Burke had acquired his fortune partially through illegal means? And not just illegal, but immoral.

After putting on a Debussy CD and building a fire, Burke settled in front of the massive fireplace in the study. The first time he'd visited this lovely hillside villa, he had chosen this room as his favorite. The furnishings were antique—big, dark, heavy pieces that appealed to the old-fashioned part of his personality. A manly man's room. Yet as elegant as any other room in the house. In this study he truly felt like the lord of the manor.

He was glad Callie approved of the villa. When choosing between this house and the apartment in Paris for their mock honeymoon, he'd decided that the villa offered more space. More room for them to avoid each other, if they chose to spend some of the next forty-eight hours apart. And if the confinement became unbearable, they could take the Porsche he kept in the garage and drive into the nearest village to do a little sight-seeing. Or they could drive along the coast and enjoy the scenery.

If this were truly his honeymoon, he would never leave the bedroom, except for necessary diversions. If Callie were indeed his bride, he would keep her occupied day and night making love to her. His sexual thoughts stimulated him, exciting him instantly. Thoughts of Callie, naked and aroused, filled his mind. Young and fresh and sweet. And somehow innocent, despite the fact that she wasn't a virgin.

Would it be so wrong to take what pleasure they could from this marriage of necessity? They were consenting adults, sexually attracted to each other and well aware that their relationship would soon be terminated. He wasn't a man who enjoyed staying celibate for long periods of time, although in the past two years, he had found himself more and more dissatisfied with meaningless affairs. But an affair with Callie wouldn't be meaningless. And that was the crux of the situation.

Burke forced his thoughts from the delights of Callie's body to the reality that she would most likely thwart any attempts he made at seduction. She believed him to be an evil man, someone she despised. Even though she wanted him—of that he had no doubts—she would fight the urge to succumb to her desire.

He heard her outside the study, the heels of her shoes clicking softly against the marble floors. Quickly he scanned the table by the windows that overlooked the sea, inspecting each item. He'd brought their dinner into the study, along with a bottle of Lambrusco, an Italian red wine. If nothing else, they could share a nice dinner and perhaps some civil conversation.

When Callie entered the study—an elegant room by anyone's standards—she found Burke pouring wine. The strands of a Debussy melody encompassed her and relaxed her immediately. The shimmery warmth from a fire in the six-foot-high fireplace mesmerized her, beckoning her into the alluring trap. An aura of sensuality and seduction permeated the atmosphere. Her common sense warned her of danger, but her body and her heart led her deeper into the enticing setting.

"You look lovely," he said, taking in every inch of her, from shoulder-length red curls, down over the silk blouse that hung loosely and yet still managed to cling provocatively to the tips of her breasts.

"Thank you." She walked slowly across the room, making her way to the table. "But then this is a Marilyn Farris original and I suppose anyone would look lovely in her creations."

When she neared him, Burke handed her a glass of wine. She accepted his offering and somehow managed not to shiver when their hands brushed against each other.

"I hope the things Marilyn packed for you are to your liking."

"The items she chose would be to anyone's liking."

Burke held the chair for her. Glancing up and over her shoulder, she smiled at him. "Everything looks delicious. And the flowers!"

Callie spotted the bouquet of yellow roses that graced the center of the table. "You're certainly an expert at setting a scene. No wonder you have a reputation as a ladies' man."

Burke sat across from her, then looked directly into her eyes. "This is the first time I've been damned for my expertise."

"Was I damning you?" She sipped the wine.

"By everything you say and everything you do."

"Then I must apologize. I realize that you're simply trying to make the best of a bad situation. And given the circumstances, you've been very kind to me. You've put my safety and my son's safety above everything else. And for that I am grateful."

"But you still don't trust me, do you, Callie?"

With nervous fingertips, she circled the rim of the glass, then set it aside. "You can't begin to imagine how much I want to trust you." *I want you to be a decent, law-abiding man,* her heart cried. *My son deserves a father whom he can respect.* "But I know about Simon, about your secret life…so how can I possibly trust you?"

"I don't suppose, just for the duration of our stay here at the villa, you could forget that I have a secret life?" Burke reached across the table and took her hand in his. "We would be good together, my darling. I know it and you know it. Regardless of how you feel about my business dealings, you can't deny that there is something powerful between us. Just wishing it didn't exist won't make it go away."

She pulled her hand from his grasp, lifted a fork and speared the spinach in her salad. "I'm not foolish enough to deny that I'm attracted to you. I realize that I'm not very good at hiding my feelings. But despite the fact that I have a child and I've never been married, my sexual experience is limited. I've told you that my first lover was my fiancé. I was in a committed relationship with him. Or at least I was committed. And that's what I want…what I need. I'm not the type of woman who wants to have casual sex."

"What about Seamus's father? You seem reluctant to talk about him. Were you in a committed relationship with him, too?"

"No. But that was my one exception. I allowed lust to… He and I were both in pain. We needed each other. What started out as comforting and caring turned into passion. And see how that turned out? I don't want to repeat that kind of mistake."

"Are you saying that you consider little Seamus a mistake?"

"Don't put words in my mouth." Callie toyed with her salad, her appetite suddenly gone. "Seamus means more to me than anything. It's just that I wish I'd been married when he was born and that he had a father to be there for him as he's growing up.''

''When our arrangement ends, I'll help you find Seamus's father, if you want me to. I think the man has a right to know he fathered a child.''

''I don't need your help, Burke. I know where to find Seamus's father. I've always known. But the man...he isn't someone I want to be involved in my child's life, certainly not as his father.''

''You're very judgmental. You don't trust me. You won't give me the benefit of the doubt. And now you tell me that Seamus's father isn't worthy of knowing the truth—that he has a son.''

''This isn't any of your business,'' she lied.

God, how had the conversation drifted from their sexual attraction to a discussion of Seamus's father? *Sooner or later, Burke is going to find out,* an inner voice warned her. *How can you stay married to this man, even for a few weeks, and keep him and Seamus apart?*

''I'd rather not discuss my son,'' she said, releasing her fork to rest on the edge of her plate. ''I should never have told you so much about my past. It has nothing to do with you and me.''

''Hmm...somehow, I think it does.'' Burke studied her closely, then shook his head. ''I remind you of him, don't I? That's it, isn't it?''

''What are you talking about?''

''I remind you of Seamus's father.''

''No! I—I never said that you... Why would you think that?''

''Was he rich and powerful? Was he about my age? Was he a womanizer?''

''Yes,'' she admitted. ''He was all those things. And

he was also the most exciting man I'd ever met and the most incredible lover.''

Burke felt his reaction to her comment from the inside out, in every fiber of his being. His nerves rioted. Each muscle tensed. His stomach tightened painfully. Pure unadulterated jealousy consumed him. She had cared about this man. He could see it in her eyes, in the expression on her face. Had she been in love with her son's father? Was she in love with him still?

A man didn't want to hear about how exciting another man was or what an incredible lover he'd been. Not when he wanted a woman the way Burke wanted Callie. Desperately. Mindlessly. More than he'd ever wanted anything or anyone in his entire life.

Wait! his memories whispered. *Are you forgetting her? The woman who still haunts your dreams? The sweet, alluring woman whose taste and scent and feel are all a part of you still?*

But she was an illusion, a faceless spirit from a night he refused to acknowledge. God, what could have possibly happened that night to have forced his mind to erase so much of it? Why had he been left with only fragments and not the whole? After that night, hadn't he tried—tried so hard—to recall her name and her face? He had thought so, but now he realized that the exact opposite was true. He hadn't wanted to know her identity. If he had known who she was, he would have gone after her and opened himself up to—to what? To love and commitment? To unequaled passion that could have left him vulnerable and easily hurt if she rejected him?

But Callie was a different woman. He knew her name. Her face. He'd even had a few glimpses into her heart. He could want Callie. He could share passion and pleasure with her. And still remain safe. Never vulnerable. She knew that their relationship came without strings, without permanent bonds. He could take her and satisfy the raging hunger without risking his heart, without being vulnerable. If only Callie could accept what was between them for what it was—desire. Not love. Nothing to tie them to each other. Pleasure for the sake of pleasure. Sexual fulfillment that could ease the ache inside both of them.

"Let's eat," Burke said, determined to diffuse the tension he had created between them. Detrimental tension, the kind that would push her further away from him instead of bring her closer.

"What?"

"We shouldn't let this delicious meal go to waste."

"No. No, we shouldn't, but—"

"I want you. You want me. But unless you're willing to set aside your distrust, even for a few hours, you won't come to me willingly. And I will not seduce you, Callie."

"I see."

"So, let's eat," he repeated.

He noted the rise and fall of her breasts as she sighed heavily. Was she relieved? Or was she disappointed? He wasn't sure. But he knew one thing for certain—whatever happened between them on this mock honeymoon would be her decision. If she wanted him as much as he thought she did, she would come to him. He would simply wait. And hope.

Feeling like a caged animal, Callie paced the floor in her elegant bedroom. She could not—would not—go downstairs and expose herself to Burke's undeniable charm. She knew what he wanted—the same thing she wanted. Sex! Hot, passionate, earth-shattering sex! For him their mating would mean nothing more than appeasing his sexual hunger, but for her it would mean everything. If she succumbed to her wanton desires, she would be putting not only her heart at risk, but her and Seamus's future.

She had reminded herself of all the reasons she would be an utter fool to give in to the lust that urged her to relive that one night—that fantasy night with Burke. The devil on her shoulder whispered enticing rationalizations in her ear. *What would it hurt to enjoy these days alone with Burke? The two of you could agree that these were moments out of time, and what transpired between you here at the villa wouldn't affect your future relationship.*

And all the while her conscience battled with her desire, she listened for any sound of Burke. He hadn't come upstairs, that much she knew. So where was he and what was he doing? After she had insisted on helping him clear away the dinner dishes and straighten up in the kitchen, she had excused herself and fled like the coward she was. If she'd stayed with him and shared more wine in front of the fire, she doubted she would have been able to resist him.

And for so many reasons, all of them sane and sensible and oh, so right, she had to protect herself from the deep and passionate yearning she felt for Burke. A man she could not trust. A man who offered no explanations for his illegal activities. A man she could never acknowledge as Seamus's father.

Memories of that long-ago night surfaced, heating her body from the inside out and igniting a deeper and more urgent longing within her. She could know again that unparalleled passion and incomparable fulfillment. All she had to do was go to Burke.

No! You can't! The war of desire versus willpower raged like two giant armies fighting for dominance.

Feeling as if she were on fire, knowing that she had to

do something to calm the battle within her, Callie rushed to the French doors and flung them open wide. The cool night air enveloped her immediately, chilling her hot flesh. Then suddenly she heard the sound of water, but not the sweet, lulling roar of the sea far below. The noise came from close by, directly beneath her. Gripping the balcony banisters, she leaned over and stared at the swimming pool. Burke swam the length of the pool and then back. She watched as he repeated the process again and again.

She knew what he was doing—working off sexual energy, trying to calm the beast. He was a man in his prime, on his honeymoon, and he wanted sex. But he would not force her, wouldn't even attempt to seduce her. Why? she asked herself. If he was such a cold, heartless monster, capable of selling weapons of destruction to terrorists, why would he balk at forcing himself on a woman he wanted?

The answer came to her immediately. The only rational explanation. Because Burke Lonigan wasn't that kind of man. Perhaps he was a bit of a womanizer. And he was certainly a self-confessed playboy. But he was not a bad man. And definitely not evil. There was a genuine goodness in him. She'd recognized that goodness two years ago when she'd spent the night in his arms. She'd seen it time and again in the two months she'd worked as his personal assistant. The picture she held in her heart of Burke Lonigan was at odds with the image of him as a global arms dealer. The two didn't mesh.

She could think the worst about him or she could choose to trust him and believe in her instincts. *You're trying to rationalize your desire,* she told herself.

Standing on the balcony, the starry sky overhead and the dark sea below, Callie watched as Burke made his last lap and then emerged from the pool. Tall, lithe, magnificent. And naked.

Chapter 10

Burke wrapped himself in a thick white terry-cloth robe and picked up a towel from the wrought-iron chaise longue. Rubbing his wet hair briskly, he tried to dislodge thoughts of Callie from his mind. He had hoped several swift laps in the pool, combined with the chilly November night air, might dampen his ardor. Dammit, something had to work. He couldn't spend two days and nights in this state of arousal!

Stay outside for a while, he told himself. *Breathe in all this fresh sea air and let the autumn wind blow away the confused thoughts from inside your head.* He was in a no-win situation—damned if he did and damned if he didn't. His instincts told him that if he went upstairs, he'd find Callie still awake. And if he pushed her the least bit, she'd give in to him. She might not want to lie down with the mongrel she thought he was, but she would. She would because she wanted him in the same crazy way he wanted her.

The primitive need that rode him hard wasn't something he'd had to deal with very often. In his youth, when he'd been randy day and night, he would have bedded almost any willing female. But this specific yearning, this desire for one particular woman was alien to his nature. With two exceptions. Once, with his mystery woman, whose face he couldn't even remember. And now, with Callie.

Burke walked to the awning-covered terrace and sat in one of the cushioned rattan chairs. The electric torchères at the far end of the pool area threw soft shadows across the dark terrace. Tossing back his head, he closed his eyes and willed himself under control. Being this close to Callie and not being allowed to touch her was sheer torture. Perhaps he deserved punishment for having inadvertently allowed her to become involved in the dirty mess with Simon. God knew there had to be a reason he was being tormented this way.

Had he been sitting there for two minutes or ten? He didn't know. But suddenly he sensed her presence, even before he glanced up and saw her entering the outer terrace. Straightening in the chair, he watched her and soon realized she was searching for something—for him! Just as he started to speak, to let her know that he was near, she turned and stared right at him.

"Hello." Her voice was soft and raspy, as if she'd been crying.

"Did you ring Enid again?" he asked, when what he wanted to say was, *Why are you here? Don't you know that you aren't safe with me?*

"Yes, I rang her, for the third time since we left London," she admitted. "But I got to speak to Seamus only the one time. He was napping when I rang from Naples, and this time he was asleep for the night, of course."

"I take it that all is well?" Burke inquired.

"Quite well. It seems that Seamus has taken a liking to Leland." Callie sighed. "And so has Enid."

"Enid and Leland?" Burke chuckled. What an unlikely pair!

"Mm. Your Mr. Perkins had best watch himself or he'll wind up wondering what hit him. Enid can be quite lethal, you know."

"That must be a family trait." Burke rose from the chair and stood, his gaze lingering on Callie.

She wore a white robe identical to his. The robes were staples in the baths, kept there for the convenience of his guests. Callie had let her hair down, and the dark, fiery mass hung about her shoulders in curly disarray. She had removed her makeup, leaving only the fresh, youthful glow of her flawless skin.

"Do you think I'm lethal?" she asked somberly.

"Most definitely. Lethal to a man's self-control. Lethal to a man's sanity." He took a tentative step toward her. "You've driven me quite mad, you know. When I'm with you—"

"You're the one who is dangerous." Callie untied and loosened the belt holding the robe together and let the lapels fall apart. "You tempt me to forget all the reasons I should stay away from you."

He caught a glimpse of her flesh, her legs, her belly, the swell of her breasts. He became instantly hard. What sort of game was she playing? he wondered. Or was this attempt at seduction no game at all?

Callie eased the robe from her shoulders and dropped it to the tiled terrace floor. Burke swallowed hard. She wore a skimpy teal-green bikini. The top was little more than two small triangles that covered her nipples and the center of her round, firm breasts. And the bottom was a thong, with only a triangle covering the apex between her thighs.

She'd better not be toying with him! The savage beast within him roared. If she thought she could expose herself this way and not arouse him to the point of no return, she was sadly mistaken.

"Do you know what you're doing?" he asked. "Do you know what you're asking for?"

Callie squared her shoulders and lifted her chin. With a hint of a smile quavering on her lips, she looked directly at him. And then, without a word, she turned and dived into the pool.

As she leisurely swam the length of the heated pool, she listened, waiting for Burke to follow her. Within minutes, the resounding splash announced his plunge into the water. *You shouldn't be doing this,* her conscience warned. *You know there will be a price to pay for dancing with the devil. But I don't care. God, forgive me, but I don't care!*

Burke caught up with her as she neared the side of the pool. With a fierce lunge, he grabbed her around the waist and hauled her to the shallow end, bringing her up so that her feet touched the bottom of the pool. Water lapped around her hips and the cool night air chilled her naked flesh. Her peaked nipples pushed against the thin barrier of cloth that covered them.

When she saw the look of raw hunger in Burke's eyes, she almost cried out in fear. Moving her backward to brace her hips against the wall of the pool, Burke slid his hand beneath her wet hair and grasped the back of her neck. His mouth descended and his lips covered hers with an urgency that took her breath away. He tasted of wine— the rich, red wine they'd drunk with dinner. Had he finished off the bottle alone, after she'd fled from the study?

This question was her last totally coherent thought, as Burke led her deeper into the sensual haze that encompassed her completely.

While he ravaged her mouth with a kiss that alternated between brutal possession and stimulating tenderness, he reached around to the ties of her bikini top and undid them. So engrossed in the nearness of his big, hard body and the devastating effect of his kiss, Callie was only partially aware that she was now almost totally naked. But the moment her nipples pressed against his chest hair, she moaned deep in her throat. The sensation spiraled through her, from breasts to feminine core and then to every nerve ending in her body.

While he explored her mouth, she clung to his broad shoulders. She allowed him freedom to do whatever he wanted and it soon became apparent that what he wanted was precisely what she wanted. All the while his mouth worked its magic spell, he held her head in place with one hand and used the other to artfully remove the thong that protected her body from his complete invasion.

The expectation sent shock waves through her body. While his hand separated her thighs and his fingers worked their way around and about and inside, her femininity clenched and unclenched in preparation.

"I don't want our first time to be in the pool," he whispered in her ear, then drew her out of the water.

Quickly he wrapped her robe around her shoulders and slipped into his, then guided her into the house through the open French doors that led into the study. Before she could protest, he tossed aside his robe and hurriedly removed hers, then took her hands in his and drew her across the room. He eased her onto the rug in front of the bright, warm fire and came down over her, his face tense with the struggle to control himself. She understood only too well the hunger that he could not disguise.

Burke was big and broad and blatantly aroused. He lowered his body just enough to brace himself on his elbows and smothered her with another possessive kiss. She expected him to take her, to enter her body and claim her. But instead he began touching her. Softly, with fingertip caresses—all over her body. From neck to shoulders. From shoulders to hands. From collarbone to navel. From hip to knee.

Mercy! He was teasing her. Tormenting her. Arousing her. This was what she remembered. A talented lover. A maestro of foreplay.

Soon his lips, tongue and teeth joined in the adventure. Tasting, licking, nipping. But he deliberately avoided her nipples, which stood rigidly erect, aching for the feel of his mouth and tongue, begging for attention.

She writhed beneath him as longing coursed through her body, heating her blood. Her breasts ached. Her feminine core throbbed.

"Please, Burke." She speared her fingers through his hair and tried to bring his mouth to her breasts.

"Please, what?" His breath was hot on her breast, but his lips didn't make contact with her flesh.

"Touch me," she pleaded.

"Where?"

"Here!" Cupping one breast, she lifted it to his lips.

As if he knew she had reached her limit, he flicked his tongue and raked it hurriedly over her nipple. She cried out as the unbearable pleasure rioted inside her. Liking her reaction, he rewarded her by focusing on her breasts. While his mouth adored one breast, his fingertips played havoc with the other. Callie moaned when sensations so incredible she could hardly endure them spread throughout her body. Need so great she would have killed to acquire fulfillment claimed her, mind and body.

She bucked her hips, inviting him, urging him. *Take me! Take me now!* her body cried.

Aching with the need to have him inside her, Callie tried to drag him down to her. She clasped his buttocks and pushed. He slid between her legs, rubbing seductively over her feminine core. But before she could grasp him and bring him into her, he moved down her body, his tongue painting a moist trail from breasts to thighs. With his head between her parted legs, he kissed her intimately.

"Burke!"

"Yes, my darling?"

"What…oh…"

When his tongue sought and found the tight kernel protected by hot, wet flesh, she shivered uncontrollably.

Momentarily ceasing his assault, he whispered, "You like this, don't you?"

"Mm…" She couldn't speak, could barely utter even the most simple compliance.

While he loved her with his mouth, each stroke bringing her closer and closer to completion, his fingers caressed her nipples, building the tension tighter and tighter. Suddenly the world exploded. In her. Around her. Waves of tumultuous release washed over her, tossing her into the throes of a climax unlike anything she'd ever before experienced.

While aftershocks tingled in and about her feminine core, Burke lifted her hips and plunged into her. She whimpered when he filled her. He was big and hard and demanding. And she loved the feel of him. The taste of him. The scent of him. The sound of his labored breathing and harsh, manly grunts as he rode her.

He hammered into her with a fury born of intense passion and a need to possess her completely. His climax came like a bolt of lightning—fast and furious and electrifying. As completion claimed him, his body draining into hers, Callie lifted against him and cried out with the unparalleled pleasure of a second release.

Sated, relaxed and totally satisfied, they lay together on the rug in front of the fireplace. When his breathing returned to normal, Burke rose to his knees, then lifted her into his arms and stood. She flung her arms around his neck and buried her face against his shoulder. He nuzzled the side of her face.

"I'm going to make love to you again and again," he said. "For the next two days, we have no pasts and no futures. There is no one else in the world, except the two of us."

"Just you and me," she agreed.

Callie awoke the next day in Burke's massive, decorative, black wrought-iron bed, situated on a raised dais. Sheer cream-colored curtains formed a canopy around them. Morning sunlight streamed through the balcony doors. She lifted her head from the pillow and glanced at the sleeping man beside her. The satin sheet covered him only to his waist, leaving his broad, hairy chest visible.

He was a beautiful man. And sexy beyond belief. A warm blush covered her cheeks as she remembered what had happened between them last night and again shortly after dawn. The things they'd said to each other! And the things they'd done! Callie had never imagined lovemaking could be so deliciously wicked and so gloriously earth-shattering.

Two years ago, Burke had been drunk and yet had made love to her with a passion unlike anything she'd ever known. But a sober Burke had taken her to heights she'd never dreamed existed. Dear God, no wonder practically every woman in Europe stood in line to get into his bed. And to think he was her husband!

But only temporarily. Only for the weekend would she allow herself to truly be his wife, she reminded herself. *Enjoy what you have for the moment. Don't let thoughts of what happens when you return to London interfere with this once-in-a-lifetime pleasure.*

"I don't like that frown on your face," Burke said as he opened his eyes and looked at her.

She smiled. "No more frowns. Not today. And not tomorrow."

He lifted a hand and cupped one of her breasts. She sucked in her breath. "Are you sore? I want you again, but I don't—"

She answered his question by whipping the sheet away from his body and shoving it to the foot of the bed. He was aroused and ready.

Before she took things any further, Burke halted her. "Remember the condoms," he told her.

She nodded and reached to the nightstand where a box of protective sheaths lay open. She slipped a packet from the box, then ripped it open and handed the condom to Burke. She watched with fascination as he slipped it over his erection.

"I'm sorry I got so carried away the first time and didn't use anything," he said. "It's not like me to forget. I'm always very careful."

"It's all right," she told him, but something deep within her heart wanted to remind him that he had forgotten once before. One life-altering night when she had conceived his child. A premonition flashed through her mind. The image of a little redheaded girl lingered in her thoughts. No. *No!* She couldn't be pregnant.

"You're frowning again."

"I'm sorry."

"If you're pregnant..."

She covered his lips with her index finger. "Hush. I'm not pregnant."

"I never asked, but are you on the pill?"

"No, but I'm sure I'm not pregnant." *Fate wouldn't play the same trick on me again,* she thought.

"If you are, we'll deal with it. You mustn't worry."

What did he mean, *we'll deal with it?* Would he expect her to give up her child? *Stop tormenting yourself,* an inner voice advised. *By the time you find out if you're pregnant or not, you'll be out of Burke's life once and for all. You'll be safely in America. You and Seamus and...*

Callie dismissed the worries of reality from her mind. She had promised herself two days of pretense, of illusion, of making enough memories to last a lifetime.

She straddled his hips, and gently guided him inside her. She eased herself over him, slowly taking him completely. He groaned deep in his throat and clutched her hips.

She rode him, slowly at first, savoring each undulation as she set the pace. But as their mating continued and her body became thoroughly aroused, she increased the tempo until she moved in a frenzy, seeking release. They climaxed simultaneously. The earth moved. Fireworks exploded. She relaxed on top of him, their flesh glued together with sexual perspiration.

Monday afternoon arrived too soon. Burke was not prepared to end the idyllic honeymoon. Moments out of time. No past. No future. Only the glorious present. Night had melted into day and again into night as they laughed and talked and made love again and again.

Burke hadn't wanted to leave the villa, hadn't wanted the interlude with Callie to end. She fulfilled him in ways no other woman ever had. Not only sexually—and he had to admit that her inexperience pleased him because she was an adept pupil who was eager to learn—but emotionally. She seemed interested in what he thought and how he felt. She wanted to know all about his childhood, his parents and his entire family. Callie was an ideal companion—friend, confidante and lover. But a phone call from Jonah prompted Burke to follow their original plan and return to London Monday evening. The arms deal had gone through, but unfortunately hadn't turned out as planned. Once again, the wily Simon had outsmarted SPEAR and escaped, not only with his life, but with a goodly portion of the weapons.

"However, we did manage to capture one of his employees," Jonah had said. "The man was quite willing to exchange information for his life. It seems the weapons are headed for L.A."

"The drug wars," Burke had commented.

"Exactly. There's money to be made in the drug trade and Simon needs money to continue financing his schemes."

"Does Simon think I double-crossed him?" Burke had asked, greatly concerned that Callie and her child might be in danger. More danger than ever.

"We handled that problem. You're in the clear. No fingers point to you as the traitor, so we feel certain that you and Ms. Severin—excuse me, Mrs. Lonigan—and her son are safe from any future reprisals. But I'd wait a month or so before following through with the divorce. Just in case Simon continues to keep tabs on you."

When they disembarked from the private jet at Heathrow, Burke felt Callie's withdrawal the moment she saw Leland and Enid, who held young Seamus on her hip. The child wore a blue coat and cap, with mittens on his little hands and a plaid scarf around his neck that hid the lower half of his face. Callie rushed forward, racing toward her baby. The moment she reached Enid, she grabbed her son into her arms and held him to her chest. The sight of mother and child touched something deep inside Burke, and a slight twinge—a pang of jealousy—tightened his gut. He wasn't jealous of the child, but of the child's father. He didn't like the thought that Callie might still care for the man, whoever he was.

Burke reached out and grasped Leland's shoulder. "Good to see you, old man."

"Good to have you back, sir."

"I'm afraid I have some urgent business to attend to," Burke told Callie, who stood facing him, her son cuddled in her arms, his back to Burke. "Leland will take you and Seamus to my house and I'll join you later tonight. But don't wait up."

"Why can't we go home with Enid?" Callie asked. "Wouldn't that be simpler?"

"You're my wife now," he reminded her. "It will be expected for you and Seamus to live with me."

"But just for tonight—"

Burke gave her a disapproving glare. "When I arrive home tonight, I expect you and Seamus to be there. You can move whatever you need from Enid's place into mine tomorrow."

"But now that the danger is over, what's the necessity of continuing this charade?" When her son whimpered, Callie soothed him and quickly said to Burke, "Go on and take care of whatever needs your attention. We'll settle this tomorrow.''

"Very well.'' Burke turned to Leland. "I'll get a cab to the office. You take Enid home and then drive Mrs. Lonigan and her son directly to Belgravia.''

"Yes, sir.''

Callie waited until Burke had disappeared from sight before she confronted Enid. "Why did you and Seamus come to the airport to meet us?''

"It wasn't my idea,'' Enid replied as she looked meaningfully at Leland. "I wasn't left a choice.''

Callie snapped her head around and glared at Burke's employee. "Did you force Enid to bring Seamus to meet me?''

"The car is waiting, madam,'' Leland said. "We should be going.''

"Not until you answer my question.''

"Very well, madam. Yes. I thought you and Mr. Lonigan would be eager to see your son.''

A shiver of apprehension raced up Callie's spine. "Yes, well...I'm very happy to see Seamus, but there was no need to bother Burke with a sleepy, whimpering child.''

"I thought Mr. Lonigan should meet young Seamus,'' Leland said, then reached over to tickle Seamus under the chin. "Such a handsome lad. We've become fast pals, haven't we, Seamus?''

Seamus grinned, that bright, baby smile that warmed her heart. Callie's gaze met and locked with Leland's, and she realized that he knew. Dear God in heaven, he knew!

"It's all right, madam. I have no intention of telling Mr. Lonigan,'' Leland said. "But if I were you, I'd find a way—before he gets a good look at Seamus—to explain to him why your son is his spitting image. I've seen a photograph of Mr. Lonigan as a lad. He keeps the picture in his study. One of him with his mother when he was about two years old. That picture could easily be of young Seamus.''

Chapter 11

Burke arrived home at two in the morning. Dead tired, but relieved that he had tied up all the loose ends on another SPEAR matter. The assignment should run smoothly, as originally planned. Jonah had seemed pleased that the new situation had turned out better than the Simon deal. But Burke had pointed out that things could be worse where Simon was concerned, especially if Callie and her child had remained in danger.

As Burke climbed the staircase in his Belgravia mansion, he wondered if Callie and little Seamus had settled in. He had ordered a hurried job on a nursery, telling the decorator to convert the separate sitting room adjacent to the bedroom Callie would be using into an area suitable for a little boy not quite two.

He wanted Callie and her child to feel at home for the duration of their marriage. In a couple of months they would be able to get a divorce and go their separate ways. But in the meantime, he wanted Callie to feel comfortable in his home. At this point, he wasn't overly concerned about the end of their marriage, only with the day-to-day and night-to-night problems that would inevitably arise. His major concern was how he could ignore the fact that his wife—the woman with whom he'd shared endless hours of sexual pleasure on their honeymoon—would be sleeping down the hall from him.

She's there now, in her bed, an inner voice reminded him. *Warm and soft and waiting. Stop fantasizing! Callie isn't waiting for you. She's probably fast asleep.* But as he reached the landing, he realized that she was indeed awake. She and her son. He heard the child whimpering and Callie singing to him, her voice sweet and soothing.

He stopped by his bedroom, divested himself of his overcoat, coat and tie and then entered the hall. As he made his way toward Callie's room, the child quieted. Her bedroom door hung halfway open. He glanced inside and found the room empty. Quietly walking through her room, he listened to the words of the old lullaby she crooned to her baby. When he reached the open pocket doors that led into Seamus's temporary nursery, Burke took a deep breath. Wearing a pair of moss-green cotton pajamas, her rich red hair hanging loosely down her back, Callie sat in the rocker, Seamus cuddled in her lap. All Burke could see was the outline of the child's chubby little body and the back of his head. Seamus had curly hair, as black as his, which was unusual for a child that age, but a definite Lonigan trait. For the briefest of moments, Burke's gut tightened. An errant thought drifted through his mind. Under different circumstances, this child could have been his.

Seamus whimpered again. Callie lifted him in her arms and laid him across her chest so that his little chin rested on her shoulder. The child's eyelids drooped and his rose-bud mouth rounded in a yawn. Then Seamus saw Burke, and his eyes widened. Blue eyes. Bright, clear, deep blue eyes, identical to his own, stared at Burke. A tight fist of apprehension grabbed Burke by the throat as he studied the lad's features. No! It wasn't possible!

Burke stepped back into Callie's bedroom. He gulped in a large breath and shook his head. He was imagining things. He'd only thought that Callie's child was a carbon copy of himself at that age. Ridiculous!

You're tired, he told himself. *You didn't get much rest this past weekend and you've missed a great deal of sleep. Your vision is playing tricks on you. Callie's son can't resemble you and you know it. Now, go back in there and look at the child again. You'll see that he doesn't look a damn thing like you.*

Burke hovered in the doorway, his gaze riveted to the child's face. Seamus stared at Burke for several seconds, then his lips curved into a big smile. Feeling as if he'd had the wind knocked out of him, Burke grabbed the doorjamb to steady himself and noticed that his hand was shaking.

''Dada,'' Seamus said, and held out a little hand toward Burke.

This can't be happening, Burke thought. *I'm asleep, having a nightmare and I'll awaken soon.* But this was no dream. This was reality. Callie's son was his spitting image. And the child had just called him dada.

With her back to Burke, Callie couldn't see him, but surely she knew he was in the room. Hadn't she heard Seamus speak to him? As his mind tried to assimilate a thousand and one thoughts, Burke found his hand lifting and reaching out to the child.

''No, precious love, Dada isn't—'' Callie glanced over her shoulder and gasped when she saw Burke. Holding Seamus in place, she jumped to her feet and made certain the boy's face was hidden from Burke. "I didn't hear you come in. Did Seamus disturb you? He's teething and a bit fretful tonight."

Did Seamus disturb you? Did Seamus disturb you? My God, he wanted to yell at her, wanted to ask her if she were blind, to demand to know how she, Callie Severin, had gotten her hands on a child that he, Burke Lonigan, had obviously fathered. But how was that possible? He never had unprotected sex. Never!

Yes, you have, his conscience reminded him. *Saturday night with Callie at the villa. And two years ago with your mystery lady.*

That was it! Seamus's mother must be his mystery lady, the woman whose faceless image had haunted him since the night they'd made love, here in this very house. But if Seamus belonged to his mystery lady, then how was it that Callie had become his mother?

"Is he yours?" Burke demanded.

"What?" Callie's eyes grew large and round.

Burke took a tentative step in her direction and she, just as hesitantly, backed away from him. "Seamus is...my God, woman, you must see the resemblance."

"Yes, I...of course, I see the resemblance. And I can explain, if you'll—"

"He's mine!" Burke said. "That's the only possible explanation."

This was the inevitable moment that Callie had been dreading. The moment when Burke would get a good look at Seamus and realize the boy was his. She should have told him. Now it would be so much more difficult to explain.

"Yes, he's yours." She couldn't deny the truth that was staring them both in the face. Seamus had turned in her arms and glanced from one tense adult to the other.

"How? When? Who's his mother? His real mother?" Burke asked.

"Oh." Callie hadn't counted on that question.

"I had a brief, er, association with a young woman a couple of years ago. I don't remember her name, but…"

"She never told you her name," Callie said.

"She didn't?"

"No, she didn't."

"And how would you know?" Burke asked. "Did she tell you all the intimate details of our night together?"

"No one told me anything." The confused look on Burke's face explained all she needed to know. "You don't remember anything about her, do you? You honestly don't have a clue as to who she is."

"I remember everything about that night," Burke insisted. "I remember everything about her." *She was kind and understanding and loving. And sexy,* Burke thought. *So very sexy.*

"You remember everything except what she looked like."

Burke's expression confirmed the truth of her statement. She realized that he truly didn't remember, that he had no idea she was the woman to whom he'd made love that night.

Burke moved closer. Callie stood her ground, her chin tilted defiantly upward, her arms holding Seamus possessively. When Burke reached out and touched the child's head, Seamus grinned broadly and said, "Dada."

"He's at the age when he calls all men dada," Callie explained.

"Only in my case, he's got it right." Burke held out his arms and Seamus went to him immediately. "He's a friendly lad, isn't it?"

"Yes, quite friendly." Callie thought her heart would

break into a million pieces as she watched father and son together, the boy a miniature of the man. "Burke, about Seamus's mother—"

"Is she a friend of yours? Or another cousin? Is that why you and Enid took the boy and you're raising him as yours, because he's family?"

"He is family. He's my child."

"Were you concerned that I'd take him from you?" Burke asked, as if he hadn't heard her declaration of motherhood. "Is that why you've kept him hidden from me?"

"You can't take him from me because he's my child. Do you hear me, Burke? I am Seamus's mother. I carried him in my body for nine months and gave birth to him."

Burke glared at her as if she were speaking a foreign language that he didn't understand. "You can't be. You and I never met before you came to work at—my God! Are you telling me that *you're* the woman from that night? It isn't possible. I would have recognized you the moment we met again."

"I wondered about that. But when I applied for the position as your PA and you interviewed me and didn't seem to recognize me, I assumed either you didn't remember that night or preferred to pretend it hadn't happened."

Burke studied her face for an endless moment, as if trying desperately to remember her. Then when it became apparent that the identity of the woman from that night remained a mystery to him, he turned his attention on Seamus, caressing the child's cheek and surveying him from head to toe.

"If you're his mother…the woman from that night… why didn't you come to me and tell me that you were pregnant with my child? Why keep him a secret from me?''

Burke sat in the rocker and placed Seamus in his lap. Father and son inspected each other thoroughly, and all the while both of them smiled. When Seamus called Burke dada again, Burke's smiled widened.

''I didn't feel that I had the right to come to you. You'd been drinking rather heavily that night—''

''I was completely plastered at first, but—''

''I had been sober from beginning to end. Any fault was mine. I'm the one who should have said no and didn't. I knew you were a wealthy man. I thought you'd assume I'd trapped you because of your money. And of course, there's the fact that you have a reputation...that is, there were rumors about your being not only a womanizer, but an illegal arms dealer.''

''I see. So why come to me for a position with Lonigan's? Why, after Seamus was over a year old, did you seek me out?'' Burke opened Seamus's hand atop his. Small resting on large. The shape the same. Long, broad fingers. Wide hands. Thick wrists.

''I knew that someday Seamus would ask me about his father. I thought the best way to get to know you was by working for you. That way I could decide for myself if you were the type of man worthy of being Seamus's father.''

''And naturally, you discovered that the rumors were true. That I have a dark secret life that makes me unworthy of being your son's father. Isn't that right?''

Seamus looked puzzled when Burke's voice grew louder and harsher. His forehead wrinkled. His bottom lip trembled. Callie swept her son out of Burke's lap and into her arms.

"You've frightened him!" She said the words under her breath.

"Sorry." Burke chucked Seamus playfully, and a tentative smile began at the edges of the little boy's mouth. "I'm your father, Seamus. Your da."

"Dada," Seamus said, as if on cue, then looked at Callie and said, "Mama."

"He's quite bright, isn't he?" When Burke reached out to touch Seamus, Callie sidestepped his outstretched hand. "Am I not allowed to touch my own child?"

"Please…" Callie's misty eyes sought understanding.

"You're right. This isn't something we need to discuss in front of Seamus and upset him."

"Thank you."

"Don't thank me for anything, Callie," Burke warned her. "I'm controlling my rage for my son's sake, not yours."

"I appreciate it all the same," Callie said. "And I know that I owe you a complete explanation and I'll—"

"As soon as you've gotten him back to sleep, come downstairs. I'll be waiting for you in the library."

Callie nodded, then sat and began to rock and hum. Burke lingered in the room for a couple of minutes, watching mother and child. His mind reeled with confusion. His emotions shattered into utter chaos. Because of his illegitimate birth and precarious relationship with his father, he had always been very careful to see that history did not repeat itself. Only twice had he let passion overrule his common sense. Once recently with Callie. And two years ago with—with Callie!

Was it possible? Was Callie truly his mystery woman? If so, it made sense, didn't it? After all, she proclaimed herself to be Seamus's mother. And from the moment

Callie had walked into his office two and a half months ago, he'd felt a connection to her.

After taking one last look at his wife and his son, Burke turned and left them alone.

Callie heard his footsteps as he walked into the hall and the sound of the door as he closed it ever so softly. She let out the breath she'd been holding and felt an ache deep in her soul. A guilt she couldn't quite control rose to the surface, and her conscience chastised her for having kept Seamus's existence a secret from his father. She'd seen the amazement, the wonder, the joy in Burke's eyes. And she'd seen the hurt, too. A hurt that she had caused. She hadn't lied to him. Not outright. But she had lied by omission.

No matter what sort of man Burke Lonigan was, he *had* fathered her child. Nothing could change that fact. And there was no turning back the clock, no retreating into the past when her son's paternity had been a secret shared only by Enid and her. Now that Burke knew the truth, she would have no choice but to deal with the repercussions. She shuddered at the thought of having to face Burke Lonigan's wrath.

Burke poured himself a glass of whiskey, but limited himself to one. When he spoke to Callie, he intended to be sober. Unlike *that night*. Focusing his thoughts on the evening he'd drowned his sorrows at the Princess Inn, Burke struggled to remember the woman's face, the color of her hair, the shape of her body. *Think! Think, dammit, man, think!* But he had thought. For weeks. For months. For two years! Why had he been unable to put an identity to this person? What was his mind so afraid of remembering? He could remember her scent, her voice and even the feel of her, but not her features. Her voice! Soft and sultry. Callie's voice? Her scent had been flowery sweet. Perfume? Not the same scent Callie wore, but then women often changed perfumes, didn't they? What about the way she'd felt in his arms? As if she belonged there. Exactly the way Callie had felt during their brief honeymoon. Their bodies had been a perfect fit. Two days ago and two years ago!

Why, dammit, why couldn't he remember?

For some reason, he wouldn't allow himself to recall with clarity either her features or the reason his subconscious feared to confront the truth. What the hell had happened that night other than the fact they'd made love?

Burke knew the moment she entered the room, but he didn't glance her way or acknowledge her presence. He set his empty glass on a side table and moved toward the lone floor-to-ceiling Palladian window in the library.

"Seamus is asleep," Callie said.

"You know that I can have a DNA test done, don't you?" Burke stood with his back to her.

"Yes, I'm well aware that a DNA test could prove paternity. And if you'd like to—"

"I'd like to have known from the beginning that I had a child."

"I thought I'd explained why I—"

"I've missed nearly fifteen months of my son's life." Burke stood rigid and unmoving, his broad shoulders tense. "If you'd come to me when you discovered you were pregnant, I would have taken care of you. There was no reason for you not to have told me."

"There were several very good reasons," Callie said, halting a few feet behind him. "We were strangers. I had no way of knowing if you'd even remember me. And if you had, you might have thought the child wasn't yours."

"Feeble excuses, Callie, and we both know it."

"Perhaps, but true nonetheless."

Callie moved closer, easing to his side and glancing through the window at the dark garden at the back of the house. Wind swayed the trees. Branches scraped the outside wall. Moonlight shimmered across the barren flower beds and the stone walkway.

"Can you prove to me that you're the woman..." Burke cleared his throat. "The woman who spent the night with me, here in this house, two years ago?"

"A DNA test will prove that Seamus is—"

"It can prove that he is our child." Burke continued staring sightlessly out the window. "But it cannot prove that you're the woman from that night, can it?"

"Where else would we have been together, except here, that night?"

"Where indeed." He turned slowly and faced her. "What do you remember about that night?"

"Everything," she replied.

"You were very...kind."

"So were you."

"I was?"

"Yes. You see, you weren't the only one in pain, the only one with a broken heart."

"You thought my heart was broken?" he asked, a mocking smile on his lips. "You misjudged me."

"No, I didn't. Your heart was broken. Your father had died while you were out of the country." Callie took a deep breath. "He...Seamus Malcolm had called for you on his deathbed, but his legitimate children hadn't contacted you. When you returned, they would have nothing to do with you, but the maid...the maid told you what had happened."

"I let the situation bother me too much," Burke said.

"I shouldn't have gotten drunk, but…why was your heart broken?"

"My fiancé had just told me that he'd been having an affair with another woman and that he intended to marry her. To complicate matters, we worked together, so I quit my job on the spot."

"Ah, yes, I vaguely remember her saying something about a fiancé who had betrayed her."

I've never been with a real man. Only with one very self-centered boy who didn't know the first thing about pleasuring me. He heard her voice—Callie's voice— echoing inside his head. Memories. She had told him about her one and only lover. And he remembered feeling very satisfied that he'd been the first man to give her sexual pleasure.

"I'd never known that sex could be so…so incredible," Callie said. "It had never been that way. I slipped away early the next morning while you were still sleeping. I felt ashamed that I'd had sex with a stranger."

"How did you feel when you realized you were pregnant?"

"Scared," she admitted. "I don't know how I would have made it without Enid. She's like a sister to me and an aunt to Seamus."

Burke was torn between wanting to pull Callie into his arms and wanting to shake her until her teeth rattled. Despite what she'd done—denied him his son—he still wanted her. She had woven some sort of magic spell around him that long-ago night, and he remained under its influence even now. But how could he trust a woman who had kept such an important truth from him?

"This changes everything," he said.

"What—what does it change?"

"My life. Your life. Seamus's life. Our marriage."

"Our marriage?"

"We should have been married before Seamus was born, but at least we've rectified that now. I'll want my name listed on Seamus's birth certificate as his father. I will contact my solicitor first thing—" he glanced at his watch "—in a few hours. And my will must be altered."

"Aren't you rushing things?" Callie laid her hand on his arm.

He glared at her hand, then jerked his arm away. "I'm making up for lost time. A great deal of lost time."

"I realize that you'll want to be a part of Seamus's life, that you'll want visitation rights after the divorce and—"

Burke grabbed her shoulders and stopped himself just short of shaking her. "Apparently you didn't understand. There will be no divorce. You and I are going to stay married."

"What?"

"We have a child together. My son will not be denied his birthright the way I was. I won't be a part-time father." He released his hold on her and turned to walk across the room.

"You want us to stay married because of Seamus, not because you and I...not because we love each other?"

"Love? What the hell do you know about love?" He turned and glared at her. "Don't try to tell me that you're in love with me because I won't buy it. If you'd loved me, you would never have kept my son from me."

I might not have loved you then, her heart cried. *But I love you now. I don't want to love you, but I do.*

"Do you honestly think I can stay married to you? The secret life you lead has already put Seamus and me in danger once. If it happened once, it could happen again. I don't want my son to know that his father is an arms dealer. A criminal. And sooner or later, he'd find out the truth. As much as I—'' she caught herself before confessing her love for him ''—I understand how you feel, you must know I can't allow you to claim Seamus as your son and put his life at risk. You can see him, of course, and be a part of his life, but not…not as his father. Not as long as you continue—''

''My son will never be in danger. I can provide him with a dozen bodyguards, if necessary!'' Burke's eyes glimmered like frosty blue diamonds. His cheeks flushed with rage.

''Listen to yourself. Do you hear what you're saying? Is that the life you want for Seamus? For him to be constantly surrounded by bodyguards?''

Damn! Her accusations hit their intended mark. His conscience.

He didn't live the type of life suitable to fatherhood. Even though he wasn't an arms dealer, posing as one did indeed put anyone he cared about in danger. And how could he blame Callie for not wanting such a man to be a father to her son? If only he could explain that he was a SPEAR agent—one of the good guys, out to protect the world from evil.

But he was sworn to secrecy. Only Jonah had the power to give him permission to reveal the truth about who and what he was.

''We will postpone making any changes in Seamus's birth certificate,'' Burke agreed. ''But hear this—I will claim my son. And if you want to remain a part of Seamus's life, then you will stay married to me. If you choose to divorce me, then I'll use whatever legal means necessary to gain full custody of my son.''

Callie gasped, shocked by the callousness of his words. Was that simply the anger speaking, or did he mean what he'd said?

"You wouldn't take Seamus from me." Tears gathered in her eyes. "He's my life."

Burke's expression didn't soften when he spoke, but his voice did, ever so slightly. "If it means getting out of the arms trade in order to give my son the kind of life he deserves, then that's what I'll do. I'm willing to make sacrifices for Seamus. Are you?"

"You'd be willing to... Oh, Burke, would you actually get out of the illegal arms trade for Seamus's sake?"

"Yes." Burke intended to speak to Jonah as soon a possible. He had given SPEAR the best years of his life. He was forty-two and a father. He wondered what Jonah would say when he told his superior that he wanted out—and soon! "What about you, Callie? Would you be willing to continue on as my wife because it would be the best thing for Seamus, to have his parents together?"

"The best thing for Seamus would be to have two parents who loved each other and were devoted to their marriage and their family."

"Well, we can't have everything, can we?"

"No, I suppose we can't."

Chapter 12

"So, it's all out in the open now. Burke knows that he's Seamus's father." Enid speared a slice of tomato nestled in her salad. "I'd say the worst is over."

"Then you'd be wrong," Callie said. "I haven't seen Burke since three this morning. He was gone when I got up, and if Leland knows where he is, he isn't talking."

"Where do you think Burke is?" Enid nibbled her salad.

"I have no idea, but wherever he's gone, I'm afraid he's doing something that's going to wreak havoc in my life." Callie shoved aside the salad Burke's cook had prepared, the first course in an appetizing lunch. "You can't imagine how angry he was."

"What did you expect? Your husband is the possessive type. Finding out that you'd been keeping his son from him must have—"

"I did what I thought was best for Seamus. Everything

I've done since the moment I found out that I was pregnant, I've done for my child.''

"Oh, lovie, you don't need to convince me that you're a devoted mother. I'm the one who's been at your side and seen you through the worst of it. And I'm here for you now. You and Seamus are the dearest things in. the world to me.''

"I know. And we love you, too.'' Callie sighed. "I need your support now more than ever. What if... Oh, God, Enid, what if Burke tries to take Seamus away from me. And he could, couldn't he? He's rich and powerful and—''

"Excuse me, madam.'' Leland Perkins appeared in the dining room doorway.

"Oh!'' Callie jumped.

"I didn't mean to startle you, madam, but Mr. Lonigan just rang and he's asked me to drive you and Seamus to Kent. We're to meet him there at Oakwood Farm.''

"Oakwood Farm?'' Callie and Enid asked in unison.

"Yes, madam. If we start immediately, we should be there within an hour.''

"Leland, what is Oakwood Farm?'' Enid asked.

"Mr. Lonigan's country estate.''

"Oh, I see. And why does he want us to meet him there?'' Callie asked.

"He didn't say, madam. But he was quite insistent. He did say for you to pack bags for you and Seamus. I believe he's expecting you to stay there...for a while.''

"What should I—'' Callie looked to Enid for advice and then realized how desperate she must be to ask her irresponsible cousin to advise her. Enid was loving and supportive, but highly unreliable. And her advice usually tended to be the exact opposite of what Callie's common sense told her to do.

"Feeling a bit overwhelmed?" Enid patted Callie's arm. "Your husband seems to be the take-charge type, doesn't he?"

"I'm feeling as if I have no say in my life whatsoever," Callie said. "Burke has completely taken over and issues orders right and left. And he expects me to jump at his command."

"Are you going to the country?" Enid asked Callie, but cut her eyes toward Leland.

"I suppose if I don't go, he'll come after me." Callie looked at Leland for confirmation. When he nodded, she sighed, resigned to her fate. "Seamus is napping, but as soon as he wakes, we'll leave for Kent."

Burke felt certain that he was doing the right thing— for all of them. He and Callie could find a way to build a marriage together, for Seamus's sake. And where better to raise a boy than in the country? His estate in Kent belonged to him, unlike the house in Belgravia, the apartments in Paris and New York and the villa in Italy, which had been bought by and were maintained by SPEAR. But Oakwood Farm was his—lock, stock and barrel. The twelve-room Georgian farmhouse dated to the sixteenth-century. A two-acre garden, a swimming pool and a tennis court were part of the hundred acres of farmland, woods and orchards.

By giving Callie and Seamus a place in the country, he could allow Callie some privacy and freedom from his constant companionship. He could live in London during the week and come to the farm on weekends. And once Seamus and he became better acquainted and Callie accepted their marriage as a permanent arrangement, perhaps he would drive down several nights a week. After all, the trip took less than an hour from his office in the city.

When he'd thought of the future, he had occasionally imagined a wife and even children. And he'd usually thought of them living at Oakwood Farm. In an odd way, he was getting exactly what he'd wanted...and yet it was only a parody of the life he had hoped to have one day. He had a wife he didn't trust. A woman capable of lying to him, of keeping his son a secret from him.

And then there was that long-ago night they had shared. Something else that should have united them, but instead created another barrier between them. What was there about Callie, about the night they had spent together, that was so disturbing his subconscious refused to allow him to remember? If he asked Callie the details of what had happened between them, would she tell him the truth or would she lie to him again?

If he couldn't remember that night, couldn't put Callie's face to the voice, the scent, the feel of the woman, would he ever be able to combine the two women into one?

Perhaps their marriage was doomed to failure, but for Seamus's sake he would do everything within his power to make it work. Given time, surely Callie and he could forge a bond of some sort. After all, it wasn't as if they didn't find each other attractive. The exact opposite was true. Whatever else might be lacking in their relationship, the sex was dynamite. But a marriage, even a sexual relationship, was based on trust, wasn't it? And he suspected that Callie didn't trust him any more than he trusted her.

She believed he was a criminal, an illegal arms dealer who used his import-export business as a front. But he hoped to soon remove that one obstacle standing in the way of the trust they needed to build between them. After his conversation with Jonah earlier today, he had every hope that he would be given permission to tell his wife the truth about his business dealings. Not only had he requested permission to be honest with Callie about being a SPEAR agent, he had told Jonah that he wanted to retire from the field. He was ready for a simpler, safer life in one of SPEAR's legitimate businesses. Hell, he was more than ready.

He'd been promised a reply to his first request before day's end, and the notification that he planned to retire had been taken under consideration.

"I believe they're here, sir," Mrs. Mayfield said as she scurried into the library. "Shall I go to the door or do you plan to meet them yourself?"

Burke glanced up from where he rested in the huge wing chair by the fireplace and smiled at his housekeeper, a short, stout woman with wispy silver hair and a pleasant smile. "I'll go out to meet them, thank you, Mrs. M."

"Very well, sir." Mrs. Mayfield all but curtsied before she backed out of the room. "I'll put on the kettle. Your Mrs. will no doubt want a cup of tea. And I'll set out the biscuits for Master Seamus. Ah, how grand it will be to have a young one about the place."

Yes, it would be grand to have a young one about, Burke thought. A rowdy, rambunctious lad who would enjoy romping through the woods and playing with the dogs and riding horses and—riding horses! He'd have to order Seamus a pony. Later today he'd ask Mr. Mayfield, who took care of the stables as well as the grounds, to see about the purchase of a gentle pony.

When he stepped outside, his Irish setters, Romulus and Remus, came running, gathering about his ankles. Speaking softly to the animals, he scratched one and then the other behind the ears. He paused momentarily and watched while Leland rounded the hood of the Rolls and opened the car door. Callie handed Seamus to Leland, then emerged and looked all around her. He couldn't help wondering what she thought of his home. Her home, now. And Seamus's home, too.

Burke hurried down the steps, the dogs on his heels, and rushed forward to take Seamus from Leland. "Hello, there, my boy. Did you enjoy the ride down from London?"

"Hi, Dada," Seamus said, a broad grin on his precious face.

"Hi, yourself," Burke replied, then turned to Callie and motioned her forward. "Come on in the house. Mrs. Mayfield is preparing tea."

"I hope there's enough for me, too." Enid got out of the Rolls and placed herself between Burke and Callie.

"Enid came with us," Callie said shyly, but her gaze remained steadily locked with Burke's.

"Enid is always welcome." Burke smiled at his wife's cousin, but a part of him resented her presence. So, Callie had brought along a chaperone, someone to act as a buffer between them.

"Doggie." Seamus opened and closed his little hands in a grabbing gesture as he watched the playful animals flanking his father.

"Dogs. Yes, indeed," Burke said. "Your dogs, my boy. Romulus and Remus."

"Rom de rem," Seamus said, and all the adults laughed. Realizing he'd amused the others, he repeated his sentence several times.

Enid laced her arm though Callie's and together the two women followed Burke up the steps and into the foyer. Mr. Mayfield came from the stables and gave Leland a hand with the luggage.

The moment Callie entered the foyer of Oakwood Farm she felt an overwhelming sense of homecoming. It was a if she'd lived here once before, long ago, in another life time. Or perhaps the feeling of familiarity came from he dreams. This was the exact type of home she'd longed fo all her life. Although the decor she saw through the ope doors in the living room to the right and the library to th left was not unappealing, Callie suspected that Burke ha done little if anything to remodel or redecorate after he' purchased it from the previous owners.

Odd, she thought, how the anger she'd felt at Burke fo having summoned her to Kent had vanished. Not that sh wasn't still upset with him. She was. But seeing him i this home—and she sensed that was exactly what Oak wood Farm was, a home—all the possibilities for thei future formed into images in her mind. If Burke trul meant to give up the arms trade and become a legitimat businessman, then there was a chance for them, a rea chance they could become a family. After all, he was nc only Seamus's father, he was the man she loved.

Callie was so engrossed in her thoughts that she didn' realize she hadn't moved from the foyer until Enid jabbe her in the ribs.

"What's wrong with you?" Enid asked. "You act a if you're in a trance of some sort."

"Sorry. I was simply thinking about how much I lik this house." It was the type of home she'd alway dreamed of as a child. Something big and old and in th country. This place could so easily become a real home not just for Burke, but for her and Seamus, too.

By the time she and Enid entered the large farmhous kitchen, Seamus sat perched in an old wooden high chai and was nibbling on biscuits. Burke sat at the oak table which looked as if it was as old as the house. Calli glanced around the room. The appliances were at least twenty years old, but the plaster walls had been recently painted a light beige and the wooden floor gleamed from a recent polishing. A brick fireplace, painted the same beige as the walls, held a roaring fire that warmed the room and created a coziness Callie found addictive. The smell of baking bread filled the air. *Home.* This house all but screamed the word.

"Callie, let me introduce you to Mrs. Mayfield," Burke said. "She and her husband take care of Oakwood Farm for me. I don't know what I'd do without them."

The round and rosy Mrs. M. wiped her meaty hands on her big white apron and with a wide smile bowed her head in a gesture of respect. "So pleased to meet you, ma'am. I can't tell you how pleased we are for Mr. Burke, that he's got himself a pretty young wife and a fine son."

"Thank you, Mrs. Mayfield." Callie returned the woman's friendly smile.

"Would you and Enid care for some tea?" Burke asked.

"I'd love some," Enid said.

Callie watched while Burke stood, pulled out a chair and assisted her cousin. Enid made a funny face at Seamus, who giggled and sent moist biscuit fragments drooling down his chin. Before Callie did more than take a step forward, Burke picked up his linen napkin and wiped his son's face. Such an attentive father. And so gentle, she thought. Somehow her mind couldn't reconcile the fact that this man made millions from selling illegal weapons to criminals with the fact that he seemed to be a doting father and was, without a doubt, a tender, considerate lover.

"How long do you plan for us to stay here in Kent?" Callie asked.

Burke glanced at her, his face void of emotion. "Perhaps you and I should discuss our future plans when we're alone. I realize I rushed you into coming here, but I thought it best if we begin our life together in a new setting."

"Begin our life together?" Was he still insisting that they remain married for Seamus's sake?

"Why don't I have Mrs. Mayfield give you a tour of the house while I take Seamus outside," Burke said. "I want to show him the stables and I think he'd like to play with the dogs a bit."

"Dogs *and* horses?" Another part of her lifelong dream of a perfect life in the country, she thought.

"I'll keep a close watch on Seamus," Burke assured her. "And I'll bring him upstairs to you in time for his nap."

"I doubt he'll be taking a nap today," Callie said. "He slept in the car all the way down from Belgravia."

"Good, then I can keep him with me longer. By the way, will he need his nappie changed before we go exploring?"

"Yes. I'm sure he's soaked to the skin." Callie came forward to get Seamus, but before she reached her child Burke lifted him from the high chair.

"There isn't a nursery upstairs, but you must choose any room you'd like and convert it into one. In the meantime, I've had Mr. Mayfield set up a crib for him in your bedroom."

Callie gave Enid a helpless shrug, and her cousin lifted her eyebrows in a sympathetic gesture as she smiled at her. When Burke headed out of the kitchen, Callie raced to catch up with him. She followed him up the stairs. The upper level of the house lacked the warmth of the ground level, and she immediately noticed that unlike the kitchen, no fresh paint had touched these walls in many years.

Burke took Seamus into a rather austere room with thick dark curtains and a massive Empire mahogany tester bed. A crib had been placed alongside the imposing antique bed. Her overnight bag and Seamus's little red, white and yellow suitcase rested side-by-side on the floor by the enormous armoire.

When Burke started to lay Seamus on the bed atop the white spread, Callie gasped. "No, wait! If his nappie is dirty..." She glanced meaningfully at the pristine coverlet. "Let me get a plastic pad and a disposable nappie out of his case."

"Daddy has a lot to learn about taking care of little boys, doesn't he?" Burke leaned down and rubbed noses with his son.

Callie's heart caught in her throat. She had to be strong and not allow these sweet scenes between Burke and Seamus to sway her resolve. She would not let Burke claim Seamus as long as he continued with his illegal activities.

After retrieving the items she needed from the case, Callie laid the pad on the bed, then nodded to Burke. He laid a wriggling Seamus flat on his back and held him in place with a gentle hand across his belly.

"May I change his nappie?" Burke asked.

"What?"

"I'm afraid I don't have the slightest idea how to care for a small child, but I want to learn. Show me how to change his nappie."

"All right. If you're sure."

"I'm sure that I want to start immediately learning how to be a father."

Burke watched carefully as she removed the nappy, which was only wet and not soiled.

"The dirty nappies are more difficult." When Burke smiled, her heart did an erratic rat-a-tat and her stomach fluttered wildly. Oh, she was such a fool. How would she ever be able to walk away from this man and take his child with her?

"Perhaps I shall leave the dirty ones to you," Burke replied, a sly grin on his face.

She handed him the new nappie and gave him simple instructions, which he followed to the letter. "Good work, Daddy," she told him as he finished snapping together the legs of Seamus's corduroy pants.

When Burke lifted Seamus in his arms and headed for the door, Callie called, "Be sure to put his coat and cap on...and his mittens, too. And don't keep him out for long. In this cold weather his little cheeks tend to chap."

"So do mine." Burke patted his beard-stubbled cheek and then ran his hand over Seamus's smooth little cheek. "I'll take good care of my son."

"I'm sure you will."

Glancing over his shoulder at her, Burke said, "After dinner tonight, I'd like some time alone with you. There's a great deal we need to discuss."

At the thought of spending time alone with her husband, anticipation bubbled inside Callie like the effervescence from an uncorked bottle of champagne.

During the course of the afternoon and evening, Callie learned that Burke had purchased Oakwood Farm five years ago and that Mr. and Mrs. Mayfield had been his employees since that time. They lived in a house on the property and together took care of the manor house and grounds. After dinner, Enid had dutifully taken Seamus upstairs and Leland had disappeared outside with Mr. Mayfield, leaving Mrs. Mayfield in the kitchen.

Callie twined her fingers together as she sat on the sofa in the parlor while Burke stood by the fireplace. The mantel clock struck once, noting the half-hour. She sensed that Burke was nervous. Not as nervous as she, but certainly not his usual calm, confident self.

"I've been expecting a phone call," he told her. "I had hoped that by now... Well, some of the things I'd planned to discuss tonight will have to wait. But we can come to an agreement about living arrangements."

"If it will make things easier for you, I'm willing to stay married for a few months, just as we'd planned." Callie glanced at Burke, who looked so utterly wonderful in the old faded jeans and heavy flannel shirt he'd changed into before dinner. From his appearance one might mistake him for a farmer. "And once you can prove to me that you've ended your illegal dealings, I'll be more than willing to allow you all the rights of being Seamus's father."

"I'm working on disengaging myself from the arms trade," Burke said. "But in the meantime, I'd like for us to begin our lives as a family here at Oakwood Farm."

"You're still insisting that we don't get a divorce?"

"I'm asking that you give our marriage a chance. A year's trial. For Seamus's sake. And then if you find the situation intolerable, we'll discuss divorce."

"Six months," Callie said.

"Pardon?"

"I'll agree to a six-month trial period."

"I suppose if that's all you're offering, I have no choice but to accept. Regardless of what has happened between us, I do want us to remain friends, whether or not we stay married."

"I agree. But do you honestly think that you and I can be only friends?"

Burke's jaw tightened. "I think perhaps we won't find it easy to be friends and nothing more. And since you brought up the subject...while we're married, I don't see any reason we shouldn't enjoy the sexual pleasure of being man and wife."

Callie closed her eyes. She couldn't bear to continue looking at him, couldn't bear to see that unemotional expression on his face. For him it would be easy enough to have a physical relationship without the emotional bonding. But it would be impossible for her. She was already in love with Burke, and if she spent six months as his wife, she'd never be able to walk away from him without taking a broken heart with her.

Burke crossed the room and sat in a chair to the right of the sofa. "I believe Oakwood Farm is an ideal place to raise a child. The fresh country air, the woods, the animals. I realize the old house needs a bit of refurbishing and I have no objections to your doing some redecorating, if you'd like. As a matter of fact, it would give you something to do while I'm in London during the week, so—"

"What do you mean, while you're in London during the week?"

"I thought it best, at least until we've settled into this marriage and Seamus has become accustomed to me, that I live in London during the week and come here to see you both on the weekends."

"You're going to live in London? And Seamus and I are going to live here? What about my position as your PA? Or have you already hired someone new?"

How dare he! How dare he ship her and Seamus off to the country while he continued his life in London? Did he want her to play the dutiful wife and mother while he had no intention of giving up his playboy ways? Did he expect her to be faithful to him, to be his wife in every sense of the word, while he enjoyed discreet affairs in London?

"Callie, I thought you'd enjoy the opportunity to stay at home with Seamus. Of course, we'll hire a nanny to help you. Perhaps I can persuade Mrs. Goodhope to move to the country."

"You've planned everything, haven't you? But not once did you ask me what I wanted." Callie rose to her feet. With her hands balled into tight fists, she stood over him, glowering. "I like Oakwood Farm and I agree that it's an ideal place for Seamus. And I'd enjoy not having to work while he's so young. But I do not approve of your resuming your life in London. Not as long as you and I are legally married. If you're going to—" Callie cut herself off and clenched and unclenched her fists, barely restraining the desire to throttle Burke. "Do not expect me to welcome you with open arms when you come to visit us. I will sleep alone in my bed and don't you dare try to—"

Burke shot out of the chair and grabbed Callie by the shoulders. His big hands clamped over her bones, the pressure tight and his grip filled with tension. "If you're determined to make things difficult, then so be it. I've never forced my attentions on a woman, and believe me, Mrs. Lonigan, I have no intention of starting with you."

Chapter 13

On Friday evening, Leland pulled the Rolls up in front of the manor house at Oakwood Farm. Lights shined brightly from all the downstairs windows, giving the stately mansion a warm, inviting appearance. When Burke had rung Callie nightly, he'd been as cordial to her as her frosty demeanor allowed. They had limited the topics of their conversations to Seamus and mundane matters such as the weather. He'd been surprised that she hadn't asked him about the import-export business or about how his effort to disentangle himself from the arms trade was progressing. He sensed that something was bothering Callie—something more than their precarious relationship. She seemed to be angry with him, but he didn't know why. His decision to stay in London during the week to give her and Seamus time to adjust to him being a part of their lives as a husband and a father had for some odd reason upset her. Did she think he wanted to spend time away from his son, considering the fact that he'd missed the first fourteen months of the boy's life? And did she think he preferred sleeping alone every night instead of sharing a bed with her?

"We've arrived, sir."

When Leland spoke, Burke realized that the man had probably been standing there holding open the car door for several minutes.

"So we have. But I don't see a welcoming committee rushing out to meet me."

"It's quite cold this evening," Leland said. "Perhaps they're waiting for you in the foyer."

"Perhaps."

The November wind chilled him the moment he emerged from the Rolls, his overcoat draped across his arm. He walked hurriedly toward the house, taking the steps two at a time. The moment he reached for the knob, the door swung open. But the face that greeted him was not the face he longed to see.

"Good evening, sir," Mrs. Mayfield said as she reached to take his coat. "A bit nippy out tonight."

"Yes, it is. How are you Mrs. M.? Did everyone have a good week?"

"A jolly good week, sir. Miss Callie, if I might be so bold as to say so, is a kind, lovely lady. And Master Seamus is a delight. Me and Bob are enjoying having the lad about, running and laughing and making this old house feel like a real home."

"Thank you." Burke glanced into the parlor. "Where are Mrs. Lonigan, er, Miss Callie and Seamus?"

"I'm afraid Seamus is asleep, sir. He's had such a busy day playing and romping with the dogs. The wee one fell asleep while eating his dinner, he did."

"And Miss Callie?"

"I served her tea in the library about fifteen minutes

ago. She had my Bob build a fire in there. Said she was sure you'd want your dinner in the library this evening. I can bring it in whenever you're ready.''

Burke nodded. "Serve it in about twenty minutes. I'd like some time alone with my wife first."

Mrs. Mayfield's fat, rosy cheeks darkened to scarlet. "She's missed you, sir. Despite the joy little Seamus gives her, I could tell that she was lonely for you."

"Hm." Burke thought it best not to reply to his housekeeper's observations. How could he explain to the dear woman that it was highly unlikely his wife had missed him? If she'd been lonely then it was probably because Enid had dashed off on Wednesday, back to London. During one of their brief telephone conversations, Callie had mentioned that her cousin had become bored with country life.

He approached the library and found the door open and Callie standing by the massive fireplace. Her gaze met his, an odd look of fury and expectation at war in her eyes. What had created that indignant feeling in her? he wondered. He believed that he had done everything possible to make the best of a bad situation. Why was she so upset with him? And was he misreading the expectation he thought he saw in her eyes? Was it simply his own hope for a warm welcome that made him think she, too, might be longing for a tender greeting?

"Hello, Callie." His arms ached to open wide and invite her into his embrace. But he waited, hoping for a response from her.

"Good evening." Her tone was neither cool nor warm, but a hint of a smile twitched her lips. "How was the drive down from London?"

"Uneventful," Burke replied as he walked into the room. "I actually dozed off for about fifteen minutes."

"Did you have a tiring week?"

She hadn't moved an inch. Indeed, she seemed to be glued to the spot. Taking the initiative, he approached her, but when he noticed her visibly tense, he stopped himself from touching her.

"Business as usual. Everyone at the office asked about you and sent their best."

The tension between them vibrated like a live wire, exposed and quite dangerous. He had missed his wife, had wanted desperately to be with her and had thought of little else while he'd been in London.

"I've missed you," he said, staring directly at her.

Callie averted her gaze, quickly staring into the glowing fire. "We…that is, Seamus has asked about you. And I—I…"

Unable to refrain any longer, Burke reached out and clasped Callie's hand. Her whole body went rigid, but she didn't try to pull her hand from his. "We must talk. I have some things to tell you about myself, about the life I've lived for nearly twenty years."

"As an arms dealer?"

Burke tugged on her hand. She followed him to the sofa and they both sat. When he released her, she folded her hands together and placed them in her lap.

"What I'm about to tell you, I share with you in strictest confidence. In order to share this information with you, I had to get permission from my superior, and he gave his permission only after thoroughly investigating you."

Callie looked at him, puzzlement written plainly on her face. "You've totally confused me. You have a superior? I'm afraid I don't understand. You own an import-export business, which is a front for your arms dealing. Am I wrong?"

"Yes and no." Burke had known explaining his complicated life to Callie wouldn't be easy. After all, where outside of novels and motion pictures did the average person come in contact with secret agents? "I suppose the best place to start is at the beginning."

"The beginning of what?"

"The beginning of my life as a, er, an agent for the United States government."

"What!" Callie leaned away from Burke, as if she was suddenly unsure of who he was and was wondering if he were dangerous.

"My stepfather, Gene Harmon, was a career soldier, and he had numerous friends in Washington, D.C. He introduced me to some men, movers and shakers on the capitol scene, and these men recruited me shortly after I graduated from college. The organization to which I belong was established during the American Civil War by President Lincoln and has an identity so guarded that even most members of the government don't know it exists."

Callie stared at Burke as if he'd suddenly sprouted an extra head. Her eyes widened in disbelief.

"This organization has tentacles everywhere," Burke continued.

"In U.S. and foreign affairs and even in the private business sector. Because I was born in England and my biological father lived here, I was chosen for my particular position. The organization bankrolled my import-export business. My home in Belgravia, my apartments in Paris and New York and my villa in Italy belong to SPEAR."

"SPEAR?"

"Stealth, Perseverance, Endeavor, Attack and Rescue," Burke explained. He had always been proud to be a part of the organization and had lived by its code of honor. But now, he wanted out of the arms business. He wanted a life with Callie and their son, and he knew, without her telling him, that the only way Callie would ever remain his wife was if he stayed out of the line of fire. And the only way to be the kind of father he wanted to be to his son was by staying married to his son's mother. He was determined to spare his son the pain he'd known as boy.

Callie continued staring at Burke, her mouth slightly agape and a look of total bewilderment in her eyes.

Burke blew out a deep breath. "I know I've given you a lot to digest, but as my wife, as Seamus's mother, I felt you had a right to know the truth."

"You're not a multimillionaire and you don't own Lonigan's Imports and Exports. Is that right?"

"That's right."

"And you aren't an arms dealer?"

"No."

"Then...then what was all that business with Simon?"

"I can't go into any details with you. I'm sorry. But I can tell you that the entire situation with Simon was directly related to my work for SPEAR." He searched her eyes for any sign that she understood, accepted and believed what he told her. "Do you understand?"

"Yes, I understand what you've said, but I must admit that I'm overwhelmed. I had no idea..."

Burke couldn't stop himself from touching her. Just the gentlest of brushes. His knuckles across her cheek. She sucked in her breath and drew back from him, her eyes round and wide with a hint of fear in them.

"No, please, Callie, don't be afraid." His hand hovered in the air, not touching her but within inches of her face. "You're safe. Seamus is safe. Neither of you has anything to fear from me or my work as a SPEAR agent." Even as he voiced the proclamation, he knew he wasn't being totally honest. Not with himself and not with her.

"I can be a father to my son. A real father. But I don't

want to have to go through legal channels to gain my rights. I want you to trust me enough to willingly let me be a full-time father to Seamus."

"I—I don't know." Callie eased to her feet and looked at Burke. "You've given me a great deal of information. I need time to think about everything and come to terms with what you've told me."

"Take all the time you need." Burke stood. Forcing himself not to reach out and take her in his arms, he simply looked at her. So beautiful. So tempting. His wife. And yet not his wife at all.

"Before you make any decisions about our future, you should know that although I'm not a multimillionaire, I am a wealthy man. Oakwood Farm belongs to me. And I do receive a healthy salary from Lonigan's Imports and Exports. You and Seamus will never want for anything."

"Your money has never interested me," she said. "Not that night two years ago and not now. But your lifestyle does interest me. You're an agent for a government organization and your first loyalty is to them, not to me. Not even to Seamus. And you've spent the past twenty years as a playboy bachelor. I will not be the wife of a philandering husband!"

Before Burke could fully comprehend what her outburst was all about, Callie ran from the room, almost colliding with Mrs. Mayfield, who held a tray containing Burke's dinner.

"Callie," he called after her, but she sidestepped the housekeeper and fled. "Damn!" he muttered under his breath.

"Shall I bring in your dinner, sir?" Mrs. Mayfield waited in the doorway, a look of concern on her face.

"Yes. Certainly. Place the tray on my desk."

"Yes, sir." She did as he had bid and turned for a hasty retreat.

"Mrs. Mayfield?"

"Yes, sir?"

"Why don't you sleep in tomorrow. Take the weekend off," Burke suggested. "Miss Callie and I can take care of things here."

"Yes, sir. Thank you. But what about Master Seamus? He doesn't have a nanny yet and the lad wakes quite early. He'll have you up with the chickens."

"I won't mind," Burke assured her. "I'm looking forward to spending the entire weekend with my son."

"Very well, sir. But you will ring me if you need me."

Burke dismissed the housekeeper with a nod and a smile. He realized that he had his work cut out for him persuading Callie to accept him as her husband and Seamus's father. For some reason, she seemed to believe he intended to continue living the carefree life of a bachelor. Perhaps if he explained to her that he had told Jonah he wanted to retire, she would see that he was sincere. But he didn't dare tell her and then have her disappointed if Jonah refused his request. Callie had been right when she'd said that as long as he was a field agent his first alliance was to SPEAR. Not to her and Seamus.

Burke woke to the sound of Seamus crying. It took several minutes for his brain to register the noise. After all, he wasn't accustomed to having a baby in the house. He shot out of bed and headed for the door, then realized he wore only his underpants. After grabbing his robe from a nearby chair, he slipped into it and tied the belt securely around his waist. By the time he reached Callie's door, Seamus had quieted. Burke hesitated for a couple of minutes, then knocked softly and without waiting for a reply opened the door and walked in.

Wearing cotton pajamas of a pale yellow with a tiny peach-colored rosebud design, Callie sat in the middle of the bed with her legs spread apart. A wide-eyed Seamus bounced up and down between them. When the child teetered and almost fell, Callie caught him in her arms and hugged him to her breast.

Burke cleared his throat. In unison, mother and child turned to stare at him. Seamus smiled and said, "Dada." Callie gave him a rather harsh what-do-you-want? glare.

"Good morning," Burke said as he trekked across the room and pulled back the curtain at the window overlooking the large garden. "The sun's up. The sky is clear. And Jack Frost paid us a visit during the night." He pecked on the frost-coated windowpane.

"Why are you up so early?" Callie asked as she tried to restrain Seamus, who was reaching out for his father.

Burke grinned. "I didn't want to miss a minute of the day with my son." And with his mother, he thought.

Burke came to the bed, reached down and lifted Seamus into his arms. "You're certainly an early riser, little man."

"Meck," Seamus said.

Burke's brow wrinkled. "What did he say?"

"Milk," Callie interpreted. "He's hungry. If you'll give him to me, I'll take him downstairs and—"

"I can take him to the kitchen and feed him," Burke told her. "If you'd like to go back to sleep—"

Callie jumped out of bed. "What do you know about feeding a child? He'll want milk and cereal and some fruit. But before he's fed, he needs changing."

"Ah, yes, a nappie change." Burke hoisted Seamus

high into the air over his head. The child squealed with delight. "I think I can handle that job, too."

"Very well. His diapers are there in the top drawer." She pointed to an antique highboy on the far side of the large bedroom.

"What would you like for breakfast?" Burke asked as he retrieved a nappie from the highboy. "I've given Mrs. M. the day off, so I'll be preparing our meal."

"You're going to cook?" Callie smiled.

Burke loved her smile. It had been awhile since he'd seen a genuine smile on her lovely face. Despite the remnants of lingering anger and distrust he still felt over Callie having kept Seamus's existence a secret from him, he couldn't deny that he cared about her. And he wanted her. If only she would cooperate with him, then perhaps they could build a good life together. After all, they were highly compatible in bed, and with a bit of work they might find that they would do all right in other areas, too.

"Nothing special," he said. "Perhaps toast and tea."

"You change Seamus's nappie," Callie told him as she lifted her robe from the foot of the bed. "I'll go downstairs and prepare breakfast for us."

She left father and son alone and rushed out of the bedroom, along the hall and down the stairs. The house seemed chilly, so she paused long enough to adjust the thermostat, then hurried into the room she had begun to think of as Mrs. M.'s kitchen. She wanted to prepare a delicious meal for her men. She would like Burke to tell her what a good cook she was and how glad he was to be home with her and Seamus—where he belonged. She longed for him to promise that his days as a London playboy were over and so was his life as an undercover agent.

She shuddered at the thought of how often Burke must have been in danger as an agent for the secret organization to which he belonged. Would he be able to exchange the excitement of undercover work for the placid life of a gentleman farmer?

Callie wanted to believe that a leopard could change its spots, but Burke had made her no promises about altering his lifestyle. He might not be an arms dealer, but he was a secret agent. And he planned to continue living in London while she and Seamus stayed in Kent. Surely she wasn't fool enough to think he would be willing to give up the beautiful, sophisticated women in his life just for her.

"Oh, Burke, if only you truly loved me the way I love you. Then perhaps we'd have a chance to make our marriage work."

The day had been a page taken from Burke's childhood fantasy, only in this version, he was the father. Nothing could ever change the fact that his own father had never acknowledged him and had allowed him to grow up a bastard. But he intended to make sure that Seamus always knew he was loved and wanted. As soon as he worked through his problems with Callie, Burke would legally claim his son. Nothing was more important to him.

Romulus and Remus trotted alongside Burke as he held Seamus's hand and led him toward the stream that bisected the back half of the acreage behind the large garden area. Burke wasn't sure whether or not there were any fish in the stream, but if there weren't, he'd see that Mr. Mayfield arranged for the stream to be stocked before next spring. He and Seamus could enjoy fishing together, a sport he had occasionally enjoyed with his stepfather. But for Gene Harmon fishing had been like everything else in his life—a competition. The man hadn't known how to relax and simply enjoy himself. But it would be different for Seamus and him.

Everything would be different for Seamus. Better. Right. He glanced at his son, and a feeling of pride and deep love swelled inside his chest. The child was such a delight. Inquisitive and intelligent. Looking at the world through the eyes of his son was like looking at the world for the first time. Everything was fresh and new.

"Don't let him get too close to the water," Callie called as she followed them. She had stopped by Mrs. Mayfield's cottage to say hello and had lingered to talk for a spell.

"I'll look out for him," Burke said. "Since we have the pool and a stream running through our property, I think we should make sure Seamus learns how to swim, don't you? I can teach him myself as soon as it's warm weather."

"Will you have time to teach him?" Callie caught up with father and son, who stood by the edge of the stream, Seamus peering into the fast-running, bubbling water. "Your business and your...your other work take up a great deal of time. Not to mention your social life in London."

Burke went down on his haunches so that he was almost at eye level with Seamus. "Nothing's more important than spending time with you." He patted the top of his son's head, ruffled his black curls, then lifted the hood attached to Seamus's coat and pulled it over his head. "It's cold out this afternoon. We want to keep you all warm and cozy, don't we?"

"Cold," Seamus repeated and grinned broadly, showing his teeth.

"A new word?" Burke glanced at Callie.

"Yes, a new word. I believe that extends his vocabulary to eighteen words now."

The cold November wind whipped around them. Clusters of dried leaves swirled in the air. A dark cloud passed across the sky and blotted out the sunlight.

"He's a very bright boy," Burke said. "You've done an excellent job with him, Callie. I want to thank you for…" Burke paused, lifted Seamus onto his hip and held out a hand to Callie. "I want to thank you for giving me such a splendid son. I'm very grateful that I can be a part of his life."

Callie accepted Burke's outstretched hand. He engulfed her hand in his and tugged her to his side. How was it possible that he couldn't remember the night he had spent with this woman two years ago, the night she had conceived his child? Callie was the most unforgettable woman he'd ever met. So why had he erased her face— her identity—from his mind?

"We mustn't stay out much longer," Callie said. "Mrs. M. said she took a pot of stew up to the house a while ago. Aren't you two hungry? We skipped lunch, you know."

"Are you hungry?" Burke asked Seamus. "Mama says it's time to go back to the house."

"Meck," Seamus said.

"Yes, milk." Burke grinned. "He associates milk with eating, doesn't he?"

"He loves his milk," Callie said as they turned from the stream and headed toward the garden. "I was afraid when I weaned him, he might not care for cow's milk, but he took to it right away."

When I weaned him. Her words repeated inside Burke's head. The image of his son at Callie's breast flashed through his mind. How he wished he could have been there to have seen her nourishing their child from her body. If he had searched the world over, he couldn't have found a more loving, maternal woman to have mothered his child.

When they reached the back door, Seamus's little hand reached toward Romulus and Remus. "Doggie."

"I think he wants the dogs to come inside with us," Burke said.

"Do you usually allow them inside?" she asked.

"Into the kitchen," he told her. "They're accustomed to me feeding them in front of the fireplace on cold nights."

Callie cupped Seamus's chin with her thumb and index finger. "Do you want to help Daddy feed the dogs tonight?"

"Dada. Doggie." Seamus squealed with delight.

On the closed-in back porch, they divested themselves of their heavy coats, hung them on the wooden rack attached to the stone wall and then entered the warm kitchen. Mrs. M.'s stew filled the room with its delicious aroma. Romulus and Remus galloped into the kitchen and plopped themselves down in front of the fireplace. The minute Burke set Seamus on his feet, he toddled straight toward the dogs.

Burke and Callie stood together and watched while Seamus wedged his pudgy little body between the two big Irish setters and wrapped his left arm around Romulus's neck and his right arm around Remus's neck.

"Doggie, Dada," Seamus said. "Meck."

Callie and Burke laughed, each enamored with their precious child and the fact that they had both understood his command to feed the dogs. Suddenly their gazes met and held. Burke felt as if he'd been hit in the stomach with a sledgehammer. Not giving his actions a thought, acting purely on instinct, he pulled Callie into his arms and kissed her.

Chapter 14

Callie waited in the hall and watched Burke as he tucked the covers around a sleeping Seamus. She thought about the kiss they'd shared in the kitchen a couple of hours ago. Indeed, she'd been able to think of little else since it happened. Heat suffused her body when she remembered the way she'd felt and the way she had reacted. His actions had been so unexpected that she'd barely had time to realize what was happening before her traitorous body responded. The kiss had gotten out of hand quickly, but passion had been subdued by their son's giggles. He had toddled over to them and inserted himself between their legs. Burke had pulled back from her, both of them breathless. When he'd lifted Seamus in his arms, they'd all three laughed. In that moment they had been a family.

"Bring the monitor so we can hear him," Callie told Burke. "And leave the door partly open. If he wakes and the door is closed, he'll be frightened."

When Burke joined her in the hall, he handed her the

monitor, which she stuffed into the pocket of her bulky sweater. "He played hard today and tired himself out."

"He should sleep the night through," Callie said as she walked ahead of Burke toward the stairs. "He usually does when he's really tired."

"There are so many things that I don't know about him." Burke reached out and laid his hand on Callie's shoulder, halting her.

She glanced at him. "You'll learn everything there is to know about him soon enough. He's still just a baby. He won't ever remember a time when you weren't a part of his life."

"I do realize that you had legitimate reasons for not coming to me when you discovered you were pregnant, but..." He shook his head and sighed. "I don't blame you. Not entirely. After all, I'm the one who was drunk that night. I'm the one who didn't bother using a condom. And I'm the one who can't remember all the details of that night."

"I'd like a cup of tea," she said, deliberately changing the subject as she moved away from him. "Would you like some dessert? Mrs. M. brought over a cake while you were giving Seamus his bath."

"Mmm. Cake and tea sounds quite nice."

When Callie started down the stairs, he caught up with her and said, "Let me help you. You fix the tea and I'll cut the cake."

Callie nodded. They busied themselves in the kitchen. Like an ordinary married couple spending a Saturday night at home together, she thought. But they weren't an ordinary married couple. There was nothing ordinary about Burke Lonigan or about her marriage to him. Her husband, whom she'd believed to be an arms dealer, was actually some sort of super agent for a secret organization.

And her husband had as many women in his life as the famous fictional agent 007. Unless Burke was willing to retire from his dangerous fieldwork and put an end to his playboy lifestyle, she couldn't be his wife no matter how much she loved him. And she did love him. In the deepest, most private recesses of her heart, she had probably loved him since the night Seamus was conceived. But even then she'd known that Burke was a lethal combination of charm and danger.

She finished preparing the tea, placed their cups on a silver tray and added the two cake plates. "Shall we take this into the parlor?"

"Excellent idea. I built a fire in there earlier, while you put dinner on the table."

In the parlor, Callie placed the tray atop the walnut table between the two Louis Philippe armchairs that still had their original cut-velvet upholstery.

Burke glanced around the room. "It's cozy, I suppose. But it needs completely redoing. New paint on these old walls is the first order of business. The floors are in good shape, so they probably need only a good waxing. But the furniture needs recovering and—"

"Are you truly interested in redecorating this house or are you simply trying to make conversation?" Callie asked as she reached for her cup.

"Both," he admitted. "I do want you to redo this house to suit your own tastes. I haven't had anything done to it since I bought it because I've spent little time here." He clasped her hand before she lifted her cup. "Trying to make idle conversation with you is difficult, when what I truly want to do is to take you to bed and make love to you all night."

Callie jerked her hand from his. "I would have thought

after half a week in London, you wouldn't need the attentions of your wife.''

Burke glowered at her. ''What the hell is that supposed to mean?''

''It means that I'm not a fool, despite evidence to the contrary. Why else would you want to stay in London during the week other than to carry on with your life as usual, and that includes all the sophisticated, exciting women you know.''

His gaze narrowed. ''You think I've been having sex with one or more of my old lovers these past few nights?''

''That's precisely what I think.'' Callie sat ramrod straight, her shoulders squared, her backbone rigid.

''Would it do any good for me to deny it? Would you believe me if I told you that not only have I not touched another woman in quite some time, but I haven't even wanted another woman?''

Callie's heart gave a little flutter. She truly wanted to believe him. But did she dare? He was a known charmer, a man accustomed to getting whatever he wanted by whatever means necessary.

She sat there, speechless, staring at him. She knew he wanted to make love to her. If her instincts hadn't told her before the kiss in the kitchen that Burke wanted her, that kiss had spoken loud and clear. Would he lie to her in order to get her into his bed? *Ask him outright.* An inner voice egged her on. *If he swears that he hasn't been with another woman, then believe him.* He had never lied to her, except by omission.

''Have you had sex with another woman?'' Callie asked boldly. Her accelerated heartbeat hammered inside her head.

''I've had sex with numerous women.'' The corners of Burke's lips twitched with humor.

"Dammit, that's not what I meant and you know it!" Callie shot out of the chair and glared at Burke. "Have you been with another woman since you and I were married last Saturday?"

Burke got up. His big, lean body leaned ever so slightly toward Callie. She drew in a deep breath and held it until he said, "You kept my son a secret. You lied to me. You disapprove of my lifestyle and you hate the fact that I've been a government agent most of my adult life. You'd think I wouldn't want you, that I'd prefer a woman who didn't care who I was or what I did. But the truth of the matter is that I haven't wanted anyone but you for several months. Not since the day you walked into my office for a job interview."

Callie released her breath. A shudder rippled over her nerve endings. "Then why...why stay in London? Why—"

Burke slid one arm around her and brought her against him. She trembled as he lowered his head and brushed his lips over hers. "Two reasons," he said. "I honestly thought it would be easier for you to adjust to our marriage if I didn't come home every night. At least not at first. And second, I do have an import-export company to run and there are important negotiations with SPEAR that need to be wrapped up."

"Business is the reason you're staying in London?"

"Do you honestly think that I wouldn't prefer to come home to you every night?" Dipping his hand beneath her hair, he grasped the back of her neck and held her face to his, only a hairbreadth between their lips. "If sex alone could make a good marriage, then you and I would have the most solid marriage in the world."

She longed to cry out her true feelings, to declare that

she loved him beyond reason, but how could she confess her love when he hadn't even mentioned the word?

"Say something." Burke kissed her jaw, then her chin and followed up with a string of soft, moist nips down her neck. "Tell me that you believe me."

"I believe you," she replied as she draped her arms around his neck and dissolved into shapeless putty. Breathless with expectation, she went weak in the knees.

His mouth descended as his arms tightened around her. She opened herself up and welcomed him. Like hungry savages ready to devour the beast that tormented them, Callie and Burke kissed and touched and quickly began undressing each other. Passion rode them hard.

Her sweater dropped to the floor. His shirt landed on one of the Louis Philippe chairs. Her blouse and bra fell over their untouched teacups. His trousers and hers pooled into cloth puddles on the floor, and they stepped quickly over them as they made their way to the sofa. Socks and shoes and underwear flew this way and that, landing haphazardly throughout the parlor.

"I've thought of little else but you while I've been away," Burke whispered in her ear just before he nibbled on her earlobe.

"I've missed you," she said, then gasped when he pushed her onto the sofa.

"We have so many problems that aren't resolved, but right now none of them seem to matter." He came down over her, scooped her buttocks up and lifted her to meet his descending body. "Nothing matters except this—" He spread her legs with his knees, then thrust into her.

She moaned with pleasure the moment he filled her, relishing the incomparable feeling of having Burke buried deep inside her. Rational thought ceased as she gave herself over completely to the sensations spiraling through her body. Whenever she was with him, she lost all sense of herself and the world around them. She existed only as a part of him, only to belong to him, as he did to her. They were one. Bodies joined. Hearts combined. Souls touched.

"Feel it all," he murmured, increasing the tempo of their mating. "Feel everything I'm feeling."

She met him thrust for thrust. Hot kiss for hot kiss. Fiery passion for fiery passion.

"I am," she whimpered. "Oh, Burke, I am!"

They came together with a ravaging hunger, fueled by a week of celibacy. Days of longing. Nights of deprivation.

Callie tightened around him, her body pulsing with tension. And then with one hard lunge, he sent her over the edge. Her climax hit her with the impact of a freight train. As she cried out, her body trembling with completion, Burke came undone. He tensed as a powerful release claimed him. Breathing hard, moist with perspiration, he slumped on top of her until his big body covered her completely. She wrapped her arms around him and kissed his forehead, his cheeks and then sought his mouth. He captured her lips, loving her anew.

The harsh pounding on the front door jerked them out of their intimate cocoon, but it took Burke several minutes to fully comprehend that someone was trying to beat down the door.

"Who—" Callie tried to speak.

Burke kissed her. "Get dressed, my darling, while I find out who it is."

He picked up his trousers and slipped into them hurriedly, then lifted his shirt out of the chair and put it on, leaving it unbuttoned. Callie rushed about, picking up her clothes and trying to dress as quickly as possible. By the time Burke returned to the parlor, she was partially dressed and had regained enough composure that she worried about who might be with him.

Burke came toward her. She glanced past him and saw a man's shadow in the hallway.

"Leland came up from the Mayfields'. It seems I left my mobile phone upstairs and we didn't hear it ringing."

"What does Leland want that is so urgent it couldn't wait until morning?" Callie asked.

"My mobile phone is how SPEAR contacts me," Burke explained. "When my superior couldn't reach me, he contacted Leland."

"Leland? I don't understand. Why would they contact—"

"Leland works for SPEAR, just as I do," Burke told her.

"Oh."

Burke pulled Callie into his arms, rubbed his cheek against hers and then kissed her temple. "There's an emergency I must handle immediately. I'll have to take the jet from Heathrow tonight. I can't explain further, but believe me, I have no choice but to go."

"Orders from SPEAR?"

"Yes. And I'm afraid I might be out of the country for a couple of weeks."

She clung to him. "You'll be in danger, won't you? Oh, Burke, please..." She sucked in a cry of despair. "Please, be very careful. I...we...Seamus needs you."

"If you need anything while I'm gone, contact Ardell Healy, my solicitor." Burke released her long enough to delve into the back pocket of his jeans for his wallet. He withdrew a credit card and handed it to her. "You're authorized to use this card. Why don't you start redecorating while I'm gone? And find a nanny for Seamus."

Callie glared at the card. Burke took her hand and laid the credit card in her palm. "You're a rich man's wife, my darling. Why don't you enjoy it?"

"Must you leave now?" She grabbed the open flaps of his shirt.

"Yes." He kissed her again. Hard and deep and powerful. And then he released her.

Callie didn't leave the parlor until long after Leland had driven Burke away. To London. To Heathrow. And from there, only God knew where. Into the wild blue yonder. Off on a dangerous assignment for SPEAR. She slumped on the floor, wrapped her arms around her body and cried. How could she live this way? How could she raise a child with Burke when she would never know from one moment until the next if his undercover work would take him away from them—permanently?

Three weeks! Twenty-one days. She'd heard from him twice since he'd been gone and both times he had assured her that he was well, but she had easily picked up on the tension in his voice. She'd filled her days with plans to remodel Oakwood Farm and had hired a local architect, contractor and interior designer. The first renovation—turning one of the upstairs bedrooms into a nursery for Seamus—was almost complete.

A week after Burke had left her so abruptly, a new BMW had arrived for her. And a few days later, a pony for Seamus had been delivered. She couldn't help wondering when Burke had ordered the car and the pony. Probably before he'd come down from London that last weekend they'd spent together.

Callie paused, taking a respite from her nervous pacing in the kitchen. Laying her hand over her flat belly, she glanced down and remembered how she had felt in the early stages of her first pregnancy. For several days now she had suspected that she was pregnant again. She'd missed her period. That was a definite sign for a woman who was as regular as clockwork. And there were other more subtle signs. She had picked up a home pregnancy kit when she'd driven into town earlier in the day but hadn't worked up enough courage to use it.

"You're eager to see him, aren't you, dearie?" Mrs. Mayfield smiled warmly as she continued kneading the dough for her homemade bread. "I believe you've missed him even more than our little Seamus has. It'll be good to have him home."

"I wish he could have said exactly what time he'd arrive."

"You're wearing yourself out walking the floor this way," Mrs. Mayfield said. "While Seamus is taking a nap there in Mr. Burke's library, why don't you go upstairs and have yourself a nice long bath."

"But what if Seamus wakes up? You'll have to stop your baking and see to him." Callie sighed wearily. "I suppose I should have tried harder to find a nanny, but after Mrs. Goodhope couldn't arrange things with her family to move to Kent, I just didn't want to rush into hiring someone I didn't know."

Using her flour-covered hands to motion to Callie, Mrs. Mayfield scolded, "We can manage fine without a nanny until you find someone perfect for our Seamus. We can't settle for just anyone. Not for our young man. You just leave me the monitor and I'll listen for him."

Reluctantly, Callie agreed. She'd been in an absolute tizzy ever since Burke had phoned from London to tell her that the assignment had been successfully completed and he would arrive at Oakwood Farm by midafternoon. She hadn't mentioned a word to Seamus about his father because she'd known he wouldn't have gone down for his nap if he'd been anticipating Burke's return.

"Here's the monitor." Callie withdrew the item from her pocket and set it on the counter. "I'll be in the bathtub for a while. Call me if you need me."

Just as Callie opened the kitchen door, she heard a resounding thump. Glancing over her shoulder, she noticed that the vibrations from Mrs. Mayfield's kneading had bounced the monitor onto the floor.

"I'll get it," Mrs. Mayfield said. "Go on now. If you don't relax a bit before Mr. Burke arrives, you'll be nothing but a bundle of nerves. And what sort of homecoming would that be for him?"

Callie smiled, nodded and hurried out of the kitchen and upstairs to her bedroom. While the warm water ran into the old claw-foot tub, she added scented bubble bath. The scent she'd worn that night so long ago when she'd met Burke for the first time. She'd stopped using that particular fragrance after her night with Burke. She had put away the perfume, the lotion and the scented bubble bath. But tonight was special. It was the beginning of a whole new life for Burke and her. Whether or not he was able to free himself from the arms business, she couldn't leave him. Not now or ever. She loved him far too much to walk away again. Especially now, when she might be carrying Burke's second child.

Slowly she removed her clothes and added them to the basket sitting in the floor at the bottom of the linen closet. Lifting one foot, she tested the water. Ah, just right. She eased into the bubble bath. Heaven. Sheer heaven.

As she relaxed, she thought about Burke. About his homecoming. About tonight. After they'd put Seamus to bed, they would have time to be alone and catch up on three weeks of loneliness. Closing her eyes, Callie drifted off into a sweet fantasy. Burke, naked and aroused, joining her in the tub. She could almost feel the strength of his big body as he encompassed her in his embrace, as his mouth covered hers and he claimed her with total abandon.

Callie's nipples peaked. Her femininity moistened and throbbed. *Hurry, my darling,* her heart sighed. *Hurry home to me.*

Burke tried to relax in the back seat of the Rolls as Leland sped out of London toward Kent. He could hardly wait to arrive at Oakwood Farm—to go home. Home to his wife and son. Home to the new life he could offer them. This lengthy, complicated assignment for SPEAR had been his last. Jonah had given him permission to retire from the field. He would continue as the CEO of Lonigan's Imports and Exports for a few years, but a new agent would come aboard as a vice president, a man who would inherit the job from Burke and would immediately take over the role as arms dealer.

Burke smiled when he thought about how happy and relieved Callie would be to learn that from now on he would be strictly a businessman. When he left Lonigan's sometime in the not too distant future, he fancied spending his days as a gentleman farmer. After all, he had more money than he could spend in a lifetime. Not billions, but several million. More than enough to give his family a comfortable life.

He wondered what Seamus thought of his pony and if Callie liked her BMW. The new SPEAR agent was due to arrive in London tomorrow, so he had alerted his staff that a new VP would be taking over some of his responsibilities while he took a much-needed vacation. He intended to spend the next two weeks romping with his son during the day and romping with his beautiful wife at night.

He wanted to be the best father in the world. He promised himself that he would have the type of relationship with Seamus that he had so desperately wanted with his own father. His stomach clenched at the thought of how much he cared for Seamus. That he was capable of loving someone so much almost frightened him. His son meant more to him than anything in the world. And he knew that Callie loved their child just as dearly. She was a wonderful mother. Loving and gentle and devoted to her child.

His feelings for Callie puzzled him. He cared for her. Deeply. He wanted her. Beyond all reason. But there was more. He wasn't quite sure what, but he somehow knew that if he could ever remember her clearly from that first night, the mystery would be solved.

A satisfied smile spread across Burke's face as he remembered that last night with Callie at Oakwood Farm. They'd both been aware of a dozen reasons they shouldn't make love, but they hadn't been able to keep their hands off each other. It had been exactly the same way the night they'd first met, hadn't it? He could recall the way he'd felt, the hunger that had pushed him to act irresponsibly, to take Callie without precautions of any kind. He wanted to remember everything about that night, but most important to him was being able to remember Callie—her face, the true essence of who she was.

Just thinking about his wife aroused him. He leaned his head against the back of the seat and closed his eyes. The image of Callie naked, her sweet body open and giving, flashed through his mind. Flowing red hair hanging around her shoulders. Tight nipples begging for his touch. Soft, pink lips longing for his mouth. Nicely rounded hips waiting for him to caress them. A fiery triangle of curls that beckoned him to enter her.

By the time Leland pulled the Rolls to a stop in front of the manor house, Burke was asleep and dreaming of making love to Callie.

"Wake up, sir," Leland said. "It seems there's something going on here. It appears that quite a few of the neighbors are running about over the grounds." Leland got out of the car, rounded the hood and opened the back door.

Burke's eyelids fluttered as he roused from sleep, then he stepped out of the Rolls onto the brick walkway. That's when he noticed Callie running toward him. The moment she drew near, he saw the tears streaming down her face. His heart stopped beating for a split second.

Callie raced into his arms. "Oh, Burke. Thank God, you're home. Seamus—" She gulped down her sobs. "Seamus is missing. We've searched the house and Mr. Mayfield rang several neighbors and we've begun a search of the grounds. Oh, Burke, what if...what if he's been kidnapped!"

Chapter 15

Burke's couldn't breathe when he heard the word kidnapped—he felt as if the wind had been knocked out of him. It wasn't possible, he told himself. There was no reason anyone connected to his most recent SPEAR assignment would want to harm his son. He was free and clear on the Simon deal, and no one else had made any threats against him or his family.

"Oh, Mr. Burke." Mrs. Mayfield wrung her hands together as she gulped down a sob. "It's all my fault. I'd sent Miss Callie upstairs and promised her I'd keep an eye on Seamus. But I had no idea that when the monitor fell on the floor, it turned off."

With Burke's arm securely around her waist, Callie reached out and patted the housekeeper on the arm. "You can't blame yourself. I should have checked the monitor myself after it fell."

In his peripheral vision, Burke caught a glimpse of Mr. Mayfield speaking with Leland. Without releasing his hold on a trembling Callie, he turned and lifted his arm in a signal to the two men. Leland came forward while Mr. Mayfield returned to the search.

"Mrs. Mayfield discovered Seamus was missing about twenty minutes ago," Leland said. "They've searched the house thoroughly, as well as the gardens. And it's odd, sir, but the dogs are missing, too."

"Do you think he's been kidnapped?" Callie clung to Burke, her voice revealing her fear.

"No, my darling, I don't," Burke assured her, but he couldn't completely erase the possibility from his mind. "But what I don't understand is how Seamus got downstairs from his nursery. Do you think he crawled down?"

"He wasn't upstairs," Callie said.

"The poor little tyke fell asleep in your library, Mr. Burke," Mrs. Mayfield said. "We thought it best not to disturb him by moving him upstairs, so we left him there on the sofa. I was close by in the kitchen and I had the monitor. But the thing wasn't working, so I didn't hear him when he woke."

"I should never have gone upstairs." Choking on her tears, Callie buried her face against Burke's chest.

"Mr. Mayfield has organized a search party," Leland explained. "We've a dozen people spreading out to search every nook and cranny on the estate. I'm going to join them and I promise you, sir, that we'll find the lad. And if Romulus and Remus are with Seamus, they'll not let any harm come to him."

"Callie, darling," Burke said. "Why don't you let Mrs. M. take you inside and I'll go with Leland and help search for—"

"No! Please." Callie gripped the lapels of Burke's overcoat. "I want to help look for him. I can't imagine why he would have wandered out of the house. Oh, God, Burke, if anything has happened to him, I'll—''

Holding her close, he placed his index finger over her lips to silence her, then he kissed her forehead and both cheeks. "Seamus is all right. And we'll find him soon."

"I'm going with you," she said.

"Yes, come along then." Burke glanced at Mrs. Mayfield. "You stay here, just in case he returns or if someone calls to let us know they've found him."

An hour later, Burke brought a nearly hysterical Callie to the house. She was cold and weary and exhausted, more emotionally than physically, but exhausted nonetheless. As he all but carried her into the house, supporting her with his arm about her waist, they found several of the other searchers huddled around the fire in the kitchen. Mrs. Mayfield served tea to warm them from the chill in the air.

"Bring some tea into the library for Miss Callie," Burke ordered.

Mrs. Mayfield nodded, then gasped silently when she saw that Callie held Seamus's favorite stuffed animal, a floppy-eared bunny rabbit that his aunt Enid had given him on his first birthday. Burke shook his head at the housekeeper, a warning not to say anything. Callie was upset enough as it was. The minute they had discovered the stuffed toy beside the stream, she had become convinced that their son had fallen into the water and possibly drowned. Burke had gone into the water himself and he, Leland and two other men had explored for a good half mile down the creek, but found no other sign of Seamus.

Burke led Callie into the library and seated her on the sofa. Suddenly she stopped crying. He looked her square in the eye and saw the numbness set in as she stared at him with a blank expression on her face.

"You should get out of those wet shoes and trousers," she said, as if she were speaking of the weather, without a hint of emotion.

"I'll be fine, my darling." *It's you I'm worried about,* he wanted to say. But he wouldn't be fine. He was far from all right.

His gut was twisted into painful knots. His head throbbed with tension. And he didn't think he'd ever been so afraid in his entire life. But he couldn't break down, couldn't lose control. He had to remain strong for Callie. She needed him.

"Oh, Burke!" she cried and began trembling from head to toe.

He knelt in front of her and wrapped his arms around her. With tenderness and compassion, he stroked her back and whispered reassurances that he didn't believe. He held her tightly, hoping to give her his strength and in return praying to absorb some of hers. Alone they couldn't endure the strain. United they supported each other.

Seamus couldn't be lost to them forever! Burke's mind reeled with thoughts of his son hurt. Drowned. Dead. A quivering sensation started in the pit of his stomach and quickly invaded his whole body.

He shook from the force of his barely controlled emotions.

Callie lifted her head and stared directly at Burke. She had seen this look in his eyes once before—two years ago. In the wee hours of that November morning, when he had awakened and was partially sober, he had sat on the edge of the bed and trembled as if he were having a seizure.

"Burke." She whispered his name.

He didn't seem to hear her. She grasped his face with her hands and said exactly what she'd said to him that night when he'd been mourning his father's death.

"It's all right. Go ahead and cry. Don't hold back your tears."

He glared at her as if seeing her and yet not seeing her. The shudders that racked his body increased.

"Cry, dammit, Burke. Cry!"

Only sissies cry! Gene Harmon said. Real men never show their emotions. It's a sign of weakness. And no son of mine is going to be a blubbering mama's boy. Do you hear me, Burke? Don't ever let me see you cry again.

Burke huffed loudly. Sucking in and blowing out deep breaths, he struggled to control his emotions. But his son was missing. Their precious little Seamus might well be dead. He hurt so much. The pain inside him was almost more than he could bear.

As he struggled to maintain control he kept hearing his stern stepfather's voice chiding him for being an emotional boy who wept easily. Since that day when Gene Harmon had taken him to task for daring to cry when the family's dog had died, Burke hadn't shed another tear. Except...

God in heaven! He had cried that night. In Callie's arms. She had held him and told him it was all right to cry. His father had died. Seamus Malcolm, who had never acknowledged him as his son, had called for him on his deathbed. *Oh, Da, I'm sorry I wasn't there. I wanted us to be father and son. I wanted...*

He felt Callie's comforting arms holding him—as she had held him that night. She kept saying, "Cry, my darling, cry."

A groan of sheer agony escaped from Burke's throat, the sound of a wounded animal in pain. Tears gathered in his eyes. Large, heavy tears, a sign of torment.

His little Seamus was missing, possibly dead. He could not bear the thought. What would he and Callie do if they lost their child? It was a punishment too severe for any parent.

Tears trickled down Burke's face. Her face wet with fresh tears, Callie held him and continued encouraging him to release his pent-up emotions. They clung to each other, weeping.

He closed his eyes and clenched his jaw. Memories flickered inside Burke's head. Déjà vu. A repeat performance of moments he had chosen to forget—to block from his mind. As those memories grew stronger, the image of the woman who had held him and had been a witness to the most vulnerable moments of his life began to take shape. He could see the dark red hair, the soft gray eyes, the warm, pink lips and the small, narrow nose. Callie! He saw her in his mind's eye as clearly as if he had opened his eyes and was looking at her. Only with her had he allowed himself to lose control, to be weak and needy. He had permitted her a glimpse of his soul, something he hadn't dared to admit, not even to himself.

Burke opened his eyes. Callie stroked his cheek with her fingertips. "I remember," he said. "I know what happened that night. I fell apart in your arms. I cried my heart out like a weak fool."

"No!" Callie said. "You cried, but you were not a weak fool. You were mourning your father. You desperately needed the release of tears that night and...and now."

"I didn't want to remember you," he admitted. "I couldn't bear to remember your face and the pity in your eyes."

"Oh, my darling Burke. It wasn't pity. It was sympathy and love you saw."

"Love?"

"I think I must have fallen in love with you that night,

but later, I convinced myself that I'd been wrong. Because silly me, I thought you'd fallen in love with me, too.''

Burke swallowed his tears, then wiped his face with his fingers. When he rose to his feet, he held Callie's hands and brought her up with him. ''You weren't silly. I did fall in love with you, but I wouldn't admit that, either. You've haunted me for two years.''

''Then our little Seamus...he—he really, truly was born from our love, wasn't he?''

Burke surrounded her with his embrace, holding her close, longing to ease her pain. ''We're going to find him. He's all right. He isn't... He isn't dead, Callie. We must believe that.''

''Where is he, Burke? Where is he!''

A group of children—five boys and three girls—walked up the road that led to Oakwood Farm, two galloping Irish setters on their heels. Burke saw them from the window in the parlor where he'd been standing for the past few minutes, pondering what action to take next. Callie sat across the room, and he knew she'd been praying continuously. Their son had been missing nearly two hours, and the search of the grounds had turned up nothing. Who were those children and what were they doing with Romulus and Remus? Burke wondered. If the children had found the dogs, was it possible that they had found Seamus, too? As they drew nearer, he noted that the eldest was probably ten and the youngest was only a toddler whose hands were held by two of the girls. A black-haired toddler. Burke rubbed his eyes. Seamus. The toddler was his *son*.

''Seamus!''

''What?'' Callie shot to her feet.

"Outside," Burke said. "There's a group of children coming up the drive and Seamus is with them."

"Oh, God!" Callie gulped in a deep, calming breath.

Together she and Burke raced out of the parlor and into the foyer. He jerked open the door and they ran outside, down the steps and up the drive.

"Seamus!" Calling her son's name, Callie broke into a run.

Burke kept pace with her, but allowed her to reach down and swoop their child into her arms. She held him so tightly that he began to squirm.

"Mama, me play," Seamus said and pointed to the children who surrounded Callie.

"Where did you find him?" Burke asked the eldest, the ten-year-old boy with a freckled face and sandy-brown hair.

"We didn't exactly find him anywhere," the boy replied. "Seamus has been playing with us. We've taken good care of him. He's even had milk and biscuits"

"I don't understand," Callie said, clinging to a wriggling Seamus.

"I'm Dennis Lloyd and these are my cousins," the boy said. "We were playing in the woods that connects your property to our grandfather's and we saw Seamus near the stream. He told us his name, but we couldn't understand much more of what he said."

"So we took him with us," one of the golden-haired little girls said. "We didn't know he belonged here at Oakwood Farm. There's never been a little boy here before when we've visited our grandparents."

"Are you telling us that Seamus has been over at Windwood all this time?" Burke asked.

"Yes, sir," the eldest boy said. "Even Grandfather was at a loss as to whose little boy he might be. He said he knew the man who owned Oakwood Farm wasn't married and had no children."

"I've never had the privilege of meeting Sir Michael," Burke said. "So how is it that you knew to bring Seamus back here?"

"Oh, Grandmother insisted that the authorities be notified," one of the other boys said. "But just as Grandfather started to ring the—"

"The gardener had been part of the search party." The eldest girl broke in to finish the tale. "When he saw Seamus on the lawn playing ball with us, he informed Grandfather immediately and so—here we are."

"Mrs. Lonigan and I can't thank you enough for taking such good care of Seamus," Burke said, smiling warmly at the group of children, not a one of them aware of the hell Seamus's parents had recently endured.

"Yes, thank you." Callie placed Seamus on her hip and he waved to his newfound friends. "All of you must come over soon to see Seamus."

"Yes, ma'am. Thank you. We will," the eldest boy replied, then turned to his cousins and said, "it will be dark soon. Grandmother told us that we mustn't tarry."

After waving goodbye to the children, Burke draped his arm around Callie and together they carried their son into the house. For hours neither of them could stop looking at Seamus, couldn't stop kissing him and hugging him. They had just lived through a parent's worst nightmare— a missing child.

After giving him his bath, Burke and Callie both read Seamus a story and together tucked him into bed. They stood for quite some time and watched him while he slept. Then Burke led Callie into the sitting area of his bedroom.

He loved this woman. He had loved her since the night he had fallen apart in her arms. Since the moment he had touched her, kissed her, made love to her. She had given him back his humanity, something he'd lost long ago. Something he'd begun losing the day Gene Harmon had chastised him for being a weakling because he'd dared to cry when his beloved dog, Skippy, had died. Year by year as he had grown into a man, raised by a stepfather who had been good to him but had been a stern taskmaster, Burke had become a hard, disciplined little soldier. Long before he had joined the ranks of the highly secretive SPEAR organization, he had taken on the persona of a tough guy.

When he sat beside Callie on the antique sofa, he caressed her face. "I realize that you're tired and I could wait until tomorrow to have this conversation with you, but... I need to tell you everything."

"What is it?" Callie asked, concern in her eyes.

"Nothing bad, my darling." He couldn't stop himself from kissing her, but he pulled back quickly and reached down to take her hands into his. "The reason I've been away for nearly a month is because I've been finishing up my last job for SPEAR. As of today, I'm officially retired."

"Burke! Do you mean it? You're no longer a secret agent?" She squeezed his hands.

"My only connection to SPEAR for the next few years will be as CEO of Lonigan's Imports and Exports," he explained. "Already SPEAR has installed a new agent as a VP in the company. He'll take over and use his position at Lonigan's as a cover for his supposedly real job as an arms dealer."

"This is such wonderful news. You can be a real father to Seamus and—"

"And you and I can continue on as man and wife?" he asked.

"Do you want to stay married to me?"

"Callie, my darling—" he lifted her onto his lap and encompassed her within the cocoon of his arms "—there is nothing I want more than to be your husband until the day I die."

"You do? You really do?"

"I do. I really do. Now the question is, do you want to be my wife for the rest of your life?"

Her chin trembled. Her bottom lip quivered ever so slightly. "You know that I do. I love you so much. I have ever since that night."

"I remember how you held me when I wept for my father. How you gave me the courage to lose control and show my feelings."

Tears gathered in the corners of Callie's eyes. She wrapped her arms around his neck and gazed lovingly into his face.

"When I cried in your arms this afternoon," Burke said, "I recalled everything about that night, including exactly what the woman I'd fallen in love with looked like. I love you, Callie Severin Lonigan. I love you more than I've ever loved anyone."

"Am I dreaming?" she asked. "Can this happiness be real?"

Burke stood, then swept her into his arms and carried her into his bedroom. "I'm going to prove to you that you aren't dreaming. By the time I finish with you, there won't be a doubt in your mind that our love is very real."

They undressed each other hurriedly, driven by the hurricane force of their desire and the long days and nights of celibacy they had both endured while they'd been apart. When they were naked, Burke took her with barely controlled passion, holding back just long enough to elicit an earth-shattering response from her hungry body. Afterward they lay in each other's arms, unable to break the physical tie that bound them.

Hours later, when Callie awoke, she found Burke with his arm bracing his body in a half-sitting position, gazing at her. Her heartbeat went wild at the sight of him.

"What are you doing?" She sighed contentedly and smiled.

"Watching you, my darling."

"Do you find me that fascinating?" she asked teasingly.

"I find you endlessly fascinating."

"Oh, Burke." She wrapped her arm around his neck and drew him down to her. "I love you so."

He kissed her, then withdrew a few inches and said, "And I love you. You can't imagine how much."

"There's something I meant to tell you earlier, but I fell asleep after we made love." She gazed into his beautiful blue eyes and wondered if their second child, the one just beginning to grow inside her body, would look as much like Burke as Seamus did.

"Not another secret," he said, a hint of a smile on his face.

"This time, I won't keep your child a secret from you."

Burke pulled free and sat up straight. "What do you mean, this time?"

"I'm pregnant," she told him. "My guess is that it happened on our honeymoon. That one time when we didn't use protection."

"My God!"

"You aren't upset, are you?"

Smiling broadly, he leaned over her. She saw plainly how he felt. The joy shone clearly in his eyes and in the expression on his face.

"A little sister for Seamus," he said. "What could possibly be better? My life is perfect."

"My life is perfect, too." Callie sighed as Burke lowered his body over hers.

"And I intend to keep it that way, Mrs. Lonigan."

He made love to her with the slow, practiced expertise that drove her mad with desire. And she returned the favor, exploring his body as he had hers, learning anew the wonders of his magnificent masculine form. And when fulfillment claimed them, they shared once again the incomparable pleasure of lovers whose hearts beat as one.

*   *   *   *   *

*Look for new books in Beverly Barton's
popular series, THE PROTECTORS, coming
to Silhouette Intimate Moments in 2001.*

And don't miss
THE PROTECTORS:
SWEET CAROLINE'S KEEPER,

*a brand-new, longer-length single title book
from Silhouette Books, available
in the summer of 2001!*

And now, here's a sneak preview of
HERO AT LARGE

*by Robyn Amos (IM1040), the next
exciting book in
A YEAR OF LOVING DANGEROUSLY,
available next month!*

Chapter 1

Regrets were a waste of time. Keshon Gray had lived as a criminal long enough to know that much.

Stepping onto the rooftop, he took a pack of cigarettes out of his breast pocket. Gray only had a minute or two before he had to go back to the pretense of being a bouncer for L.A.'s trendy nightspot, Ocean Sand Castle Lounge. As he struck a match and held it to the end of his cigarette, a strange sensation washed over him.

Before his break he'd helped move a shipment of cocaine, but that wasn't what was pushing against the edges of his conscience. Nor was it the crates of semi-automatic Street Sweeper shotguns stacked in the storeroom beside the paper cups. He released a short puff, and as he watched the blue smoke curl and blend with the cool November air, it hit him.

Each guise he'd taken on over the years—and there had been many—left a new layer of grime clinging to his soul. He may not have chosen the right path in life, but he'd done it for survival—not his own, someone else's. He'd made up his mind to do whatever he had to, but he hadn't been quick enough or strong enough then, and someone he'd loved like a brother had died.

Even now, he couldn't think of that episode in his life with the numbing cool he was able to apply to everything else. For that reason, Gray had never failed again—at anything. He approached each new challenge as though someone's life depended upon his success—and more often than not, it did.

Since he'd returned to L.A., he'd reconnected with the remains of the gang he had belonged to. Those that weren't dead or in prison had been floundering on the edges of the L.A. drug trade and getting nowhere fast.

He herded them off street corners where they'd been hustling, and yanked them out of basements where they wasted their days getting high. It was time for them to move from petty street dealing into the big time. Making real money in this business required contacts, which he'd been cultivating carefully. Add a little weapons brokering into the mix, and they had an organized operation with the flashy L.A. club scene as the perfect cover.

The agency Gray worked for, SPEAR, was on the trail of a traitor named Simon. He was willing to do whatever he had to do to bring down the enemy, but the fact was, he'd been hiding in shadows for so long, he no longer knew what he looked like in the light.

However, when Gray hurried down the stairs to return to work, he couldn't know that after nine years he was about to look into the eyes of the only person who had ever known the real Keshon Gray.

In the split second it took for Gray to register Rennie Williams's presence before him in the Ocean Sand Castle

Lounge, several emotions jolted through him like bolts of lightning.

Some of the sensations he was feeling were reflected in her eyes, like the surprise and excitement, the regret…and especially the pain. The sight of her brought an immediate and stabbing ache ten times more intense than what he'd felt each time he'd thought of her over the years.

He pulled her to him in a brief embrace. He still didn't know how to process her sudden appearance. When he'd come back to L.A., he hadn't believed for a second that he might run into Rennie. When she left him to go to Texas, he'd been certain she wasn't coming back.

As a teenager, Rennie had been a pretty girl with lots of potential. As an adult, she was heart-stopping. Especially in that short, clingy little dress she was wearing.

Gray smiled down at her. "It's good to see you."

"So, how was prison? I mean, how have you been?"

Gray flinched before he could stop himself. He felt his whole body go cold. "You want me to tell you it isn't true, right?"

She seemed to be holding her breath. "*Is* it?"

"Sorry to disappoint you, sweetheart."

Of all the clubs in L.A., why did she have to pick this one? If she'd stayed in Texas, she might never have known if he were dead or alive, but that would still be better than returning to find her worst fears confirmed.

"I guess a lot has happened since the last time we saw each other," she said.

Gray expelled a harsh laugh. "You can say that again."

Rennie stared down at her hands; they were trembling slightly.

Instantly, he felt terrible for upsetting her. None of this was her fault. He couldn't say anything to change her mind about him. Lying to her was surprisingly easy, but it was killing him that he had to.

"You look beautiful...and successful," he said, noticing the diamond studs sparkling in her ears. He was glad she'd moved up in the world, but part of him still wished she hadn't had to leave him to do it.

"So you're...what...a bouncer here?" Her tone was imperious.

"That's right. You know there aren't a whole lot of options for an ex-con."

Tension filled the air. "I'd better get back to my friends," Rennie said. "It was...nice seeing you again."

"Not as nice as it should have been. But, like you said, a lot has happened since we last saw each other, *Rainbow,*" he said, using his old nickname for her.

He could tell he'd caught her off guard. The change in her demeanor was immediate. The line of her lips softened, and her eyes became dewy.

In that split second, they were transported back to a time where only the two of them existed. Before she had a chance to recover, he leaned down and brushed his lips against hers. He needed to be close to her for just a moment. He had to have a memory to carry with him.

"You take care of yourself," he said, pulling back.

She nodded and bolted down the stairs and, most likely, out of his life.

INTIMATE MOMENTS®
™ *Silhouette*®

presents a riveting 12-book continuity series:

A Year of loving dangerously

Where passion rules and nothing is what it seems...

When dishonor threatens a top-secret agency, the brave men and women of SPEAR are prepared to risk it all as they put their lives—and their hearts—on the line.

Available November 2000:

HERO AT LARGE by Robyn Amos

Keshon Gray was on a dangerous undercover assignment that demanded all his attention, so when his true love Rennie Williams reentered his life, Gray had to do everything in his power to keep his eye *on* a deadly traitor named Simon—and *off* Rennie's enticing curves!

*Available only from Silhouette Intimate Moments
at your favorite retail outlet.*

Silhouette®

™ *Where love comes alive*™

Visit Silhouette at www.eHarlequin.com

SIMAYOLD6

#1 *New York Times* bestselling author

NORA ROBERTS

introduces the loyal and loving, tempestuous and tantalizing Stanislaski family.

Coming in November 2000:

The Stanislaski Brothers

Mikhail and Alex

Their immigrant roots and warm, supportive home had made Mikhail and Alex Stanislaski both strong and passionate. And their charm makes them irresistible....

In February 2001, watch for
THE STANISLASKI SISTERS: Natasha and Rachel

And a brand-new Stanislaski story from Silhouette Special Edition,
CONSIDERING KATE

Available at your favorite retail outlet.

Where love comes alive™

You're not going to believe this offer!

In October and November 2000, buy any two Harlequin or Silhouette books and save $10.00 off future purchases, or buy any three and save $20.00 off future purchases!

Just fill out this form and attach 2 proofs of purchase (cash register receipts) from October and November 2000 books and Harlequin will send you a coupon booklet worth a total savings of $10.00 off future purchases of Harlequin and Silhouette books in 2001. Send us 3 proofs of purchase and we will send you a coupon booklet worth a total savings of $20.00 off future purchases.

Saving money has never been this easy.

I accept your offer! Please send me a coupon booklet:

Name: _____

Address: _____ City: _____

State/Prov.: _____ Zip/Postal Code: _____

Optional Survey!

In a typical month, how many Harlequin or Silhouette books would you buy new at retail stores?

☐ Less than 1   ☐ 1   ☐ 2   ☐ 3 to 4   ☐ 5+

Which of the following statements best describes how you buy Harlequin or Silhouette books? Choose one answer only that best describes you.

☐ I am a regular buyer and reader
☐ I am a regular reader but buy only occasionally
☐ I only buy and read for specific times of the year, e.g. vacations
☐ I subscribe through Reader Service but also buy at retail stores
☐ I mainly borrow and buy only occasionally
☐ I am an occasional buyer and reader

Which of the following statements best describes how you choose the Harlequin and Silhouette series books you buy new at retail stores? By "series," we mean books within a particular line, such as Harlequin PRESENTS or Silhouette SPECIAL EDITION. Choose one answer only that best describes you.

☐ I only buy books from my favorite series
☐ I generally buy books from my favorite series but also buy books from other series on occasion
☐ I buy some books from my favorite series but also buy from many other series regularly
☐ I buy all types of books depending on my mood and what I find interesting and have no favorite series

Please send this form, along with your cash register receipts as proofs of purchase, to:
In the U.S.: Harlequin Books, P.O. Box 9057, Buffalo, NY 14269
In Canada: Harlequin Books, P.O. Box 622, Fort Erie, Ontario L2A 5X3

(Allow 4-6 weeks for delivery) Offer expires December 31, 2000.   PHQ4002

a Year of Loving dangerously

If you missed the first 3 riveting,
romantic Intimate Moments stories
from *A Year of Loving Dangerously*,
here's a chance to order your copies today!

#1016	**MISSION: IRRESISTIBLE** by Sharon Sala	$4.50 U.S.☐ $5.25 CAN.☐
#1022	**UNDERCOVER BRIDE** by Kylie Brant	$4.50 U.S.☐ $5.25 CAN.☐
#1028	**NIGHT OF NO RETURN** by Eileen Wilks	$4.50 U.S.☐ $5.25 CAN.☐

(limited quantities available)

TOTAL AMOUNT	$ _____
POSTAGE & HANDLING	
($1.00 each book, 50¢ each additional book)	$ _____
APPLICABLE TAXES*	$ _____
TOTAL PAYABLE	$ _____
(check or money order—please do not send cash)	

To order, send the completed form, along with a check or money order for the total above, payable to **A YEAR OF LOVING DANGEROUSLY** to: **In the U.S.:** 3010 Walden Avenue, P.O. Box 9077, Buffalo, NY 14269-9077; **In Canada:** P.O. Box 636, Fort Erie, Ontario L2A 5X3.

Name: _____

Address: _____ City: _____

State/Prov.: _____ Zip/Postal Code: _____

Account # (if applicable): _____ 075 CSAS

*New York residents remit applicable sales taxes.
 Canadian residents remit applicable
 GST and provincial taxes.

Silhouette®

COMING NEXT MONTH